The Saleswoman
And The
Househusband

David Ross

ISBN 1500495255
ISBN 13: 9781500495251
Library of Congress Control Number: 2014912805
CreateSpace Independent Publishing Platform
North Charleston, South Carolina

Part One

Chapter One

WHAT I HATE IS THINKING about it.

I have to sit down. I prop myself on the edge of our metal kitchen stool with both feet on the floor and shake my head to stop the worry inside me. But the worry won't stop because we're almost completely out of money. And the worry won't stop because we'll have to move and because it's been over a year. Stuart and I have actually been unemployed for over a year.

So I have to call my brother and beg for a Goddamned job?

Dim horizons beckon and beckon.

I push my hair back behind my ears and check the rice and slice the carrots and chop the scallions and celery and mangle the damned garlic. The pan's heating up for the trout and the fake range hood is blowing the electric stove's hot air back into the room. I have to ignore that. It is the middle of July and it's been too hot during the day to go out. For weeks now we've kept these cheap canvas shades down to block the sun, and we're all inside a big broken vacuum cleaner. It's the same lukewarm air and moldy dust blowing around with the groaning of the old window air conditioners.

We trudge on with Stuart getting Keith to set the table in the tiny dining room and all of us carrying in plates of food.

And the air conditioners keep groaning on through dinner and I'm trying to be here with my family. I just can't get myself to talk and even ignore Keith pushing food to the side of his plate.

Stuart doesn't. "No, Keith, try to eat your carrots."

Keith winces and pokes his fork at bits of warm orange rubble covered by warm maggot rice. Stuart's eyes flicker toward me, then away.

I don't laugh. I don't even smile. My remoteness is plenty of warning to Stuart that something's up. I push my plate away, lean forward to pick up Ally from her highchair, bounce her a few times on my knees, kiss her head, sit back and wait.

And wait.

Stuart's cleaned up the kitchen and I've played with the kids and finally I say, "I'll call Ron after the kids go to bed".

Standing at the bottom of the stairs with Ally on his hip and Keith at his side Stuart doesn't say a thing back, maybe because, obviously, he's already taking the kids to bed.

Stuart walks upstairs.

Standing at the kitchen sink I can hear them up there above me. Ally was already asleep on his hip, so Stuart will just tuck her in and then read to Keith. But I saw that tautness, that awful look of shame on Stuart's face as he walked upstairs. He knew if he walked away, I'd be forced to phone my brother.

But maybe necessity is the brother of all our shame right now. After dumping the rest of my glass of water into the sink I walk to the most far removed space, the narrow back summer porch, to make the call.

A few minutes later I'm standing, waiting for Stuart as he walks back downstairs. I'm leaning against the door jamb with my back to the small living room as the front hall ceiling light is sinking into the grayness behind me. I just remembered it's Friday night.

"I called him."

"What happened?" Stuart stares at me as he walks by to sit on one of the striped armchairs. I take a few steps to sit across from him on the other armchair. Neither of us puts on a light.

"You okay Lisa? What happened?"

I slowly take in a deep breath. "Well, he has a job for me, but wait till you hear what it is, where it is."

A few seconds later. "Yeah?"

"I'd be selling small engines to Amish and Mennonites."

Stuart laughs, jerking his head back. "No. What do you mean? Amish and . . . what?"

"Yup."

We sit still. We're both half grinning, not moving, mouths open like we're waiting for the next punch line.

Stuart asks, "But Lisa, really, what is the job?"

"I don't know. No, I talked to Ron for less than like, four minutes. The Amish must use the little gas engines for cutting hay or something. I mean, they're not allowed to drive trucks or tractors" I feel my eyebrows raise, then lower.

Stuart's still motionless.

I straighten my back. "All I know is, the job my brother's offering is selling little gas engines to farmers in eastern Pennsylvania. And it's mostly in the counties where all those Old-World Amish and Horse and Buggy Mennonites are."

"Old-World," Stuart echoes.

"Yeah. Holy shit. And I think from the little bit he said, small engines are one of the few modern things allowed by those religious sects. So I guess there are lots of little shops where Amish and Mennonites sell them and repair them. I don't know. I can't believe it."

"You think this was the job he was offering you last Christmas?"

"I have no idea. Maybe. I didn't let him get into it at all back then before I just said no. I shunned him."

Stuart lowers his head, eyes up at me. "Okay, funny, but obviously there's no way you can do this."

I say nothing.

"Lisa, what the hell, really, I should call Ron and try to get a job from him."

"First of all, he's saying there aren't any other jobs. This is all he has, for his sister. And Stuart you can't do commercial sales. You hate sales. You love not-for-profit sales."

"But what the hell are we talking about then?

"A job.

I'm tired and want to just go to bed and sleep. But I see Stuart's wobbling mentally over there, his face flaccid. He's in some kind state of disbelief, so I draw in a breath. "I forgot to ask him how much it pays. It was such a short, weird conversation. It was just me telling him I needed a job and that we'd be fine with relocating and then he said this was the only position available. So I was sort of, you know, obviously flabbergasted. And I asked him how big these Amish engine repair shops are. And he waited and then he said, 'Small . . . yeah, they're small.'"

I've always been good at doing my brother's very deep, very slow, flat voice.

Stuart's whole face dilates more and more and we both laugh out loud for a few seconds and then moan. After a minute of looking around the room and shaking our heads, I continue, "I asked him how the Amish actually use engines and he said, 'Yeah . . . what they do is . . . they use horses to pull the tractor . . . the tractor holds our hay cutting engine'."

Eleven the next morning Stuart's walking away with the kids, out into the wet heat of the morning's shiny yellow back yard. Stuart and I finally decided. Basically, I decided, and a very skeptical Stuart shook his head and stared at empty space. Now I'm waiting, phone to my ear.

"Ron. Hi. Yeah, that'll be fine. I'd like to take the job."

"Okay. Yeah, good."

"What's the salary?" Now I ask.

"Uh, seventy-five thousand. There'll be a bonus. Yeah, I'll give you a bonus, if things are good at the end of our fiscal year. That's the end of June."

"Okay." Awful job, but okay money? "A bonus?"

"Yeah . . . usually around . . . forty thousand."

"Okay." I'm numb and can't even add up these figures. "Uhh, and when would I start?"

"Yeah, we should get you in there September fifth. Right after Labor Day. Yeah."

I can't think. If I don't ask questions the conversation will just end. But I can't think.

Nothing. I say nothing, just goodbye and when he says goodbye, that's it.

I walk into the kitchen following the muffled outside sounds of Stuart and the kids. I look out the window and there they are, caught in the small backyard, because I asked Stuart to give me some room to talk to my brother. My brother's just offered me a lot of money, if I get the bonus. It's not a lot of money for Ron, but it is for Stuart and me.

I walk through the kitchen, through the little dining room, the little living room, then back to the kitchen again. I sit on the stool and shake my head.

Ronny Allingham. We were never close. We were never close to being close, but I was older and I was preoccupied. He had a bunch of friends and a girl friend or two, but I didn't know them. He was a whole five years younger and I always figured it was just standard sibling alienation, but he was my only sibling and here I am still alienated and so is he. He's lived his whole life in suburban Pittsburgh, and I escaped. So now what do I do with him? What will he do with me? Ron Allingham. I wrote that letter to him years ago when he dropped out of college after only one year. It was a sad, dull looking local college and I wondered if he couldn't move on to a better one, maybe farther away. Instead, he went back home and lived with Mom and Dad and worked at the family company. He never answered my letter.

Then my smart little brother made a tidy bundle, somehow in the last ten years or so. It was last Christmas when Mom told Stuart and me Ron was worth around ten million. She said he did it by investing in stocks and bonds and real estate, or something. Mom didn't have the details.

And here I am, staring out the kitchen window at Stuart and the kids. I forgot that we have to sell our house. God! Then we have to find a new house. Stuart will go nuts. We have less than two months.

Stuart and Ally are watching Keith running in circles kicking a soccer ball. I'm staring, not really ready to go out yet. I'm thirty-eight, almost nine years younger than Stuart and I'm starting to feel a little old and so how is he feeling? Tired and beaten down? I know I'm tired of sitting around recounting how brave and cool we were running our rarefied nonprofit center in Boston. It was too rare for this damned world.

The point is, after almost a decade of our Art Collections Care Center struggling to bring in any money, Stuart and I had to watch it slowly die. And the postmortem's been all the more and more hopeless, vapid time this last year; both of us sending out resumes and meeting with all those people and making pointless phone calls, chasing jobs and never getting jobs.

Now I seem to have a damned job. I'm standing here in this stale, groaning mid-summer air and obscene yellow light and I'm squinting through the small kitchen window at my husband and two little children outside. They're waiting for me.

A long night's shaky sleep and it's Sunday morning, a little after nine and we're all in the little kitchen. I can't help it, I'm staring at pictures of Amish and Horse and Buggy Mennonites on my phone. It rings. I jump and I know before answering it that it's Mom. It's her weekly phone call. I'd like to stay here with Stuart and the kids, making scrambled eggs but I have to take the phone and me to the living room. Leaning on the back of the striped chair, I tell her about the job right away to get it over with.

"Oh, that's great! I saw Ron yesterday at the CVS in Northhills but he didn't say anything." She sounds raspier than usual. It's her usual low, almost muttering sound, just raspier because she's excited. She never uses much air in her voice even when she gushes.

"Well, maybe he's just saving it for a better time," rumbles out of me.

"But that's wonderful news. I know how hard the job search has been for you guys. So Stuart will look for work, or work out of the house?"

"Yeah, work out of the house and take care of the kids."

"Wonderful. He's such a good father. Oh, I'm so glad. Really, I'm just speechless. It's wonderful news."

I usually cruise through these weekly conversations. But the little airless, muttering, Pollyanna voice of my mother might drive me berserk this morning. She doesn't like Stuart. She thinks he's an arrogant, fancy-pants twit. But she thinks I am too.

I massage the back of my neck with my phone-free hand. "Well, we'll see. It's a pretty, extremely weird job, Mom. I mean, Mom, you did hear me say Amish and Mennonite farmers?"

"Oh, I'm sure you'll do a great job and Ron will take care of you."

"Take care of me? Mom? Mom? Really? I am the older sister. And how's Ron going to take care of me exactly, with him up in Pittsburgh and me three hundred miles away in Amishland?" I stop my rant.

"I know. I know. I'm sorry the job market's so tough. It's terrible."

"Yeah."

"How does Stuart feel about it? Do you think he can find a way to get work down there?"

I wait, then say, "Yeah. He'll try. He feels trapped, I guess. He has to do this the way I have to. It's six of one, six dozen of the other."

"Sorry?"

"Yeah, I don't know." I suck in the last of the air in the dull little living room. The few decent pieces of furniture, like the two armchairs we invested in back in Boston years ago, are too big for the tiny room with the low ceiling and small windows. Stuart calls this our Diane Arbus house.

Toast and coffee smells are coming in from the kitchen, but I sit down.

"Well, I've been so worried about you and Stuart and the children. Do you need more money? I can send you a check."

"No. Thanks. No, we appreciate the money you sent the last time. We're all set." Subservient, is what I should say. She sent that two thousand dollars about three months ago and I should just be thankful, instead of pathetic and envious. She has a couple of million invested somewhere and her house and car are paid for and she's never worked a day in her life, except summer jobs for her father as a teenager.

I've barely heard the words coming through the phone from Tricia. It's something about how proud she is that Stuart and I held up during the hard times.

"Well, I just really wish you the best of luck. Are you worried that you won't be able to do the job?"

"No. I think I'll be able to do it."

"No, I know. Ron wouldn't have given you the job if he didn't think you could do it. And if you have trouble, you can always call him. That's what family's for. That's what I meant before, Lisa."

I'm stuck. It's that feeling that nothing I say or do will make a dent. I'm hungry and just want some of what I can smell – scrambled eggs and toast and coffee.

"You'll have to sell your house in Connecticut and buy something."

"Yeah."

"Well, I'm sure that won't be a problem. Stuart likes doing that. He's so good at that."

I say nothing back at all.

"I tell Ginny how great Stuart is at being a father."

I sigh, "Yeah. He is."

Now I can hear Tricia sigh. It's contagious, like yawning.

She says, "Well, I have to go. I'm playing golf with Paul and Lee and having dinner…"

"Okay." I hope I'll stop her there. I don't want to hear about her playing expensive games right now.

"Sorry I have to get off so soon. We'll talk again soon. Give my love to Stuart and Keith and Ally. Oh, I'm so glad you'll be working for Ron. That's really so great."

"Okay. Bye Mom."

Chapter Two

AT LEAST TODAY I'M ALONE for the first time in over a year. Ally's right upstairs there, taking her late morning nap, but Stuart's gone and Keith's playing at his friend, Jamie's house. Standing here in the kitchen packing I just have to try hard to not think about Amish and Mennonites shunning me.

Stuart's doing his bit, driving to Pennsylvania to look for a house.

I stop wrapping and boxing china. It's eleven o'clock. Instead of staring at pictures of those Old World people online, I'm walking around the little house, finding windows to stare through. The sad row of little wooden and vinyl boxes across the street are the mirror image I've avoided for the past three years. And I don't see them now. I see Pennsylvania farms with things looking like broken engines of some kind in the dirt, out in some field. Jesus, how am I going to do this?

I half listened when my father talked about his job. It was usually to strangers at a party during an introduction or something. He'd keep it short. He worked for the family company that sold small engines wholesale to retail shops.

I've never known much about our little family company. I know when Mom's father started it after the Second World War, he called it, *OhPa* Distributors. Funny name and chuckled over many times. I think it slowly made a bit of money for the handful of bosses in the offices and the fifty or so employees. Grandpa died in his late seventies and it all passed on to Daddy and two other guys who had worked for Grandpa for years. It was some sort of three-way partnership. Daddy made a comfortable, low six figure salary and I noticed he always just looked really bored by it all. He always said he couldn't wait to retire. Then Daddy did retire, and Ron was put in his place.

But just to add a zany yowl to the family story, it was just over two years ago, right after Daddy's funeral, that Mom let me know women couldn't be owners of the company. Zany.

It came up during the conversation Tricia organized for Stuart and me back at the house, after the last of the ceremonies -- two days of standing in one place and shaking people's hands very, very slowly. Tricia wouldn't sit down. She was agitated, walking around her living room while Stuart and I sat on the long, cushy sofa. Keith was down in the basement family room watching a movie and Ally wasn't even a thought yet. We still had on our dark clothes and were raw and tired after the church service, the finale; all but Mom who was outlining the provisions of the Laurence Allingham will. She kept saying she wouldn't state the actual amount of money entrusted to her, and Stuart and I kept nodding, stating we didn't need to know.

Tricia's sashaying went on as she mumbled, airlessly, "Ron will continue running the company with Teddy and Rick and their sons, but, of course, women can't be owners anyway, but so that just means everything will just go on the same way." She was moving to the baby grand piano to put down her glass of white wine. No one played the piano, so it was a gigantic end table.

I just stared fish-eyed at my mother for a few seconds. I wouldn't get pulled into a scene, especially after my father's funeral. Anyway, I knew. I went away to Boston to indulge in the cool life while Ron slugged it out for years in the old company.

That ugly taunt from my mother back then has coughed-up occasionally from inside me, well before this new, nightmare job offer. Now it's stuck along with all the rest of my anxieties, a large lump in the middle of me.

It's still July twenty-fifth. The kids are in bed. Insects are buzzing outside the sheer black screened walls of the porch, and the air's thick but cool enough to breathe. My head's back on the pale green wicker chair, an almost empty glass of beer next to me, and I'm trying to picture Stuart. All day, there he was, driving and driving on and on, moving straight ahead in a group of forward prone vehicles on the most concrete linear perspective life provides. Person of action, person on a mission, person facing straight ahead into space that escapes behind him. The five-year-old Jetta on cruise control and him safe, I hope.

I think he wanted to get out of here. So when did Stuart say, "At least we can move out of Woodstock"? Last week some time? Stuart knows I never wanted to move here and I know he didn't. He loved living in the center of Boston so much. He was such a city boy. We just couldn't afford the city and kids and we really, seriously wanted to have kids.

And if you can afford it, Woodstock, Connecticut does seem to be a fine series of old country roads nonchalantly connecting beautiful antique wooden houses. Stuart and I could only afford the suburban looking clump closer to the small strip, near the highway, that takes you north and then east to Boston. It's a clump of three streets with shrunken, imitation

Colonial or Cape or Victorian houses built after the Second World War. These little wooden houses sit on little lots, sub-clumps. And it was supposed to be temporary. We'd move when there was more money saved. Then we lost our jobs.

"We went from self-employed to self-disenfranchised." Stuart said last year, before we'd been shut-ins for too long to joke about things like that.

But the air's cool enough now, to ebb and flow with wood and cement and grass and beer off-gassing around me. I'm just stationary here on the porch, still sitting, waiting for Stuart to stop driving and tell me he's stationary somewhere in Amishland. The night drags on. And on. I jump at the sound. It's my little cell phone vibrating and imitating an old-fashioned ring on top of the pile of magazines covering the small wicker coffee table.

I reach for my glass of beer. "So, how's the house husband's house hunting?"

"Funny. I just got here to the motel. And yeah, we have no idea what's available down here. We shouldn't assume it's even as good as, let's say, Woodstock? It might be mostly parking lots and strips."

"Okay. I hope not."

"Yeah, but anyway, we're in a hurry, partly just to get Keith settled in a school. The thing is, I might not find us an area we want and the, you know, house in it, this quickly."

"No, I know. It's okay. Relax. I know we have to sell our house here first, but I guess Keith can go to school here for a while."

I gaze through the mass of screening at the cloudy shades of black in our yard. I don't want to make the conversation more phobic by mentioning again that I'm supposed to be in Pennsylvania, working on the ground, right after Labor Day, about a month away.

"I'm putting a bid on the first house I see for nine hundred thousand," Stuart says.

"Um, better not or you'll never see the end of me again." Odd elliptical phrases slip out of my mouth every now and then.

Stuart grunts loudly, then laughs. "Ahh, Lisa . . ."

"Really, I'm worried that we're in too much of a hurry."

"What?"

"There's no huge hurry."

He grumbles, "But there is a hurry and Keith can't go to school there for a while. He needs to start with the rest of the kids at his next school. You said that."

I'm stymied. There are no words, just muffled, burbling sounds through the tiny phones back and forth for a few seconds.

He says, "Anyway, it's okay. There are those great old stone farmhouses down here."

I say, "You'll do fine. You're an ace."

"Yeah, well I hope you knocked on some damned wood. Because I found us the ugly little house we're in now."

"There. I knocked on the ceiling with my head."

He laughs. "Funny. Yeah, funny, and the joke's on us."

There isn't a lot I can say. He found us really great apartments in Cambridge and Boston and fixed them up to be amazingly gorgeous. But we got tired of paying rent and not investing in real estate. Three years ago, when Keith was almost school age, Stuart said we should move out of Boston to find a house we could afford, to raise a family. Now our family is all we have. I tell him whatever he finds us out in the country will be fine. We say goodbye.

Chapter Three

We're here slowly. It's almost seven at night and furrowing toward dusk. After those sun glaring, long highways all day, now little charcoal country roads are twisting and twisting in the Pennsylvania countryside. Boston's way, way behind us, gone. Allison's asleep, then awake, then asleep. Keith's silent, watching strange, wild adult things unfold.

Stuart's been driving all day as a favor to me.

"That's it." He points, tapping his knuckles on the side window.

There is something small but heavy looming out there. It seems to be a crude, pale white lump a hundred feet from the road, lost in some trees in a big dark field. After we pull into the even darker shadows of an overgrown driveway, fifty feet to the side of the house and get out of the car, I look warily at the building off to our left. The white, rough-pebbly stucco manages to glow in the gray air. It's a small mid nineteenth century stone box with a small open front porch. I remember Stuart's lecture. In the late nineteenth century a shed kitchen was added, a stucco over wood structure attached to the right side of the original house.

There's a big cement slab covering the ground to the right side of the shed kitchen, spread before us like some ramshackle, hideous patio or something.

Before now, in pictures, it looked like a poor farmer's cottage you'd find in rural Scotland or Ireland. Maybe Stuart was reaching out to his ancestors. Now it just looks like a dingy old hut and my heart sinks.

Stepping inside after Stuart wrestles with the key and then turns on an overhead light, I see a bare bones kitchen on the right, rough to the point of looking grim and shabby. There are only four wall cabinets with no doors. There's a smell of mold. The appliances look heavily used and the floor's some sort of ugly self-done job of cheap red and blue vinyl squares over cement. And everything's filthy.

Straight ahead is an exposed, heavy, gray field stone wall with the original doorway on the left, cut into the side of the building. As we walk along, Keith and then me, then Stuart holding Ally, we pass through the stone wall. It's like a cave. It's like a tiny stone frontier fort. Then my eyes take in the old, wide pine floors and then the thick gray-white plaster walls and all the whitewashed rafters running along the ceiling. To the right, as I turn, is a huge fireplace at least seven feet long with a very plain wooden mantle on top that's over five feet high. And everything has that coat of grime.

"This was the kitchen, originally. Now it's a dining room, right? It's eleven feet by twenty-one," Stuart says, then blows his nose.

I walk slowly, looking up, down and around. Across from the fireplace there are two doorways seven feet apart, without actual doors, leading into the next room. It's the living room and it's the same size with the same floors and walls and ceiling. Now I'm walking through the second doorway back into the dining room. The wall next to the dining room fireplace is that same mustardy khaki color as all the wainscoting and window trim. It's an original nineteenth century wood paneled wall, Stuart's saying, after waiting silently.

"Like it at all?" he asks.

I take in a breath. "Uh, well, it's a little extreme." I take Ally from Stuart's arms.

Stuart stiffens. I'm trying to not be too negative, but my God, it's not easy.

"Sorry. I know you want some drama in our lives right now. Our last house didn't have any. But this. How are we going to live in this place?"

Stuart sneezes, then says, "I'll fix it up. It'll look a lot better after I paint it. Really."

"Okay."

It's a done deal. Jesus, I have enough worries and just needed a moderately normal house.

Stuart sneezes and blows his nose. He's allergic to mold. Great. He turns away and leads the way up the narrow old stairway to the second floor, announcing that the realtor told him it was a classic old Pennsylvania staircase. It's very steep, almost ladder-like, and paneled and turns in a spiral to take up less room. Each narrow, smooth pine step is worn away in the center. We're creaking a lot. At the top, the boxed-in stairwell opens to a tiny landing with one bedroom ahead, another one to the left and a bathroom to the right.

One glance into the small bathroom is enough. There's a tiny, slimy plastic shower stall and very small plastic, imitation-porcelain sink. To the left of the landing is a minute bedroom that Keith will have to call his own for a while. It's only ten feet long and six feet wide. I walk into the larger bedroom and it's actually fairly large, twenty-one by sixteen feet according to Stuart.

Looking around, I say, "So, sure enough, it actually is a one-bedroom house with no closets and almost no bathroom or kitchen."

"Yeah. For now," Stuart says.

I shrug slowly, looking around. There are the same rough wooden floors with half their varnish worn away and the same thin white paint on the rafters and the same graying old white plaster walls, with more than a hint of mold.

I sit in one of the deep windowsills with Ally asleep in my arms. Stuart looks anxious and continues sneezing.

"I like it without any furniture." I sweep the room with my eyes trying very hard to be charitable. Then I look out the window to the front view. The hut feels like it's more than a hundred feet back from a narrow dark country road.

Keith has been running from one room to the next listening to his seven-year-old echo, excited about this tiny medieval castle his father found.

I hand Ally to Stuart and take in the view out the back. There's a big, rough crab grass lawn leading to a half painted, white wooden fence, beyond which is a field of wild grasses a couple of feet high and then way back, woods. There are no houses anywhere that I can see. It's looking very dark back in those woods. So who will the kids play with? What the hell will winters be like? The lawn drops down at a slight angle in the back, but the field is flat. Flat was important to these farmers hundreds of years ago. None of this is important to me and my family. There are trees on both sides, and I notice a little stone building to the right side of the back lawn. That must be the spring house that Stuart talked about. It's too much to take in and what I want to do is stay on this windowsill and not look around anymore. I close my eyes and try to relax.

Stuart's staring at me. "It'll look much better after I fix it up. I'll start building closets and painting next week. Trust me, it won't cost much at all."

I just nod but know I'm communicating how much I hate this little Goddamned hut or fort or whatever it is. I'm filled with new-nasty-job fear, but it isn't a house.

Chapter Four

THIS IS MY DAY, THRUST into an exclusively male world, because how many women want to work with little filthy lawnmower engines? It's the latest in obsolete nineteenth century technology.

I look over at Stuart who's all flushed with some sort of nervous energy as he drives us away from the Comfort Inn. He has to deal with the movers today and he's probably a nervous wreck about trying to find some work way out here in the wilderness and having to tidy-up that ridiculous old hut he bought and take care of the kids by himself. And, I hope his car holds up. He plans on driving Keith to school for now, because it's less than ten minutes in the car and an hour on the stupid bus. Plus, Stuart has to find food somewhere. So the car has to hold up.

Jesus, I have to try to hide from the detritus storm in my brain.

Becker's Hill forms around us at the top of a long rise and at the meeting of roads and Stuart is pulling into the shallow gravelly parking lot of, *Phil's Convenience Store*. I kiss all three of them and get out and watch as they pull away. The gravel crunching, the kids chirping, the car humming -- all the sounds are driving away.

It's quiet. I'm, exposed and abandoned, standing somewhere on dusty gravel in the warm sunny morning breeze. They're all just gone and no one else is in sight. I had no idea how to dress for this, but I just went for a conservative look. Yup, a white cotton button down collar shirt with narrow brown khakis, oxfords and a dark gray thin linen sports jacket. My hair is in a neat twist behind my head, knotted in a half-inch wide black velvet tie. A few strands always drift free at my temples. Stuart always gets very enthusiastic about my hair. Very enthusiastic. I have to relax.

Only two cars have passed me since I was dropped off over five minutes ago and it's rush hour in this non-place. Derelict fields surround me, enclosed by old wooden fencing enhanced by barbed wire. There's a sense of wet morning earth rising and drying upward into sunny air. My nose is feeling more and more encrusted and I didn't bring any tissues.

I look at my watch. It's twenty after. They have my cell phone number, this Joe and Bobby. That little convenience store behind me and post office next to it look ossified in the direct, dusty morning sun. And that little church across the road has a castoff feeling to it, like so many churches. The large dark cut stones are long term but the red wooden trim around the windows is looking almost weathered away.

I'm sweating. It's probably in the mid-seventies and overcast, but bright. I always perspire when I'm tense. There's a minivan and another one behind it. Of course, I'm the only person out here. The first van is silver and puts its turn signal on and slowly pulls in near me, with the dark blue minivan right next to it. They're almost half an hour late. The guy in the silver van waves and unbuckles his seat belt. He's bald on top with a rim of dyed black hair and looks like he's in his fifties. He gets out and comes around the front of the minivan smiling with his hand out. He's stocky and exactly my height, five-five, with a five o'clock shadow already.

"Hey. Lisa?"

I shake Joe's hand and then Bobby's. Bobby's at least seven inches taller than Joe and slightly overweight and blond and baby faced making his age hard to guess, but definitely at least ten years younger than Joe. The contrast is extreme. Bobby's ethereal fairness, with thin, short wispy blond hair and pale, almost hairless skin, looming, like a cloud above its shadow, above the dark eyed and black rimmed little Joe.

"Boy this is in the country. You live way out here?" Joe yelps this smiling, moving his head toward the collection of weeds and old buildings. I'm smelling lemony after shave from one of them.

"Yeah, we just moved in, down the road a little." I point my head at my new, narrow country road.

"Where'd you move from?"

"Boston." That just comes out.

"Boston!"

Joe rotates his head and shoulders looking around at the pastoral scene. He turns to me with his face red, then looks up at Bobby who was smiling the whole time and who now repeats Joe's gaze of astonishment, at me. They're trying to comprehend the female conundrum standing there, all pristine and from distant worlds, standing out on this ragged dirt, white trash parking lot.

I sense we all need direction.

"So I don't really know if you can help, but I don't even have a list of clients, just some maps I downloaded with dots where some businesses are. And I don't really know much about engines."

"Yeah, that's okay. We're the OhPa technical services team. We may look stupid, but we can sound smart." Joe gives up a throaty laugh and Bobby follows again. This cloud follows its shadow.

I manage a smile. "Yeah, well I'm going to look and sound really stupid if I don't know anything."

"No. That's why we're here. I have a phone for you with your dealers logged in it. Baby Bear did that yesterday and that's in the minivan. And we can travel with you today and introduce you to a few dealers. Then, I'll be in the office any time you need help. Bobby answers technical questions too. We call Bobby, *Baby Bear*. I'm just, *the Bear*. Most of the dealers know us and they call in if they have questions about promotions or new features on products, or about warranty issues. Dumb stuff like that."

They both have on baggy tan khakis and white soft collared, short sleeved shirts.

"Did Dale like this territory? He's up in Bethlehem, now?" I ask.

"Dale? Yeah, up in that area. Yeah, Dale was fine with leaving here. He had some shit to say about these Old-World guys, though. Sorry."

So Dale had problems with the Amish and Mennonites? I don't trust these guys to be willing or able to tell me much, so I just shuffle toward the car, nodding to confirm for them that I don't take offense at the use of the word, shit.

"No, *shit's* a word I like to use too, on special occasions."

"Special occasions!" They both laugh about that and I join in as much as I can.

The silver minivan isn't awful. At least it's all paid for. It has sixty-four thousand miles on it and it's pretty dirty inside. There's a layer of grime on the dark gray carpeted floor and the dashboard. The second backseat was removed to make room for a bunch of things. After asking, I'm told what's back there. There are examples of engines and small generators and backpack blowers and chainsaws and chain for those saws. There's a fairly pungent odor of oil, metal and new plastic coming from back there.

The Bear's driving and Baby Bear's in the backseat and I'm their passenger, to the heart of Amish Country. I suggested that. I figure I can use help there the most.

The GPS tells us to take route 82 north for five miles to route 322 west. My eyes feel bloody and strained looking out the window. The Bear is still trying to be jovial but it's a little frantic while I'm trying to stay calm and while the GPS is chirping progress reports.

"There are other people here too, you know. Even Catholics." Baby Bear says this, reading something on his phone.

"Yeah, good. Let's hear it for the church of Rome," the Bear cackles.

"So there are modern Mennonites, right?" I turn back to Baby Bear.

"Yeah. Dale said the Mennonites sometimes drive cars and, you know, have electricity in their houses and even computers and cell phones, some of them. Some of them. Some are just like the Amish, with none of that. Dale wasn't so great with all the differences. He said it was all bullshit to him and he was an atheist."

"Yeah, let's hear it for the atheists. They mow lawns too!" The Bear barks this and he and Baby Bear roar laughing. These guys laugh a hell of a lot.

After half an hour of driving, we arrive in Hinkleville. It's about the size of Becker's Hill but even less attractive. Actually, it has serious periodontal disease, with decaying old stone houses and then some gaps where there's only a foundation. The GPS leads us to a gas station. We don't need gas. It's a small standard looking Sunoco. The Bear looks confused and lowers his window for the attendant, who looks back blankly, waiting.

"We're looking for *Reinhart's Lawnmower Supply?*"

There's still no end to the blankness of the middle-aged thin man in dirty jeans and a dirtier baby blue sweatshirt with *Dickenson College* on it in wrinkled, faded black letters.

The Bear looks down at the sheet of paper on his lap.

"Enos Reinhart?"

"Enos? He still doin that?"

"Thanks a lot. Bye a lot." The Bear ducks his head and turns away, trying to not laugh. Baby Bear is leaning over in the back seat as we drive away. Then, the Bear is trying to imitate banjo music and I can barely smile.

"Is it hard to find these dealers?"

"No, not usually. I mean, right Baby Bear?"

"Not up in Ohio. No, that was just funny, that's all."

"Ohio's not up, numb nuts. Oh, sorry . . ." The Bear pulls over next to a field of very tall corn. He glances at me, then faces the GPS to type in the next address. "Down here, in this part of Pennsylvania, is what Baby Bear means, is where the shops can be small. And kind of hidden away. Not all of them, but some."

"But back there, that was all the smaller they get," Baby Bear says from the back seat.

"Thin air," the Bear says.

And we drive on and I try to be their audience. I can't shun them. I want to, but I can't.

Eventually Route 322 south is softer on the eyes, with trees lining parts of the narrow road and fields beyond and beyond. The Bear drives along following the loud repetitive directions of the GPS. Of course, as I tap into my new phone, I see there are over fifty dealers in Lancaster County, a lot more than anywhere else in my territory. Jesus. The Bears banter on and my face freezes facing the landscape.

The Bear shouts, "Beartown!" Immediately, Baby Bear shouts the same thing, both of them pointing at a road sign that says some place named, Beartown is five miles away. This is happening as we turn, with the GPS saying again and again, "You have reached your destination." We go up a gravel driveway into a farm. On the right facing the road is a one-story white cinder block building with a small, half paved parking lot in front. Half of the old cement is covered with grass and weeds.

Zimmerman's Repair, is in five inch black plastic letters over the glass and aluminum door.

"Marvin does a lot of business with us. Marvin Zimmerman. He's Horse and Buggy Mennonite and does a lot of business with outsiders, according to Dale," the Bear says as we all get out of the van.

The Bear and his tall blond buddy stand at the door with outstretched arms to allow me to enter the building first. There are three hulking, orangy-yellow stand-on lawnmowers on the thousand square foot cement display floor with some generators. On one wall are a few backpack blowers sitting on shelves and on the opposite wall are four chainsaws. In the back of the dimly lit room there's a counter running straight across the width of the room with two men behind it looking at me and the two Bears. Mostly at me.

"Marvin, hey, how are you? Been a while." The two Bear's step forward and I stay a few steps behind. "Joe from OhPa. You know Baby Bear from the phone."

Marvin is about six-two, in his late forties. He looks like a cross between the two Bears, dark haired but large. Unlike the Bears, he doesn't project a toothy, broad grin, but does smile. It's a reserved, wary smile. He's wearing a plain, button-down green and blue checkered standard old-fashioned shirt. He has on jeans with suspenders and a beard with no mustache.

"So, anyway, Lisa Macnayer is taking over for Dale."

I step forward and shake Marvin's hand across the counter. He's very slow to offer his own hand and then it's a brief, only fingers handshake. I then get the same thing when I shake hands with Marvin's son-in law, Silas, who works as Marvin's assistant. This isn't about germs.

Silas is thinner, younger and dressed almost the same way, but not quite. He has on suspenders and a black cotton narrow brimmed hat. The same beard, with no mustache. The latest style in 1750 for mountain men.

"Marvin, you order stuff and what? Do you fix engines and repair things, still?" The Bear seems to want to gather some information but also to show me how to engage.

"Some. Silas, now does a lot of the repairs." He has a German accent, sure enough.

"Oh, so you get to sit back and boss Silas around."

The Bears both laugh loudly enough to fill the silence as Marvin and Silas gently shut them out with plastered-on smiles. I feel myself shrinking and cringing, stepping back, wanting to escape as the little pushy Bear asks how business is and how the family is and each time he gets, "good" and nothing more. He asks Marvin how his inventory is holding up. Marvin says it's good. He doesn't need to place another order. Marvin and Silas stay planted behind the counter staring at us and the Bear and Baby Bear shuffle backward and begin wandering around the shop, with me trailing behind. I'm sweating on top of sweat. After a couple of minutes of wandering and looking at big lawnmowers, it's time to leave as far as I'm concerned, but I stand and wait as the Bears banter with each other and poke at some equipment. I try to follow them to listen to any words about these products I have to sell.

They mumble a few names and I ask what they're saying.

"Yeah, you don't have to worry about this stuff. These mowers are end products. We sell the Foster and Knolls engines for pumps and seeders and all sorts of things these farmers use. But up here . . ." The Bear points with his thumb to the wall next to us. "Those small end products are things we sell too. You have four different models of Nuco back-pack blowers and three different sized chainsaws. They're on our website. You just yak with the dealers and if they need anything you take an order, or they do it themselves at some other point."

In a few sentences the Bear just told me how easy my job is. I'll spend all my time, forty hours a week, yakking at Amish farmers about engines, yakking at these sociopathic males who won't even talk to the two Bears. I hate this place. I want to go home to Stuart and the kids.

With me festering in the dingy, gray air surrounding me, the door opens and three men with long beards enter, slowly walking to the counter. All three might be in their late twenties, but who knows because they have on shiny, narrow brimmed black hats, baggy cotton pants with suspenders and soft looking, slightly wrinkled, collared shirts. Two of them have on white sneakers and one has on black tie shoes. They gaze at me and move on. They're speaking their form of German now, to Marvin. They keep glancing back, looking at me. Sure as hell, this isn't men admiring me and I'm feeling extremely estranged. They're speaking in a foreign language and it sounds like them venting some sort of ugly, deep seated alienation.

"What? Are no women allowed in these places?" I hiss to Baby Bear, who happens to be standing near me at the front of the shop near the small plate-glass window. The sun's intensely bright and hot.

"No. I think you see women here. Why?"

I don't want to try to explain reality to the damned simpleton. I just shake my head and move away, the knot in my stomach combining with the strong sunlight and making me lightheaded. I didn't eat enough breakfast.

The bear walks near. "Should we head out?"

I nod, my jaw clenched.

I follow him back to the counter, trying not to look at the three men who are all looking at me.

"So when you need any more blowers or generators or parts, you can call Lisa on her cell phone," the Bear says. Okay? Anything you need."

I have to snap out of my deep funk suddenly and reach inside my jacket pocket and step forward to hand Marvin and then Silas a business card. They both take my card, then just recede somewhere, far away eyes vaguely aimed in my direction. The other guys have turned away. And that's it, no Goddamned yakking at all.

"Well, that sucked," I whisper as I step past the two Bears and out into the motley little hot parking lot.

Inside the van I release a bit more anger. "That sad little place was a typical Mennonite shop?"

Baby Bear answers from the back seat. "Yeah. I guess. I mean, he's pretty conservative and doesn't drive a car and doesn't have a phone or computer. So, but, yeah . . ."

The Bear is unsure what to say.

Baby Bear seems too dumb to shut up. "Yeah, the guys who came in, I don't know what they were. I think they were Amish. They did have beards, so they were married."

I bob my head. According to what I saw on my phone, that was one of the biggest dealers I have. The Bear is driving and poking at the GPS.

"Okay," I say. "I've been wondering. If they don't have phones or computers, I can't get in touch with them without driving to each one, every time?"

The Bear points his eyes at the road, saying, "They use phones sometimes, or a bunch of them do. They can't have them in their houses or businesses, but they have them out in sheds, out in the back somewhere, or in a barn. They'll call you."

I take some time to partly digest that, then ask him, "That guy, Marvin, sells to what? He sells to Amish and Mennonite farmers exclusively?"

"Yeah, mostly, I think. But those big mowers were for, I don't know, the rest of us," the Bear says, in a calm, quiet voice. He wants to steady me.

Baby Bear grunts from behind. "They probably get some new people coming in here now. People moving in. English, that's what they call outsiders. We're all English."

"English?" I cough out a dark laugh, vaguely remembering something about that from some book.

"There's a Bob Evans up by the turnpike." The Bear is staring at the results of tapping, *restaurants*, into the GPS. "It's a twenty-minute drive, but worth it. You for it?"

He's excited and so is Baby Bear and I just nod trying not to scream at the sky and off we go.

Chapter Five

I GET DROPPED OFF AT Becker's Hill and nod goodbye to the Bears. Finally, I'm alone in this old polluted, stinking silver van, and I'm supposed to be all set to do this job. I'm supposed to be all set to go, not a wreck, trembling as I drive; hours and hours of feeling ragged, pushing me now, slowly along the road toward the hut.

Should I tell Stuart I can't do this insane job? Can I manage to wait a week before telling Stuart I can't do it? What the hell else can we do for jobs and money?

I stink of perspiration, the tense, angry, worst kind of smell. The sun is in my eyes on this, Knicht Road. It's only four in the afternoon but the Bears are going to drive all the way back tonight and wanted to get going. It was pretty obvious they didn't want to visit any more Amish or Mennonite shops for a long time. And they could feel my alienation, so I was on my own. It's a nightmare. We only managed one dealer visit after lunch. Rufus Stoltzfus. Yeah, that guy was just as hostile, barely saying a word to us and his shop was a small pole building next to his barn and he looked like the pictures of Amish men I've seen online, with a beard and no mustache and a wide straw hat and suspenders and homemade clothes. He shook my hand very reluctantly and never said anything to me after, hello, in a thick accent. Clearly, these guys hate women, or the English.

Even harebrained Becker's Hill seems almost current and normal and welcoming in comparison. I just want to embrace my family again. Then a shower. Pulling into the driveway that's a little less shadowy and forbidding in the daylight, I pull next to the ring of six foot high and four foot wide yews and park next to Stuart's dark gray Jetta and gaze for just a second out my windshield down the long slope of land out to woods, about five acres back. I just get out. A cement sidewalk leads at a diagonal line to the corner of the little stone block that's now our house, about fifty feet away. I can feel myself sinking with the weight of it all.

As I start to open the side door to the kitchen, Stuart, with Ally in his arms and Keith a step ahead, all come out of the front door yelping at me from the porch. Everyone hugs and trades questions on how school was, how the job was and how the move is going. Keith's cheek tastes so good and Ally is leaning toward me with both arms and I take her from Stuart, and we go inside. It's fantastic holding Ally.

I say, "So, wow, how did the movers do?"

"Fine. They got lost and were two hours late. It'll look a lot better when all the boxes are cleared out," Stuart says.

"Yeah. The whole place will." I try hard to sound positive. I walk through the dining room, glancing at the living room through one doorway and then the next doorway. It's filled with boxes and our old chairs. It will never all fit. I head up the stairs, winding and creaking my way to the second floor, with Ally in my arms and give her kisses on her little pudgy neck and shoulder. Ally smells so good. The rooms up here are just as jammed and confused now as downstairs.

"Great. you put the beds together." There's our beautiful antique bed in the middle of the mess.

Stuart's behind me. "Yup. One of the movers helped me. Keith helped too. Keith helped me put the sheets and covers on."

"Oh-noooooooo!" Keith runs back downstairs. I sit in a windowsill facing the front. Keith is out there climbing up one of the thirty-foot-tall evergreens that form a row along the sidewalk, five or six feet out from the house.

"So tell me, how was the job?" Stuart's standing next to the fireplace.

"It was strange. Weird."

"That bad?"

"Yeah, you know what? I don't have any idea."

Stuart's unable to respond. He probably has nothing to offer but condolences, so he stands very still and says nothing. I hate piling onto his guilt.

"Right now, I'm tired. Should we get pizza? Do we have any food in the kitchen?" I ask.

"Yeah, there's a Wegmans on 100, about twenty minutes away and we got milk and eggs and bread. And I put away some food that we had boxed-up."

"Okay. They serve good Chinese food in Wegmans. Let's go there for dinner and we can get more food for here."

It's the morning, Wednesday, as I wake up the way I fell asleep, tired, staring at the ceiling until I can see it more and more. Between all the whitewashed rafters are old wooden planks that are all whitewashed. All that rough grain fixes my eyes to the wood that turns the white paint into the color of raw wool. I smell the dust in the room and remember the sensation of breathing it in all night, waking up almost on the hour, blowing my nose to get air. Stuart seemed to be awake too, not saying anything with his arm behind his head, not breathing in his steady sleeping rhythm. I had my back to him partly to give him space because he didn't say much to me during dinner or during any of last night.

The damp morning swollen light is coming in from the back windows and Stuart gets up as soon as Ally stirs in her crib in the back corner. So do I.

Moving around boxes of clothes and books, Stuart quietly picks-up Ally while I tiptoe to the shower. We want Keith to sleep until seven and it's barely after six. I check on Keith, next door in his tiny room, that his single bed almost fills, and he looks fine, asleep on his side facing the wall. His cheeks are all flushed, and he looks so adorable I want to grab him and squeeze him, but I'll let him sleep.

Stuart put a new shower curtain in the bathroom that at least makes-up a bit for the old streaked, stained plastic shower stall. Just like yesterday after work, the shower takes a few minutes to get hot, but eventually I get clean and then dressed, standing on a couple of towels to avoid the filth of the floors. Down I go, into the mustard-khaki wooden Pennsylvania staircase, down and through the old dining room and then left to the mess of a kitchen. There are two stacks of boxes and utensils and plates and pots and pans all in different phases of being unwrapped on the counter and floor. Stuart's holding Ally who's holding onto the hair on the back of his head. Stuart bends his legs, leaning back, apparently waiting for her unconscious grip to relax. I walk over and take her.

Hugging Ally, I walk into the moving box conflagration of a living room and sit on the sofa's one clear spot to breast-feed her. Stuart brings me a glass of orange juice and a slice of toast and then he heads back to the kitchen to get food ready for Keith.

Twenty minutes later I'm back in the kitchen with Ally. With few words, Stuart and I alternate holding the bouncy, almost eight-month-old and getting out bowls and cereal and milk. It's easy to find things with the few cupboards lacking doors. After ten minutes I'm eating while Stuart rocks Ally on his hip, standing, looking around. I notice Stuart's hair seems thinner and grayer than a year ago. He is bald, so it's the sides and the back I'm looking at. The gray is in streaks and looks good. It just makes him look older.

"Where are you going today?" he asks.

"Into the thick of it. The heart of darkness. The thick, hick, heart of darkness. I think I'll go see a couple of Amish dealers and see what the deal is. But I'm not going until later, after Keith's off to school. How about you? What are you doing?"

Stuart smirks briefly and shrugs. "Me? I'm going to put things away. That's about it."

"Well, Ally appreciates your efforts and so does Keith, and so do I."

Stuart looks at me straight-faced, then raises his eyebrows. "Good. Thank you." He shrugs again. "Yeah, I don't know about mowing all that grass. When do we get that big mower?"

"I have to find a dealer. The grass is pretty high."

We both take turns looking out the front kitchen window that mostly faces the tall evergreens four feet away and where we have to look over to the right and up to the lawn and then the road. We both walk to the other side of the kitchen, where the sink and cupboards are, to look out the back window at the large back lawn.

Stuart is holding Ally and nuzzling her in her baby neck. Ally coos and wiggles. Stuart and I both love the baby aura.

"The big mower will whip right through it," I say, trying to be cheerful. "It'll take you an hour."

"An hour. Right. So we're going to get one that goes fifty miles an hour?"

"I have no idea." I shake my head looking passed Stuart and Ally, at what appears to be a wild and very expansive lawn we're supposed to keep as tame as possible. It's over two acres of weeds and crab grass with the occasional boulder. Stuart and I shrug and turn away.

Getting well behaved little Keith up and going to second grade is standard enough and Stuart drives off with him. I'm getting to be with Ally for half an hour. I kiss her head while I walk out to the open front porch and then breathe in the fresh fall morning air. What kind of school is Keith going to? I may never know.

There isn't a building in sight and there's no sound until a few birds cause a slight breeze through distant trees. Ally reaches, moaning, for the ground as I walk on the grass of the front lawn. As soon as she's placed down, she begins her sideways crawl, her "hermit crab" crawl, as Stuart describes it. She leans on one elbow only and pushes with her other hand and foot. A car passes and I look up at it. From the distance it looks like an older woman driving by, not looking at me or Ally.

It's already become eight-fifteen and I've tapped, *Yoder Engine Repair,* into the GPS. There are a bunch of places closer, but I want to see what nasty crap lies in the middle of my territory. Blind loathing, or whatever it is, seems to have me moving along. The dealer list in my phone said Lucas Yoder ran a shop at 1454 Route 772 in Elstonville, fifty-nine miles west. The GPS just said it would take me seventy-four minutes to get there, so now I'm poking at my radio and looking at the landscapes, down 562 to 82 to 23 and pushing on and on in my grimy minivan. Meanwhile, I've stopped looking at anything in particular after fifteen minutes. I have to drive right through my fears. That's my mantra. *Drive through fear.*

I'm picking up a radio station from Philadelphia.

Farms are dominating for the last fifteen minutes. There isn't anything else. Now, as I pull down a dirt road-driveway, shutting off the GPS, I see a large tan stucco over stone farmhouse with a larger half stone, half wooden barn next to it, and, in front of the barn, two parked horseless black buggies. It's barely mid-morning but it's muggy-hot and bright when I step down from my minivan. The smell of hay and manure surrounds me, just barely wafting. It's a flat, fertile, sun filled universe filled with endless organic matter. I notice two tiny figures way out in a broad field. I just stand.

Two dogs bark at me, coughing weakly into the enormous damp sky. They're both behind a wide planked unpainted picket fence that's next to a large vegetable garden. Laundry, on a long line strung from the side of the house to a tree, billows slowly.

The metallic sound of my car door closing goes nowhere and I'm almost too heavy to move but do. How can this be an actual business? I walk toward the little hand carved sign, *Yoder Engine Sales and Service*, over the small door to the left of the two large doors of the barn. The barn is a hundred feet away. The packet of information is stuck to my hand. The weak, sporadic barking goes on and I look to see if the two guys out in the field notice me, but they don't. Should I go in the open door, even though it's dark inside?

I lean my head in. "Hello."

Nothing. I hear some movement and realize it's the sound of horses shuffling somewhere in there. I just said hello to them.

"Yah?" A man's voice makes me jump. I gaze in again and barely see the form of a man facing me from ten feet inside. I have to decide whether to step inside or not. I stay put.

"Hi. I'm Lisa Macnayer. I'm the new Territory Manager for Ohio and Pennsylvania Engine Distribution. You might know us as OhPa." It blurts out of me toward the doorway.

Nothing, then, "Okay."

I gaze in.

"I just wanted to introduce myself and ask you if you need anything. Or have any questions." I'm speaking at blurs.

"No, I'm okay," he grumbles in a thick German accent.

I get the hint. "Okay, well can I leave a new price sheet and our latest product booklets?" I just step forward, one, then two steps into the dark barn. There's a dark gray haze with enough light from a couple of small distant windows to show three dimensional images hovering here and there -- two hulking, swaying, snorting, dark gray horses in stalls forty feet back to the right -- some hay bales -- some old tools hanging from a beam -- an old worn wooden bench in the back, to the left, with a couple of old engines on top, surrounded by tools and parts. The dense smell is hay, horses, manure and motor oil.

The man is taking on more and more detail. He's wiping his hands with a rag. Sure enough, he has a beard, a wide brimmed straw hat and baggy, slightly wrinkled, homemade looking clothes with suspenders. He's about fifty and has a reddish tint to his gray hair. Otherwise, he looks like Abraham Lincoln. And Abe is standing very still looking at me like I'm something that just dropped out of the sky into his distant private time and space. His re-past. He then steps forward, and I expect to shake his hand but instead he reaches with his left hand for my glossy packet of information. Amish men, apparently, don't shake hands with women.

"Okay," he says after he steps back a few feet.

"Okay. My number's on the sheet." I'm stopping there. This guy probably doesn't believe in phones and things. "Uh, I can come by again in a few months."

"Okay."

I back away and sidle out the barn door. "Bye." I walk away. When I turn, ten steps later, the man's not at the door. I get in my car and drive away.

I pull over on the narrow shoulder when I can a minute later and put my head back. I'm so damned frustrated and jittery. What can I do? Go home? I reach over for my phone and scroll down the list of dealers in Lancaster County. There's one in Penryn. Elam Bruener of *Bruener's Repair*. I grimace and shake my head and tap that into my GPS and drive on. It's just five miles away on country roads, and, before I can think, I'm there. It looks like a smaller version of Earl Yoder's farm. There's a small stone house with a smaller white stucco addition, a combination I think is beautiful, for a second, before I regain my bearings. The barn is backed into a hill so it must be what's called a bank barn. When I pull down the dirt driveway a couple of hundred feet, I have to decide whether to drive to the barn, fifty feet to the right, or stop and park and assume the house is where to go. There's a building, a shack really, in between.

Just driving onto their properties in a car feels like a violent invasion.

As I pause with my van in park, a bearded man appears from the barn. It looks to me like he's in his fifties. He's short and solid looking, not thin, not fat. He stands and stares at me, dressed in a wide, flat-brimmed straw hat and suspenders and I turn right, drive over slowly and park.

I grab some information and get out and start walking toward him.

"Hi, Mr. Bruener? I'm Lisa Macnayer. I'm the new rep from OhPa distributors?" I feel like I'm yelling.

He's nodding at me, not moving a muscle otherwise.

"Can I give you some brochures we have? I think we have a couple of new items you might be interested in." I'm three feet from him.

Nothing back but a hostile stare.

"We have a new Foster and Knolls engine that's more powerful and lighter."

"Don't need any. We're just cleaning a baler, so I gotta go."

"Okay. Want any brochures?"

He leans forward and reluctantly takes my handful of information.

I try to think. There are special prices for backpack blowers. The Amish wouldn't have anything to do with those.

"There is a fall special on chainsaws." I'm pointing at a page in a brochure with pictures and stats. "If you buy three of these new larger models, we can give you the same price as the old models and a year's dating."

He flips through the brochure for a few minutes and I shut up.

"Okay. Don't think so."

"Okay. I'll just go. I'll see you again some time."

He barely bobs his head and I retreat to my car. Pulling away, I look in my rearview mirror and see another man in a wide flat straw hat, younger, beardless standing in the broad doorway of the barn, watching me. Elam is nowhere to be seen. At least these guys are all committed to nonviolence.

I drive down the road slowly, trying to think. They hate the modern, messed-up, Goddamned world, so they won't even talk to me? It's a little after eleven. I pull over onto a narrow side road, not seeing any traffic anywhere, and scroll through my phone, trying to calm down, fighting tears.

Maybe I'll just find ways to screw-off. How would Ron ever know? Screw-off doing what?

I have to steady myself. After five aimless minutes, parked alone between the fields of grain or whatever they are, I relax a bit. I should get something to eat. Where? I brought some tea in a thermos and a banana and some almonds. The tea's still hot and tastes good and the rest does too, but I have to find some place with a bathroom. Ms GPS will tell me.

Eleven miles. There's a large gas station-convenience store at the corner of Cumberland Street and Route 30, so I stop for lunch. I don't need gas and I'll just park and walk into the store.

It's hugely air conditioned and reflecting morgue white everywhere and has the old Rolling Stones song, Midnight Rambler overhead, a song about rape and murder. Do these people know what they're listening to? I have to shake it off, but this hard white tiled, sanitized glare is jarring after the humid, old, pungent barns I've been in and I have to squint and fold my arms, trying to follow the sickening-cute signs to the Womenfolk's Room. The music follows me, now the soaring quaverings of Taylor Swift, on and on. Leaving the Womenfolk's Room, I make my way to a long counter with at least ten people waiting for or reading about a list of sandwiches posted on a white board above the counter. I'll take a chance on a, *small turkey, red pepper and lettuce sandwich on a short baguette.* I can't believe this place will have a good sandwich, but I'm taking it out through the broiling parking lot to the next pocket of air conditioning, my van.

And the thing tastes really good. I'm feeling forced to stare through the windshield at cars pulling in and out, but try to feel comfortable eating alone in this van. Civilized Boston is very far away.

Chapter Six

I'M FINISHED EATING AND THIS parking lot's glare is hurting my eyes, even with sunglasses. It's hard for me to see but I manage to tap a name from my dealer list into the GPS: *Stoltzfus Engine Repair*. The guy's Aaron Stoltzfus, so maybe he's a cousin or brother of the Rufus I saw yesterday. I've already seen names repeated a number of times.

The drive reveals the same spread of old, then new houses along the road and sometimes out into what were clearly farm fields just a few years ago. Without housing developments, the fields are fallow with scrubby looking patches of rose-hip thorn bushes and small red cedars. As I drive up 322, it becomes more and more spare. The land is fairly flat and open with only a few trees, cedars usually, along roads and separating fields of scrub. It's the fields that are visible for miles. Soon enough, the GPS says that 1768 Route 322 is next on my left.

Again, I'm driving down a long dirt driveway, about three hundred feet long. Ahead of me at the end of the driveway is a bank barn. Straight ahead is a large, white stucco-over-stone farmhouse. To my right is a new clapboard garage, painted white and instinct tells me the garage is the place to head for and, sure enough, there's a small sign over the door. It's the size and style of a four car, two story contemporary suburban garage, but they don't have cars, so I park in front and try to peer in. Still in my van, I see light through the small garage door windows, and it seems dim and flickering a bit.

I park and get out. I'm hearing a voice inside, I think. I open the door slowly. It's dark inside and I can barely make out any forms, but I step in, tentatively, and close the door. There's a coursing, singeing sound and a smell of something like burning oil. I make out two flames shooting out of metal pipes to my left. Two sky light widows are open above them. That's a relief but it still is hot and smells rank. Just as my eyes adjust, after turning away from the torches, a man greets me from about twenty feet back and I jump. He's standing behind a wooden worktable and, sure enough, he's working on a small engine. He was working. Now he's stopped, looking at me.

"Can I help you?" he says again, in a Pennsylvania Dutch accent, looking cow eyed.

I introduce myself and at the same time suddenly make out a whole series of eyes staring at me from behind a counter to the left of the door I just came in. Five kids, all in a row decreasing in height, are staring at me and not moving and not making a sound. Bright blond bowl-cut hair on all three boys and black bonnets on the two girls outline their faces, their gorgeous faces. None of them is over the age of ten, all silently staring, speechless, at me. The boys have on straw hats, blue shirts and black pants with suspenders and the girls long black dresses. I want to continue staring back at them but the man in the back of the room speaks again in his strong accent.

"I'll get Aaron here soon. He left for just a minute." He walks to the counter and, as the motionless children watch, he taps at a buzzer that must be connected to something somewhere – the house or the barn. It's a handmade gizmo that might be battery operated somehow. There aren't any electrical wires from the road to any of these buildings. He goes back to work, eyes on me at times while I stand waiting and staring back at the line of children. The metal pipes continue to singe the air inside, offering some light. The air isn't exactly healthy, but I'm oblivious, lost by the sight of the row of kids. Since these adults don't see outsiders much, kids probably never do. They don't watch TV or movies, the internet or even see magazines. Then, if they do see the occasional outsider, this way, a salesperson, they see men. I notice that they're looking at my clothes and at my hair. Old Order women cover their hair. Trying to not smile too much, like a crazy person, and wary I could frighten them away, like they're pixies, I step to the counter, nodding and smiling and say nothing. They gaze back, saying nothing, not moving.

"Hello."

Nothing back.

There's movement out the open window that makes me look the same moment they all do. A man dressed like the kids, but with a beard and straw hat, is on a child's kick scooter, scooting down the hundred foot path from the house toward us. I've read about them using scooters, but still can't believe it. Scrapping and a squeak or two from the scooter precedes the door opening and a tall, gaunt, late forties Aaron Stoltzfus enters and introduces himself, filling the interior's silence with his deep, German accent.

The abrupt sounds of his voice and mine stops and only coursing sounds remain for an awkward second or two. I collect myself enough to address the kids, the beautiful kids.

"I see you have some helpers."

"Yah." He looks at them and says something in German. All five of them stream in single file from behind the counter, barefooted out the door.

"It's after three o'clock and they have their chores," Aaron says.

"Right." I speak slowly. "Well, I'm Lisa Macnayer and I'm the new Territory Representative for OhPa. I wanted to come and say hello and ask if you need anything."

"No. I'm okay for now."

"Okay."

Silence, except for the other guy moving his engine around. Some crackling sounds coming from the counter and Aaron excuses himself and walks to a white plastic plumbing pipe running out the window and up a hundred feet to the house. He yells into the pipe in Pennsylvania Dutch, then listens with his ear to it. Some female crackling back and he has a few more words with the person at the other end and I guess it's about the kids because I think I hear the word, *kinder.*

He's back to facing me, wishing I'd go away, and I've had a day of that, so I say goodbye and head for the door.

Outside I say, "If you do want to place an order, do you mail it in or . . .?"

He's standing just outside the garage with me twenty feet away, next to my car door.

"Yah, I have a telephone there." He points to a small wooden building halfway between us and the road, plopped in the middle of his long, wide front yard. Jesus.

There's nothing I can say, ducking my head, getting in the van, and leaving as quietly as I arrived.

It's just after four-thirty so I push the button on my cell phone for Stuart's cell phone.

"Hi. How's it going?"

"Fine, I guess, out here in the bush. How are you?"

"Okay. Getting some unpacking done."

"Good. No, I'm fine. I'm just unfolding myself talking to you. I can't wait for the weekend, two days away. How was your day? How are the kids?"

Stuart says, "They're fine. Yeah, I got a few things done, even though it doesn't look like it. Allison, no-no. Don't touch. Not safe, not safe. Yeah, she wants to put her fingers in the sockets."

"God! We need safety plugs. They're packed."

"Yeah, I haven't found them yet, but there are still about seven boxes I haven't opened. But, so, what did you do today?"

For the next five minutes I relay what I did, spending most the time on the last visit. Part of the time, I can hear Stuart wrestling with Ally. It sounds like he's carrying her now.

"So you're driving around in a Winslow Homer painting," he says.

"Yeah, in his late, hate period."

He doesn't laugh. "Yeah, it actually sounds fairly dark."

"A little. I was just hyperventilating some humor."

No laugh, again. He clears his throat, mumbling, "Anyway."

"Well, I'll be home in twenty minutes. We can have pasta with that sauce we bought. How's Keith?"

"Okay, I'll start boiling the water in twenty minutes and get the pasta going later. Keith's great. He's outside in his tree."

"Any friends yet?"

"Yeah, I don't know."

"The school still seems okay?"

"I think so, so far, yeah. But who the hell knows?"

"What are we going to do if it isn't?"

"Send him to an Amish school. I don't know. We. . . yeah, I don't know."

"Okay. I'll see you in twenty minutes."

"Okay, drive carefully."

Stuart used to talk about all sorts of things before he was a shut-in. I drive on.

Why did we move out of Boston? It was back there, me just out of Boston University, where I met Stuart. There he was -- tall, lean, straight backed, thinning blond hair, Stuart, in his elegant white shirt and dark stripped silk tie, meeting me at the back door of the Museum of Fine Arts.

Before I arrived, I thought, whoever this guy is who's going to interview me, he'll be much too conceited to hire me. Obviously, BA's in art history are a dime a dozen and I was nervous. Then, there he was, looking just as old fashioned and self-possessed as I had fantasized. But he was polite, really polite, as he asked me questions and described the position of matting and framing works of art on paper. And I got it. I couldn't believe I got it, and then I called Mom and Dad and told them I wouldn't be moving back to Pittsburgh. My life was my own and my life was so amazing. I raved to them about how Stuart worked for curators who chose prints, drawings, watercolors and photographs for exhibitions. Stuart prepared all those exhibitions and my job was to help him. The parents listened quietly until I stopped raving and then we all said a short goodbye. I half knew I was annoying them, saying bye-bye blah-blah Pittsburgh.

Stuart and I talked a lot while we worked, about everything. He talked about wanting to start an art conservation center for all the small museums in New England and I said he should do it. I knew he was dating one of the conservators in the museum and, of course, he heard about my problems with my boyfriend, but Stuart and I seemed to avoid flirting. He was a lot older. He was the most mature and insightful person I knew. He actually seemed to like hearing about my family and my ambitions, and I needed that.

I liked hearing bits about his past. Stuart Macnayer, born in Brooklyn, moved up to Liverpool, a village outside Syracuse, New York when he was almost six. He was the youngest of three. He described his family, basically, as corroded and he had very little to do with his parents or his older sisters. There was that time when he said he was, "the only neurotic hick in a family of neurotic Brooklynites."

He wouldn't say much about it back then, but I got that his father had a drinking problem that kind of ate up his family. He referred to his family in the past tense. I pointed that out, after we worked together for a year or so.

So he went to Syracuse University, then Tufts for graduate school, then spent two years in Oxford at the Ashmolean Museum doing what he described was a, "haughty version of a museum studies internship." He spent half of each day there with the paper conservator and the other half matting old master prints next to a retired English army Colonel. Sounded like iconic coolness to me.

I finally got rid of my stupid, immature college boyfriend, and Stuart was no longer dating the sorry bitch from Conservation. Thank God for all that. But I was going to leave the museum. The funding for my job was drying-up and I told Stuart I was applying to insurance companies and various manufacturers around the country for jobs in sales. After two years, I was leaving icons for the real world.

It was one day around that time that Stuart and I were having a pizza lunch across the street from the museum, like so many times before. I asked him if he liked Syracuse University. He always talked about high school and Tufts and Oxford, never Syracuse.

He said, "Yeah. I was really lucky to go there. My parents paid for it all and it's not like they had a lot of money. But I was such a lousy, immature student. I bombed some courses in high school and then went to a community college and finally did some work. And then, there I was somehow at Syracuse, on a sumptuous college campus surrounded by thousands of permanent adolescents inside those artificial boundaries, not reading a tenth as much as I did in high school, not enjoying the parties, feeling like a stupid brat when I wanted to feel accomplished and important. Then senior year, I started to fail a bunch of courses and I got a girl pregnant."

I was used to intimate conversation with Stuart, but this was suddenly weighed down, heavyhearted. I waited.

"Yeah. I did. I was an idiot. She was just a girl I dated a couple of times and so…"

"What happened?"

"We got married." He was looking passed me somewhere. "We thought it was the right thing to do. Then we tried to get along for almost a year, but we didn't really like each other at all. And then someone else married her and adopted the baby. A guy who actually liked her and knew she and I were not at all serious, yeah, he married her. And college ended and we all moved away. They had a bunch of kids and live in Rye, outside New York City."

"The child?"

His eyes met mine for a second, then we both looked away. "Martin…Marty. Uh, I haven't seen him for years, about twelve years. The last time I saw him he was just a baby. I spent a few years writing to him through Lucy and Greg his stepfather. They sent me some pictures. After a few years they very politely let me know they didn't want to confuse Marty with too much noise about some biological father who was off somewhere else. Marty was a part of a family and I'd only make him think he wasn't. I dematerialized since it seemed like the best thing to do for him and I just made it clear in a last letter that he could see me if and when he wanted to."

I was stunned and just sat, trying not to stare at him, neither of us finishing our pizza.

"Anyway, sorry. I don't know why I just said all that to you."

"Syracuse University?"

"Yeah, I guess. I grew up a bit after that. I hate dating for fun and chronic sex. Sorry."

We both flinched and I was speechless, and he saw that. He said, "Sorry, sorry. Really, I didn't mean to get weird." I nodded.

He said, "I know I'm not responsible for Western Civilization decaying."

"I don't decay Western Civilization."

Stuart gave me his puzzled smile. That got me laughing in a twitchy sort of way.

Hardey's Pub, where we were sitting, was almost empty. It was a nighttime hangout and always so dark and almost empty in the middle of the day. I could hear the Green Line trolley cars clanking past us outside, but the windows next to our booth were painted or something. Maybe just covered in grime. It was May and sunny but all I could hear was the trolley and the cheesy pop music coming somewhere out of the stains in the cheap old hung ceiling. I'd be leaving the museum and probably Boston in a month. I really noticed he wasn't looking at me. He seemed to be trying to not look at me for the previous few weeks.

"Anyway, I'm a lot older than you and I've messed up and so you have to listen to me lecture you, whether you want to or not."

"You're not that old. You're not that much older than I am."

He grinned at that, which embarrassed me, and I said, "What? Why are you laughing at me?"

"Uh, I'm not laughing, Lisa. Wow, you actually have to learn the difference between laughing and barely smiling. No, it's just that there is a big difference between being twenty-four and thirty-three. Hell, I'm well on the way to being bald."

"Oh. Well, I'm not so immature."

"No. No, you're not immature at all. Nope, you're . . . yeah, no you're fine."

He was stumbling theatrically despite himself and I had expected a pithy response.

I said, "Emma Zondag offered me her condo in Portsmouth, New Hampshire for this weekend and I don't want to go alone." It was suddenly airborne.

It hit the table between us like a two-ton carcass. He went pale and so did I.

"No, just as friends. Sorry," I added.

He was looking at me now. "Uhh, yeah . . ." He was just barely shaking his head, starting to frown.

I must have looked crestfallen because he turned himself around. "Okay. Let me see if I can."

"I didn't want to do anything," came out of me.

Jesus. Could I be any more insipid? Now I was insulting him?

He took on a stern look, the way he'd get sometimes. His eyes got bluer, much bluer and the skin on his face tightened. We stopped talking and just left the ugly damned pub.

But there were some dragged out, painfully quiet hours back in the museum. Endless dead air. Just as we were ready to finally leave for the day, he asked me if we could talk. Jesus.

The paper conservators in the next room were gone for the day and we were totally alone. I knew he had some heady issue with me, something to do with my sad, little degenerate weekend invitation. I could feel myself stiffen and blush as I nodded at him and stood still, wondering what his actual problem was.

"Yeah, Lisa, we have to talk." He paused to get my full attention. "I mean we've worked together for two years and you're leaving, right? You're moving away and then you asked me if I wanted to go away for the weekend with you. And that's fairly tricky. Sorry. It's important for things to be a little more, uh, clear or something."

"Oh. Clear?"

"Yeah. Also, because we're friends but I'm a guy and I don't think there's any way we could be just friends going to Emma Zondag's place in Portsmouth. Sorry. You might think I'm really old fashioned or something, but maybe you should ask Beth or someone."

"Oh, okay. That's fine."

Beth? I could barely talk to Beth. We had lunch a few times because she was my age and worked in the museum's Registrar's office. Who cared about Beth? I hated the way this had turned into him scrutinizing everything, fussing so much.

I said nothing and he just looked unyielding and said nothing, shutting down. He turned away and started poking at a few things on the matting table. I was grinding my teeth, getting really bugged, moving a few things on my own matting table. And I knew he was right. I was going away, and the invitation was just plain stupid. What was I, ten?

Stirring that way for a minute got me to say, "I'm not used to guys talking about things this way."

He stopped poking at things and turned to me. "Yeah, sorry. I know. It's okay. I told you I'm old and stuck in the mud. I just like a few rules of some kind. You know, I live and pray for even the tiniest bit of clarity in the mud. And going away on a trip with someone of the opposite sex is usually a date in my dying little world."

Now I liked the way he was being funny. This was the Stuart I was used to working with and yapping with every day.

"Usually?" I said.

He smiled just a bit, looked down, waited, then said, "Yeah, I don't know. There are women I hang around with in that nice, friendly way. Sure, I've been friendly once or twice. But I don't want to be that friendly with you. Sorry."

I said nothing.

He added, "You'd have to actually be a little boring."

I liked that a lot. We were staring right at each other from fifteen feet away.

"Maybe we should go somewhere and talk about how boring I am." It came out of me gently, but it did come out somehow, my heart pounding.

Mouth opened, he nodded at me. "Okay," he said quietly. "Okay."

We both looked away. We walked through the basement of the museum fairly quickly, making it out onto the street toward Simon's Brew House in Kenmore Square, near Boston University. We did it in about twenty minutes. We didn't look at each other and the bits of chatter were slim on content. I had never walked this far from the museum with him. Then, at the Brew House, and maybe because I sensed he wouldn't violate some antiquated gentlemanly code, but I reached my hand to touch him once we sat down, just on his arm for a couple of seconds, because he was sitting across from me in the booth and I wanted to point out the list of beers posted above the bar. I knew Simon's and he didn't and, now that I thought about it, the place seemed a little silly with him there. He was being reserved and seemed too old for the stupid, noisy little college world around us. Then again, maybe he was shy and hid it behind smooth Brooks Brother's white shirts and ties and amazingly beautiful, expensive shoes. We did talk, but just aimlessly and I just felt that high blood pressure pumping and churning everything. Something had changed between us and just changed in general. Later, after half-eaten club sandwiches and a beer each, as he stood in my Bay State Road apartment and I leaned near him to put on a light, I put my hand on his arm again. I really wasn't vain or deluded, and I knew he was very responsible and cool, but I was sensing just then that he might like me. Maybe really like me. Then I sat on my cheap college couch in my knee length skirt, feeling available and looked at him. He smiled into my eyes. I reached up and gently touched his leg and we looked at each other, all guards down. As I started to stand up, he started to sit down and we were on the couch around each other.

I really, seriously, did not want to move away from Stuart and he really, seriously didn't want that either. It had been a two-year long date and, together, it was seriously time to move on together.

Chapter Seven

HOME IN STUART'S AND MY driveway, the small stone hut's sitting over there like all the boulders around the property -- primordial accents to our frail little human family. This is just all very far from everything, even neighbors, whoever or whatever they are. The huge old evergreens in front and the huge old hickory trees in the back make the hut look stunted in the daylight.

A long, meandering Wednesday settles down and it's after dinner. The pasta tasted good. I want to sit out here on the front porch longer, I guess. The inside's a mess. Here, the porch roof over us keeps the mosquitoes to a minimum. There are bats flying high and low and crickets and the occasional high-pitched howl of a fox off somewhere in the dark woods or fields that surround us. The air is blowing clear and almost brisk, so maybe fall will come soon.

Stuart says, "I'll get started on the closet in the attic Monday. That should take me a week or two, fitting it in between time spent with Ally and Keith."

"You don't want to build a closet in our room?" I hate any talk about a future here.

"No, not really. Uh, if we leave that open, we can put a bathroom in there someday, you know, by extending the bathroom that's there now a bit. Then, we can have a closet and a decent sized bedroom with windows looking out back. Someday we can add onto the house."

"We have to pay our mortgage and credit cards. I don't know how you think we can afford anything else."

"I know. We'll just see in six months or a year or two."

I moan, "A year or two. Jesus." Sounds like forever to me.

Stuart glances, concerned. "I know. I just have to think about possibilities. Just in case scenarios. I'll stop talking about it."

"Yeah, really, please just go ahead and do some things but don't spend any money."

"When do I ever spend any money?" he says slowly, in a low voice, leaning forward and down.

"I know. I know. I'm just tired and wondering what I'm going to do tomorrow. My third day of work and I'm becoming totally unclued."

Stuart grunts a laugh at my word choice, but he doesn't say anything, and I hate my mood. We sit back and I try to shut up and try to enjoy the marauding biosphere around us.

Mount Zion in Lebanon County is up and over for me the next morning. The GPS wants me to drive on a highway, but I turn off its whining and look at a map.

No Amish today. The *Mount Zion Lawn Care* business is about the size of Marvin Zimmerman's and similar in look, except it's close enough to Route 422, so that it should attract a fair amount of business. According to my phone, the business buys a couple of hundred thousand dollars of OhPa stuff a year and is run by Lonny Huss. There are snow blowers and mowers out in front but I'm noticing there are no signs outside that say what products he sells. I go in the front door to a showroom filled with mowers and leaf blowers and chainsaws on the walls with Foster and Knoll posters. It's the standard design again with the counter in the back. There's a youngish looking, but probably middle-aged guy, possibly in his early forties, standing there gazing at a catalog.

I introduce myself and he shakes my hand warmly. Finally, here's a friendly person.

"Wow, so what gets you mixed up in a business like this?" he asks.

"Well, my family owns part of it. And I needed a job."

He shucks out a nervous laugh and I do too. He's around six feet and not lean, but not too hefty. He has thick dirty blond hair with some ginger roots that might reduce his age, but he has bags under his eyes that add years to his age, when you get close. He's wearing old jeans and a faded red *Mount Zion Soft Ball* sweatshirt.

"Yeah, well, that's how I got into this. My parents started this back in the sixties. That's them there."

I look at the picture on the wall behind the counter of Bobby and Louise, looking like the hair styles of the nineties, slicked back hair on both of them. There's a lot of brown and gray in the picture, in their clothes and even the wallpaper behind them. I find myself wondering why tastes change so radically over time.

"Great. So you run it now?" I put my folder down and lean one hand on the counter.

"Yeah. My father comes in still, but I pretty much run the show now."

"Great."

"Yeah, well business is tough. And customers get stuff at the big box stores or on the Internet. Yeah, they do their best to do-in smaller businesses like this. My Dad didn't have that shit around until he was older. He was it and everyone around came here."

"So, but, you repair engines for people too."

"Yeah, stuff they buy for cheap at those discount places that get it bulk and the manufacturers sell it to them for less. Then these customers, they bring it here to get fixed."

"That's not good."

"Sucks."

Lonny leans back when I'm silent.

"Yeah. So yeah, where you from?"

"Uh, my husband and I live in Becker's Hill, over in Berks County now. We just moved there."

"Becker's Hill? I think I've been there. You moved from where?"

"Boston. Yeah."

He raises his head. "Yeah? Huh. So, you're an owner of OhPa?"

"No. No, just working for it. My brother's an owner, along with a few other guys."

He looks at me with a blend of admiration, embarrassment, envy, frustration and I know probably some other urges and emotions. It's obvious this isn't an Amish man as he horny-gapes at me constantly.

He leads me back for a walk around the building. I'm feeling nervous. It's all behind the wall that's behind the counter in front. Back here is where Luke stands at a workbench bent over some engine parts.

"Luke deals with our computer system too. I'm good at that stuff, but I don't have time and Luke here is really good at it."

I make a point of shaking Luke's hand and looking at him for a second. I know, from seeing it at OhPa years ago, that people in back rooms get ignored. Luke looks like he hasn't washed in a while. He's around Lonny's age, forty, and short and thin and gray faced. His shy glances at me are almost morbid. I notice his teeth are mostly decayed away and what's left seem to have tobacco stains, since he's obviously chewing on some.

Lonny walks me twenty more feet to the rear of the building to his office, which makes me more nervous. The office is only big enough for a desk and two chairs. There are no windows. The old brown metal desk was designed to imitate wood grain, but just looks like streaks of fecal filth. I sit down across from him as he shuffles behind the desk, trying to sit down in his chair, wedged next to the unpainted cinder block wall. As I turn to check that the door's still open behind us, I see pictures of naked women all over the wall, cutouts from some magazine.

"Have any kids?" I ask.

He nods. "How about you?"

"Two. A seven-year-old boy and an eight-month-old girl."

"Well, I've got two girls, both teenagers. But I'm divorced. And, yeah those alimony payments are killing me. That, and I have to pay off my parents for this business. Yeah, I just got divorced last year." The bags under his eyes tremble and darken.

I want to get away from his eyes. "My husband and I were going to get a mower from somebody. Can I get it through you?"

He just stares, waiting for more.

"You have those Wright Standers. Can I get one from you? No discount, but could you deliver it?"

"Yeah."

I sit and listen to him describe the relative merits of the different models of mowers and their prices. I already know I want the mid-sized one because Stuart and I looked them up online and decided a week ago. But finally, thank God, we're leaving his office.

Lonny repeats his pitch again in the showroom and I'm hoping this transaction won't mean a lot of interaction. Standing and nodding, it's hitting me how awkward it would be if any of these guys ask me what my husband does for a living. This isn't exactly politically correct Boston or New York.

He takes me outside to one of the display models and shows me how to stand on it and start it. He rides it around on his large side lawn. The gleaming hunk of yellow machine roars. He's mowing in long, fifty-two-inch-wide, swaths, back and forth. I watch, standing in the shade of the side of his building. The sun's at a late afternoon angle but I'm not admiring the golden fall light and colorful leaves off in the distance. I'm wary of being alone with this guy. He drives toward me, his metallic, mobile sculpture machine cutting the six-inch-high grass effortlessly, growling.

"Try it."

I feel like a goof, but I step forward.

"You stand there on the platform, right over the wheel-base." Lonny points, one hand on my hip, standing very close to me. Soon I'm standing over the damned trembling wheel-base feeling like I'm almost over the middle of the thing.

"Yeah, get on it like it's a horse or your boyfriend."

This guy's in a lather and I've gotten myself standing in this position, but I'm getting the thing to lurch forward and now I'm worried that I'll jerk and spin out of control, and do a bit at first, but I just want to get away. The big machine below me has amazing torque and moves around so well and at least now I'm fifty feet away from the letch watching me. I mow like a pro for a few minutes and then manage to stop the thing and get off in front of him.

"Yeah, you got a little sweaty," he says.

Yeah, he's out of control.

"Nope. That's enough."

"Want it?"

I look at the mower and nod as I say, yes, and walk away quickly, back to the front of the building and, with him ten feet behind me, we enter his shop. He goes to the counter and I stand back looking at a similar Wright mower on display. I'm trying to pretend he's not a sad wreck and wasn't hitting on me.

I fix my eyes on the heavy orangey-yellow metal and, of course, I don't sell big, beautiful commercial mowers. Nothing this cool.

Some customers come and Lonny helps them for about twenty minutes as I wait. I leave after being there for almost two hours, half depressed for the sad state of Lonny, half for me.

Chapter Eight

TWO MORE WEEKS HAVE GONE by for me. At least today's Friday. I'm driving around in big circles, looking for momentary peace of mind. If I'm going to survive, I'll have to just go through the motions, driving around slowly in these large circles, showing up at Amish dealers, saying hello and leaving. If I want human contact, I'll call Stuart. Same as it's always been. Stuart and me versus the world.

Because Mom's coming for a visit. Later today. Zany yowl Tricia. I'll do my best to get along with her, but Stuart seems anxious to get Keith's room cleaned up. I wonder how much anxiety Stuart has building up over having to face his mother in-law with the fact that he isn't working right now. He is working, but he doesn't have what's called, a job. Tricia's never had a job in that sense, but still, Stuart has to know Tricia's not going to be impressed with the hut or his not working -- at a job.

Anyway, I told her she could sleep in the pull-out sofa in the living room.

Now I have to stop driving nowhere and finally pick some dealer to visit.

It's after five and Tricia's here.

She has on heavy white sneakers with just visible white socks and a light blue linen skirt an inch below her knees. Above that is a matching blue linen jacket and a peach colored blouse with a long, pointed collar.

Stuart gets her a glass of white wine and we all settle down, sitting here and there in the living room around her two large suitcases. Stuart bounces Ally up and down on his knee.

"Oh, I think she's a daddy's girl, isn't she?" Tricia uses a gravelly voice and flat vowels. "I was a daddy's girl too. It's wonderful being spoiled."

"She likes anyone who feeds her. No loyalty at all yet." Stuart squeezes Ally with his arm and Ally puts her head back against his chest, looking at her grandmother. This seems to confirm my mother's view.

"I tell everyone what wonderful parents you guys are. You love your kids and that's so great. I love it."

Stuart and I shrug, embarrassed, thanking her and I stand and walk into the kitchen to check the soup on the stove. Keith follows me. He doesn't know what to do with himself. I take another big swig of red wine from my glass. I hear the low murmuring voice of my mother from two rooms away just as I'm heading back with my hand on Keith's shoulder.

"I love seeing you two together. You make such a terrific pair."

"Thanks. It's great to see you too and great for the kids," Stuart says, stiffly.

"Oh, I wouldn't miss it for the world."

I sit down in the old striped upholstered chair near Stuart and across the room from my mother on the sofa.

There's a full gaping gap, then Stuart says, "So, you had good weather today, right? It's been beautiful here all week. This is a great time of year in Pennsylvania."

"Um. You're so visual, Stuart. I know you'll make this place look great." Tricia stares directly at Stuart until it's so awkward he looks away. Tricia drinks some more and sighs and puts her head back on a cushion. After a second, she lifts her head again and, after a few more minutes of chatting, mostly about the latest news about neighbors back in Pittsburgh and a few relatives in Florida, she tells me she's ready for the tour.

The word, *tour*, is absurd for the hut, but I shuffle on. And Stuart looks happy to take Ally and Keith outside as I begin to tell my mother about how the dining room would have been the kitchen a hundred and seventy-five years ago. We mount the old Pennsylvania staircase and there's the tiny bedroom that will be for Ally in a few months and there's the big bedroom. She says, "Uh-huh", after everything I say. There's the very ugly, but temporary bathroom, followed by the climb to the raw, very rustic attic. Back down, all the way down to the bleak kitchen I'm stirring the homemade vegetable soup and my mother's looking out the window at the expanse of back yard and beyond.

"I'm so surprised that you want to live so far away from things. You and Stuart always loved the city."

"Well, we do. We can't. At least we can't now. My job?"

Tricia seems distracted and waits a few seconds. She grumbles, "Your father would have hated this place."

I grit my teeth and stir the pot not saying anything as my mother walks around the kitchen. My father might have disliked the hut, or he might have even liked it. My mother's little caustic dig was more about my mother.

She shifts around, moving from the middle of kitchen to the far wall to look out the window facing the front yard. I don't want her to evade me.

"It's okay if you hate this place, Mom. Mom? Really, I have to ask. On the phone every week you constantly ask me if I can do this job, but what's the deal with this company? I mean, it's our family company, or it was our family company, and I've always had the feeling we weren't allowed to talk about it. No questions, but then you said that no women could be owners that time. What the hell?"

Tricia's face goes pale and flattens out. Her mouth slackens and she walks to me awkwardly.

"Oh, sweetie, I know you can do the job."

She reaches me and hugs me and looks straight into my eyes. I turn to rock maple, totally hating the cloying and deflection.

I manage to step back. "Yeah, thanks Mom, but please, really, answer my question. Women can't be owners?"

"Oh, that was years ago. I don't know how it is now."

"But what don't you know?" I don't want to just vent. "Never mind. Please, let's back-up. You never had the option of owning the company?"

"No. Oh-no, I never wanted to, Lisa. Daddy wanted that sort of career. I wanted to be at home with you kids."

"Right Mom. We've had this part of the conversation tons of times before. What I'm trying to ask you is, were you ever offered a serious position at the company? I mean, it was your father who started it and ran it. Daddy was married to you. What was going on?"

"Oh, nothing. You have to understand. We were all less . . . oh, I don't know what the word is . . . ambitious then. Everyone wants to do so much more now."

I feel my temperature rise. I hate the way my mother slithers sometimes. It's just another form of Goddamned shunning.

"Want to or have to?" I pause. "But Mom please just answer the question. Why were you never given the option? Please, please stop only saying you didn't want it. Was it offered to you? Because it wasn't offered to me. I might have looked uninterested, but the right thing to do would have been to offer something to me, or at least discuss it with me."

"Oh, I'm sorry Lisa. You were so happy in Boston."

"No, Mom! Please answer the question."

"What? Why are you so upset? Is it all the pressure?"

"You won't answer the question, will you?"

"Oh, Lisa I don't even know what you're asking me. You seem so..."

"Were ... you ... ever ... offered ... ownership ... of ... the company!? Jesus Christ!"

Tricia shrinks and steps back. Looking like a wounded cherub, she just shakes her head, and no one, including Tricia, knows all the things she's shaking at.

I sneer. "Can you answer the question?"

"No. I was not offered the company. I wanted Daddy to have the job."

"But . . . what? Daddy was never offered full ownership. What the hell?"

"Daddy didn't want that. He couldn't run the whole thing. It grew and your grandfather knew it would take more people to run it."

This is my mother's constant refrain, even said to me as a kid when my father was still alive, but not in the room.

"Jesus, Mom. I can't believe it. It's so insulting. Plenty of people run businesses a hell of a lot larger than that."

My mother looks exhausted and just shakes her head. "Daddy was wonderful, but he couldn't run the whole company."

"Wow. I can't believe you say that. Clearly, he was more than capable. But your father didn't want that, did he?"

I'm staring at my mother, who now has that pinched angry expression she gets when she feels threatened. The cherub is just a bitter little girl.

I have to push, or I'll never get her to answer anything. "So Grandpa made a point of not offering you anything. Amazing. And you claim he and Grandma spoiled you. And you claim he even stated that no women could be owners and then no one objected when he split up the company three ways. Does Ron complain about any of this?"

"Oh, Lisa, Ron loves doing his job and he's done so well. He never complains that he doesn't own the whole company."

I hate this dead end.

"Why not?"

Tricia straightens up at this. "Lisa, I don't know how things work in business. I'm going to wash up. I know you're very upset and I'm sorry, but I think we need to cool down before we say things we could be sorry for."

Chapter Nine

LYING IN BED WITH STUART feels better, tucked in and away from my mother below. At a little before twelve, that compressed wax and wood pulp log in the fireplace has been burning for twenty minutes at least. I'm glad I told Stuart about the argument and glad we both just shrugged it off, and that we're not talking about it now. Repression works sometimes.

"What are we going to do tomorrow?" I'm whispering, looking across the room at the orange and yellow light from the fireplace flickering on the light gray and white shadow speckled walls.

"The Philadelphia Museum of Art?"

"No. It's too far."

"Okay, then how about a drive through Amish Country?"

"Yeah, that's good."

"But Keith might get bored. I'll try to spend some time with him while you do things with your mother."

"Great. I'll have to be extra, extra nice to her now, since I went at her like a piranha today."

He grumbles a laugh and grabs me and then he leans forward as I wait and he whispers how gorgeous I am. I push back against him, but there isn't anything I can do right now except drift away with him. Mom's right below. Maybe watching the light from the fire show will anesthetize us.

The drive in Stuart's car has taken an hour and basically the rest of this drive should eat-up the middle part of Saturday. We've seen some landscapes, a lot of other tourists and had lunch in a Panera Bread on Route 30. And now we're seeing a few horses trotting up roads pulling buggies. Stuart's driving us to Lititz. Sure enough, there are some Amish out in front of a small shopping center and Tricia asks Stuart to stop so she can buy some lozenges for her drive home on Sunday. Stuart parks as far away from the buggies as he can, and we get out of the car.

I have my arm around Keith's shoulder and lean down to whisper, "Try not to stare."

Stuart has Allison facing him, but as we approach the buggies and a group of about ten Amish women all in their traditional clothing, Ally turns and looks. The women have on long dresses and bonnets.

Tricia veers toward the group. They're all either focused on talking to each other or purposely ignoring us.

"I just love the way you dress," comes out of my mother. It's aimed at a small group of three or four young and middle-aged women, who look startled and turn and nod at my mother, who stands grinning at them with the vaguest gaze possible. She repeats her statement, this time adding that she thinks, "It's wonderful". They nod again, vaguely, and turn away.

Stuart, the kids and I are twenty feet away by now trying not to participate in any way. My mother lumbers to us as we wait. I'm mortified and Stuart's an odd shade of blue and he's walking away quickly, with Allison in one arm and his hand on Keith's back, pushing, moving toward the CVS pharmacy door. Stuart has low tolerance for goofball public displays.

"You two look like it's embarrassing to do anything with your silly old mother," Tricia says this to me nudging me with her elbow as we walk into the bright indoor lighting of the pharmacy.

"Yup. People usually try to leave them alone, Mom. They probably don't want us doing that."

"Oh, I just thought I'd be friendly. Why not? And I do love those old-fashioned dresses. I think I'll start dressing that way. How about that? That a good idea?" Her low, gravelly voice and then chuckle is aimed at that part of me she really doesn't like.

"Uh-huh. I think you just reduced a whole culture to a stupid fad." I step away after saying this.

"Well, Stuart, don't you think I'd look good dressed that way? That's what I'll do, is ask them where I can buy some clothes just like that?" Her voice is still low but she's grinning at glowering Stuart who's only a foot away. "Oh, I'm just kidding. I won't embarrass you anymore. I know you're both so sorry you have to take me out. I'll be quiet for the rest of the day. Okay, Keithie, you want your grandmother to stop being so friendly to people?"

She has her arms around Keith from behind. He smiles as she hugs him. Then she's off, down an aisle with him and then another looking for lozenges.

Moping along, we've spent this next day in a series of forced, guarded conversations mixed with walks and naps. Finally, it's dinner time. Tricia has invited us to the Olive

Garden on Route 100 and after an hour in our slimy little bathroom, Tricia's downstairs ready to go. We walk out over the cement slab toward the car.

"I think it's so good that you have this big cement piece here already. I like your idea of building over it," Tricia says this to Stuart.

"Someday."

"Oh, I'm sure you'll do something with it. You're the magic worker and I know you'll work hard to make all this nice for your family. It just takes time. We all have to start small and work for what we have. We never know what life's going to throw at us. It's tough, but that's life." The last bit's said to her skirt as she brushes at it, walking.

She's all dressed-up in a long yellow, pleated cotton skirt and a cream colored, crew neck sweater over a blue collared shirt. She has on low cream colored heals. The rest of us, including Ally, are a few degrees less dressed-up. I have on jeans and a green turtleneck and Stuart has on tan cords and a charcoal sweater. We go in her car and Stuart sits in front to point the way.

Stuart takes Ally from me as we walk slowly across the parking lot. Stuart always wants to beat people to the front of lines. I always want better parking places. We're both thwarted this time. Mom drove slowly around the lot three times, while the line grew, and the parking spaces got filled. Realizing we bug her as much as she bugs us, doesn't always help.

We get into our spot against the inside wall with what Keith calls our, "alarm light. He's excited the square plastic device will blink lights and vibrate when, finally, it's our time to be seated. Guessed at by the restaurant staff to be around twenty minutes. I'm not waiting for the fun to start.

"Here, let me take Ally for a diaper change."

Stuart hands her over and I walk away from the conversation about smoking led by Tricia. A young woman was standing on the sidewalk outside having a cigarette, triggering Tricia's story, one more time, that she quit decades ago and hates the smell and hates the sight of cigarettes.

I was already lost in my own private doldrums.

We wait and we wait, then we sit down. Eventually, we order. Ally is not having fun. If she isn't crying, she's wrestling to get free from this boring booth, this soft padded feeding pen we're all wedged into.

"Yeah, this is why we don't go out. One reason. We don't know any babysitters where we are now and it just all gets too expensive," I say, watching Stuart try to rock Ally to sooth her.

"Oh, I think she's a testy one. Umm. Crabby Ally. Is that what they call you?" Tricia's already on her second glass of white wine and looking a bit spacey.

Stuarts steps right in. "No, she's just too young for this. Plus, she missed her nap today."

"Um, it takes work and sacrifice. You two work so hard at it. It's wonderful."

Stuart and I nod.

I want to rebuild. I sit forward and glance around, sprightly. "This is great, a really nice break for us and we really appreciate it, but I've never seen cooking as work. I eat lunch out every day, even though most of the time I take stuff to eat on the road, and then I like to get home and make something."

Mom bobs her head gently, solemnly. "I know. You work so hard and it's not easy these days. I remember all the work and it gets harder and harder as kids get older. Sorry to tell you that!" Her little lilt at the end is like sandpaper across my spleen.

"Okay. But we're not complaining," I say, urgently, not wanting anyone in the group, especially Keith, who might or might not be listening, to think I'm a reluctant mother in some way. Jesus Christ.

Mom says, "I know. Just enjoy them when they're little, even with all the work. Later on is when it gets more challenging than fun." She's taking another sip of wine.

"This is what we're doing," Stuart says. "That's the point. There's nothing else we want to do but raise a family." He says this the way Stuart says things sometimes, pointedly aiming his face straight at Tricia.

Mom's busy eating now, looking annoyed. We're all eating, looking annoyed, except Ally. Ally likes the apple slices I gave her. Keith's just tired of being hemmed in.

Mom says, "Well, kids. All I can say is, it's your turn now. Yup. Sorry, but I did it and I'm finished. I did my bit and now I get to watch you do it."

Tricia's doing her sassy bit. We chew through dinner, thank her for it and finally all get to bed around nine-thirty.

The next morning I say goodbye to my mother in a hushed voice, leaning over the convertible sofa to kiss her on the forehead.

She moans, "Um, it was wonderful seeing you. I hope you can come home for Thanksgiving."

I stand back up. "Yeah, we'll see, but I guess we can. I don't think we can do both Thanksgiving and Christmas. Just one."

"No? Oh, that would be too bad. You just decide and tell me. Bye-bye. I love you. Good luck with your job today. I know it's really hard and you work so hard. I'm so proud of you." Mom's still lying flat, throwing some kisses with her fingers as I step back, waving and saying goodbye. Then I turn, ten feet away.

"I will be able to do this job. Don't worry. Bye."

I walk away quickly.

Chapter Ten

I'M WALKING INTO MARVIN ZIMMERMAN'S, remembering the last time with the Bears. Marvin's behind the counter again, but there's a woman there. She has on a small thin white bonnet and a long, wide wool dress with a shawl wrapped around her shoulders, looking like a woman in a Civil War photograph.

They stare at me as I step up to them and introduce myself.

Marvin knows who I am. "Yah, Lisa this is my wife, Ester Mae."

I'm surprised. We all nod and nod again.

"Ester Mae works with me when she has time."

More nodding.

"I do have the pricing on new Foster and Knolls engines," I say.

"Good."

"You said on the phone you needed to order some more things? Some parts?"

"Yah, if you have some time, we can place an order today? Silas and Gideon need me to help with some repairs in the back. So can you help Ester Mae?"

I nod, wondering what I'm getting myself into. I put my backpack on the counter and pull out some order forms while Marvin walks away, and Ester Mae continues writing down notes on a pad of paper. Nothing is said for a few minutes. I wait by shuffling around, glancing at the showroom mindlessly.

She coughs and asks me if I'm ready. She reads from her pad and I fill in the order. It takes twenty minutes because we're not interrupted. The one customer who comes in is just picking up an order he's paid for.

As I'm packing up, I hesitate asking, but can't resist. "How many children do you have?"

She seems startled. "Four sons and three daughters."

I'm amazed at so many kids, even though I know a lot of Amish and Mennonites have even larger families.

There's a pause before she asks, "And you?"

"Yes, two. A boy and a girl." I feel very spare and modern revealing that.

She smiles, her crowfeet accents softening her hazel eyes. And we stand wordless. It occurs to me that she's probably only a few years older than I am. She doesn't wear any makeup. I only wear lipstick, but I wear streamlined, expensive clothes in comparison and I've only had two kids.

Some customers come in and I walk around the showroom while she deals with them. They're all men and most of them have long beards. They all stare at me at times with that far away gaze that I'm almost getting used to.

After fifteen minutes of fairly leisurely conversation in German, the three men leave with their engine parts.

"Is that it for today?" I ask.

"Yah. Marvin and I did an inventory and that is it for now. Thank you. You could have gone."

"Oh, that's okay."

She stands and waits.

"Well, so it's good that you can work here. Your children are at school?" As this dribbles out of me I want to stop myself but it's too late. I have no idea what she wants to do or has to do, or what she thinks of English wenches like me roaming her countryside.

"Yes, I only work here some days while my young ones are in school and when I don't have work in the barn. The animals." A pause with both of us lagging. "And, you? This is your family business?"

"Uhh, sort of, yes. My grandfather started it." There's no way I could tell her anything about my life.

We smile, still in a holding pattern, and I should back away and leave. But I don't.

"Can I ask? Does it offend Amish or Mennonite people to have a woman doing what I do?"

Her face tightens and turns red. She lowers her head and shakes it. "No. No, I hope no one has been rude to you."

"No. I just worry that I'm stepping on everyone's toes a bit every time I do this job."

She looks transfixed. Her tense face and narrow eyes are making me really regret knocking on this door.

"Sorry. I shouldn't put you on the spot," I say, flushed.

She shakes her head. "I work, like this." She opens her palms and gestures with her hands and pointing her head out toward the room we're in. "I work in my house and in the barn and here. We live by our work. Without it we don't live. And I'm most content when I work with my family and my community. Is that making sense?"

I delay all expression.

"It's honest work, like what you do, that makes us a part of the world."

I feel myself start to tear up. God, I have to take a step back. This woman will think I'm some sort of strung out psycho. I bite my lip and nod a few times, speechless. She's staring, looking concerned.

"The Amish and Mennonites too, will be careful with you. I can tell you something."

She leans forward and lowers her voice, "The person, Dale, said some things. He told a joke. I don't know what the joke was but Martin and Silas didn't like it, and there were some Amish customers here and they did not approve. They said it was very bad language and disrespectful about sex. When others were told, Dale was shunned. Martin still would buy things from your company, but not from Dale himself, if he could. That was, I think, two years ago."

"Oh. I'm so sorry."

"I don't think Dale was ever comfortable with us. Maybe he told that joke out of anger."

I stare at her. I apologize again and say I have to go. I want to leave. I find myself politely thanking her and backing out the room.

I'm driving on the farmland roads, weaving in and out of thought about that cramped conversation with Ester Mae. I'm sorry stupid Dale offended them, but I'm more and more convinced I'm never going to last in this arcane, awkward position. I can't actually talk to these Old-World people at all. It's bad enough Stuart and I have no chance at a social life but being so close to being shunned by the people I work with every day is living way too far beyond the pale.

It's seven in the damned morning and my phone's buzzing in my jacket pocket. It's mid-October and cool out so I'm wearing my old Ralph Lauren dark green tweed sports jacket. This is the jacket I wore in Boston years ago.

I walk outside through the kitchen door.

"Hello."

"Hello, this is Rufus Stoltzfus."

"Hi Rufus." Where does he have access to a phone?

"Hi, yah. I need your fall promotions. Last year we had them much earlier than this. So I don't know what to tell the customers is the cost. And I don't know if some new products are coming from the factories."

"I'm sorry Rufus. I really am. I'll phone OhPa right away and tell them."

"Okay." He grumbles something. It might be in Pennsylvania Dutch, or it might just be a guttural sound. Then he hangs up.

I stand there staring at the ground. There's a sensation all around me of pushing and pushing – forces around me, jamming against me with more and more force. I'm having a hard time breathing, hoping I'm not having a heart attack. I'm only thirty-eight. I'm sweating. I shuffle away from the house, still looking down. Stuart might think I have to get something out of the car. I go to the back of the car and lean against it, out of sight of anyone. It's not smart. Nothing I do can be smart now.

After a few minutes I begin to breathe more regularly. I have to make a doctor's appointment.

At a little after seven-thirty, standing in the middle of the old ragged kitchen, with Keith shouting something from the dining room and Stuart walking back and forth through the stone tunnel doorway, I thumb-click frantically on my phone.

"Bear – I haven't received any of the fall Foster and Knolls programs yet. Any chance they'll get to me soon? Some of the dealers have been asking. Thanks – Lisa."

I know the Bears get into the office around seven every day and work until four -- or five or six. They put in long hours. Everyone does at OhPa, including Ron.

"So, what happens for you today?" Stuart asks, as he winds up Ally on her swing. Ally's holding a white baby sock in one hand and a spoon in the other and she begins to swing back and forth trying to decide what to put in her mouth first. Stuart helps her by taking hold of the sock when she's forward on the swing. The swing cranks back and Stuart stuffs his thumbs into the little white folds and manages to get it back on her left foot without getting baby feet in his face.

"Ma-ma. Dee-dee, Da-da, ma-ma, eh-eh-eh. Yeah, Daddy took your sock away," Stuart's murmurs baby talk, mesmerized. He's looking at Ally like he wants to eat that cute little sock and the delicious little foot in it. My awful job situation, that's tipping toward critical, is beyond him and he has kid issues, cute little kid issues, to grapple with all day.

I announce, "I'm just driving over to the Lititz area. There are a few dealers I haven't seen there."

My phone dings a text and I look down as Stuart stands and waits.

"Hey, Lisa. Donny's still on it. He's been very busy, but the programs will be emailed out any day now. Got a phone call from Elam Breuner late yesterday with a warranty question on a Z Range Engine. Can you look at it?"

I feel myself get cold, my heart pounding. "Jesus. The Bear wants me to answer a question about some engine warranty. Shit. Elam Breuner."

Stuart watches my anxiety grow. "Is there a problem?" He stays next to Ally.

"Ugh! Yeah." Distracted, I walk to my laptop on the counter. I tap at it with my index finger, a technique I resort to, ironically, when I'm in a hurry and too frustrated to type. The page with Z Range Engines shows me pretty pictures and useless selling points and very little data even as I tap away, revealing other pages, until, finally, with Stuart watching and

Keith back downstairs from brushing his teeth and even Ally seeming to watch from her cranking swing, I find the page with warranty information. I mumble that fact to my audience.

"Good. Is that what you need?" Stuart's voice is tentative, trying not to be.

"Uhhhhh, no. It's just part of it. I'll have to tell this guy, this Amish man, whether whatever's wrong with the engine is covered by the warranty. I don't know anything about these engines."

Stuart leans down and stops the cranking swing and pulls a startled and disappointed Ally out of her canvas seat. That noise ends. He puts Ally on his hip facing him and walks slowly back and forth across the kitchen. Ally mutters, starting to complain a few times because she wants the swing, but each time Stuart increases the pace of walking or swings his body around to amuse her. Ally leans over and starts to gnaw on her father's shoulder, entirely pacified. I need to get away.

"I have a long drive."

"Okay. We're all set. Drive carefully. Call when you want," Stuart says looking at me and then Keith. Then he looks at Ally and bounces her up and down. I really have to calm down, by leaving. I know Stuart knows enough to keep his mouth shut, because I'm on the verge of quitting this Goddamned job.

Off I go and it's a long drive of fields and old houses passing by, some ugly. Gretzing. That's the Pennsylvania Dutch word for complaining. I can only gretz in my head. I just drive and drive and drive along mostly narrow country roads. I have to try to relax. I should make a doctor's appointment. I've already added almost ten thousand miles on the van. The breaks squeak when I press down with any force, so I'll have to have that looked at, somewhere.

It'll be my second time at *Bruener's Repair.* Elam Bruener needs technical information from me? Well he won't get any of that.

Part Two

Chapter Eleven

I GLANCE OUT THE LIVING room window. It's snowing out lightly. I hope the roads are all right. It was snowing early this morning but then it stopped so it probably won't amount to anything. That was the prediction on the radio. But I guess I won't take Ally out in it since I have to finish cleaning up. So no outdoor escape today until I pick up Keith at school. That's our adventure in space for today. Meanwhile, I just hope Lisa's okay driving all over hell out there, somewhere out there.

She said something about Willard somebody. Christ, the Amish names alone are from another Old-World time and place.

I dip the mop into the red plastic pail and stand still, looking out again. I'll call her later. The weather doesn't look like a problem for getting Keith from school in a few hours. Ally's looking tired to me over there. She's bored, sitting on the floor near the stairs, finished with the wooden train set and the cloth books. I'm back to mopping the living room floor. The dining room and kitchen are clean. Ally's crawling to me.

"Eh-eh, eh, da, de, da."

"I'll just take a minute, Allison. Allison A. Macnayer. Ally's a Macnayer. Ally, Ally Mac-mac-mac."

She stops and stares for a second, then complains and tries to kneel at my feet and reach up. She's almost ten months old and can crawl quickly and kneel and climb. She's been very patient for the last ten minutes and so I'm pushing the sponge quickly in another direction and put it in the plastic bucket. I pick her up. She leans toward the handle of the mop and I move us away.

We head for the couch at the far side of the living room wall and sit down. I put her on my knee and bounce her to her favorite, "Ally-Ally, Allingham-Macnayer, sat in her chair in order to stare, at all the world around."

She has her fist in her mouth and looks at me for more of that. So I hug her with my face in her neck and then repeat the same thing, the bouncing and rhyme.

She laughs, so I repeat it. She laughs harder, so I do it again. She loves repetition. I'm not wild about repetition but I love her laugh. I do it about ten times until she's drooling and no longer laughing, just needing something else. It's only a bit after twelve so at least an hour too soon for her next nap. She likes to be tired for her naps, or she'll make a racket instead of sleeping, and then, she'll get overtired and my life and hers and, maybe later Keith's and Lisa's, will be a long roller coaster ride in the dark.

As I'm walking into the kitchen with Ally on my hip facing forward, she's chewing on her right hand.

I aim her at the window looking out to the front, where the sidewalk separates the house from the three tall evergreens. The road is up a hundred plus feet away. It's a cold, gray November day with no movement.

"Eh, eh, eh, eh, no-no-no-no, na-na-na." She's bored and getting antsy.

I walk a few feet over to the kitchen door and we look out at the side view. First, there's the foundation, or what Lisa calls the, "cement slab", that extends about twenty-two feet out. Why did the previous owners start to build an addition and stop?

"Ally? See the big tree? Daddy's going to clear all that poison ivy out of there in the spring. Yeah, bad poison ivy. Bad. It'll smother that big old walnut tree."

She's wiggling, wanting something else. I'm walking around the kitchen, wanting something to eat, knowing Ally should eat something. I don't want to put her back in the swing. She spent half an hour in it while I cleaned up the kitchen and even longer in it when we were all up first thing in the morning. It can't be good for a baby to be in a thing like that, cranking back and forth for hours. I'll wait and eat after she's in her crib taking her nap. I'm hungry.

Another early November day with Ally, alone on our hill in the woods. We just got back from dropping off Keith at school and I'm walking up the front yard at an angle toward the far-right corner of our property. All this raw space. Ally fits on my right hip like it's her chair, looking out at the morning haze of sun and cool damp air. Somewhere in the dense growth of lawn and trees beyond, birds fly by, high and slow. Finnegan, our orange cat walks behind us. It takes four or five minutes to reach the corner, where the lawn meets the road and the invisible neighbor's woods begin. I calm down this way, get into a rhythm, and so does Ally. If I'm her rickshaw, she's my compass.

The walk is already a morning ritual. Ally wiggles and moans and points to the grass. Her pudgy little fingers are stretched down and out.

"Nope, nope. Can't get down. Sorry, the grass is wet. It's cold and there's poison ivy around here."

If I stand still, she wrestles more to get free. We both turn to face back toward the downward sloping yard that supports the little solid white stucco-over-stone house and Ally and I pass on by a dilapidated wooden shed on the left and a stone spring house about seventy-five feet over to the right. The crabgrass lawn's more brown than green from the early November frosty nights. The lawn ends at an old wooden fence where the downward slope ends too, and the flat fields begin. Five or six acres of fields all lead to acres of woods way back. Fourteen freaking acres.

I head for the kitchen door. Glancing back for Finnegan, who's an indoor-outdoor cat, I see a raccoon walking, rambling toward us from the exact spot we've just been. I stare.

"See the raccoon, Allison? See? The furry animal?"

The raccoon moves toward us. It's a hundred feet away, hobbling awkwardly the way they do, but I begin to worry about it. They're nocturnal animals, so why's this thing out in the daylight? Why isn't it afraid of us?

The raccoon keeps coming. I turn and walk quickly twenty feet to the kitchen door. I get inside with Ally and look out the front window as the raccoon approaches and then slowly hobbles on by. I walk to the kitchen door and look through its window. The raccoon has made its way to the side yard and eventually stops at the boulders that border the property on that side, right before the thicket of woods that belong to the Calhouns, another invisible neighbor, with sixteen acres somewhere next door. The raccoon moves haphazardly around the large rocks, a few feet one way, then turns around and wiggles a few feet back.

"Okay Ally, how about sitting in your swing for a minute." Scuffling around the kitchen, I reach behind her and wind-up this cheap old thing Lisa and I found at a yard sale a few months ago. I hope she'll like it as much as she usually does. I give her a bottle and then head outside.

"Scram! Go!" I clap my hands and yell at the raccoon, fifty feet away. It slowly turns and sidles toward me. The damned thing looks big and fat. I'm moving quickly to get some stones from the driveway. I run back and get within easy reach for accuracy, about twenty feet, and throw as hard as I can, missing once, then hitting the raccoon on its side. It jumps an inch then ambles closer. I hit it again and it's the same thing. It hops up, then stands, then moves toward me. I hit it again, miss a couple of times, then hit it. Same thing, it hops a bit. The freaking thing's getting close.

I throw the last few stones as a group and head quickly back to the kitchen door. Inside I look out, and the raccoon isn't moving toward the house, but isn't moving away.

Ally's making her sound, "Eh. Eh."

"Okay, Ally," I say looking out the window. "We have a crazy animal out there. It's rabid, maybe, so what do we do? Damn."

I place her bottle back in her hands. She tosses it back onto the floor.

I wind up the swing again and go back to the door to look out and the raccoon is at the boulders again and so is Finnegan.

I open the door as quickly as I can. "Jesus cat, get out of there!"

Finnegan, who is on top of a boulder looking down at the raccoon and hissing, arches his back as the raccoon starts to reach up for him. Finnegan makes a few fantastically quick swipes at the raccoon and then jumps over it and runs away, down the yard. I have to think. We have nothing to use as a weapon. A rake or a shovel? There's no way that I'm going to attack a rabid raccoon with a shovel.

My phone's ringing.

It takes me few seconds to register who's on the other end. It's Gordon Zeagler, next door. I'm picturing the sixty something round guy and his wife who drive their pick-up truck past us once or twice a week without waving. He calls himself Gord.

"Seen a raccoon over there?"

"Yeah. It's in our side yard."

"Good. Yeah, it was over here after Jack, our dog. You gonna shoot it?"

"Well, I threw some stones at it but that did nothing."

That gets a grunt of disgust.

"I got a shotgun I can bring over. We don't need some fucking rabid animal biting Jack or one of your kids over there."

"Okay."

I have no time to think before he's off the phone. That one time I spoke with Gord was in the back woods and he thought I was hunting on his land. Then he quickly sized me up as an *upy* who probably didn't pose that kind of threat. Ally's finally bored and crying for release from the monotonous fifteen minutes in her swing. After picking her up and balancing her with one arm while preparing some food for her, I see the bent, oblong form of Gord out the kitchen window, walking across our back yard, toting a big black rifle. He's wearing baggy old jeans and a camouflaged hunting jacket, same as the last time I saw him. He passes the spring house.

I go out and stand on the cement foundation.

"Hi." I want to be friendly, but I don't want Ally near some crazy guy with a rifle. The raccoon's gone. I stand there ready to say that it's past worrying about, but Gord's on a mission and not paying much attention to me or Ally.

"It went behind the rocks. It saw me coming." he says without looking up at us and keeps walking to our side yard to where all the three or four-foot-long boulders rim the woods. I'm looking for the raccoon, but don't see it. Some of those boulders continue into the woods. Gord reaches the boulders about a hundred and fifty feet from Ally and me and looks behind one, aims his shot gun and, BAM! The noise surprises Ally and she jumps. Then, BAM! Gord shoots again.

"It's okay, Ally. It's okay." I was already covering her ears. I'm about to tell Gord that I have to put Ally inside when he turns and looks up at us.

"Got a trash bag? A heavy one?"

"Yeah. I do. I'll get one."

"Get two. This thing's big."

I'm living off my wife and just hanging around all day. There's something morally wrong with me. I've basically been telling these two police officers that as they fill out their report. Then I had to tell them again why I attacked a raccoon. Now I'm standing here with Ally on my hip and the two Reinhart Township police officers, one middle aged, stocky male and one slightly younger very stocky female are looking at me and at Gord as if we're their idiot concerns of the day.

"Raccoons come out during the day sometimes. They're nocturnal, but they forage for food during the day sometimes and this time of year they wake up sometimes on a warmer day like this." the older officer says calmly, tempering his disdain.

"Yeah, this one was sick. He kept going after my dog and my dog's big and mean," Gord says.

"Yeah, it probably could be rabies," the younger female officer says.

Gord turns away, barely able to hide his contempt. He's probably still angry I called the police. As I walked into the house to get the heavy black plastic bags, I imagined Gord and me picking up the dead, bloody rabid carcass and I still think it was smarter to call someone. The police arrived just as Gord was doing all of that alone. He did have on heavy work gloves.

Sure enough, one of the first things out of the male police officer when they arrived was, "Yeah, probably better if we throw out those gloves along with this raccoon. We'll call Animal Rescue and they'll send somebody out here to pick this up and test it."

They both have so many important bulges all throughout their dark blue tightly uniformed bodies. Both have a thick holstered revolver, next to mace or something, a wide black vinyl belt, special phones that crackle on and off, a notebook in their shirt pockets, badges, sunglasses and hats, all stretching around body parts I don't want to see.

"So, well, okay, you probably have to get shots for rabies. Your baby too. You had contact with an animal that might be sick. We don't know yet," the older officer says.

"What? Rabies shots?" I was assuming only Gord would have to get shots. "Ally, the baby, has to get rabies shots? Why?"

The young female officer speaks up, "Any contact at all with you…there could have been blood on you, and you picked her up." Her face of freckles darkens almost matching her red hair, a frizzled halo of red hair that wants to eject, en mass from some tight hold inside her police cap.

"The shots aren't bad. They're just regular shots. But you have to get a bunch. You don't want to get rabies." She shakes her head at me and then at Gord.

"No." The older officer shakes his head solemnly too. "Next time call us first. Or call Animal Rescue."

"Yeah, call Animal Rescue." She's proud to know how to do the correct thing and not have a stupid fit over a minor, natural occurrence.

I just stand penitently waiting for them all to leave. Ally's getting restless on my hip. Staring at these three strangers is no longer quite so interesting to her.

"Your wife...you said you have a wife working and another child in school today?" Mr. Officer asks.

I nod apprehensively. "Yeah, why?"

"They'll have to get shots too. Yeah sorry . . ."

She says, "Could be traces of blood on you. You track some in the house..."

"Oh, God. Really?" I step back wanting to get as far away from the bloody plastic bags as possible.

She says, "And, we have to quarantine your properties for a month. Board of Health requires that."

"Oh my God? You're kidding. What the . . .?" As I say this, Gord grunts.

Gord's storming off, cursing. They're standing, staring at him, probably wondering if he's a public safety concern. After all, he's carrying a shotgun and has just used it rashly. Nothing's said for a few minutes until Gord's on his own property entering the woods. They look at me. They've already asked me a bunch of questions about how and why I attacked a raccoon. Here I am holding a baby. Now they have to decide if it's safe to leave. I know. Day in, day out they have to watch losers of one kind or another lose control, flip out and descend into some form of reckless endangerment.

Why are there so many sorry jackasses unable to avoid being a danger to themselves and/or others? They're watching me standing there.

I try to relax. They're leaving, walking slowly up to the driveway. There will be a sign posted on the telephone pole at the foot of the driveway with the word, "QUARANTINED" on it. What a joke. Lisa might not think so. No friends over for a month. We don't have any friends.

Chapter Twelve

THERE'S THE JAGGED LATE AUTUMN dark gold light that shifts on the pumpkin colored antique floorboards. It holds my eyes for a long time. Something like clouds or maybe the curtain makes the uneven, moving pattern. I lie on my stomach the way I like to sleep sometimes and watch and listen. The wind outside our bedroom brushes through miles of woods on all sides, louder, then softer. It's so cold outside and Lisa and I like to sleep with a window open so it's almost as cold inside – a five-thirty in the morning damp cold. I get up quickly at that realization. Walking quietly but quickly, I have to get an allergy pill. I remember seeing the small plastic container on the bathroom sink in the night.

The bathroom's just as cold. I never had allergies before this. This damned house has me coughing and coughing, especially at night. It was a month ago that I went through those bouts of blowing my nose and sneezing non-stop. I could hardly breathe at times and got up and sat down-stairs so Lisa and the gang could sleep. My eyes watered and turned red, sore around the edges. I was barely getting any sleep. Mold and whatever other dust particles overwhelm the immune system of some people at certain times of the year. Doctor Philips told me a lot of people in the area were allergic to stone buildings, especially in the fall or spring. Lisa was sure the porous old field stone and mortar walls were, "the flushest possible living quarters for spores of every kind." Lisa claimed she read that somewhere online.

It's raining out, freezing enough for the windows in the kitchen to streak with wide gelatin stripes. I glance at Ally in her swing, cranking away and then look back out the window over the sink to the back yard. I have to look between the icy stripes. There's a large puddle where the yard meets the back fields. It must be at least ten feet by twenty and a foot deep. Damn, I'll have to do something about that. What?

Lisa walks in with Keith ahead of her. She comes to the same window, stands next to me and looks.

"Oh, God, is that rain or sleet?"

"Uhhh," I lean forward, looking out. "It's sleet. Can you stay home and do some paperwork and make some phone calls?"

"No. Not today. Leroy Toth at Penn Small Engine Supply is having an open house. Yeah, believe it or not, even in this weather. He sent out the invitations and he cleared his show room. No one will show up."

"But you will?"

"Yeah, I told him I'd be there, just yesterday on the phone when he was telling me the weather was supposed to be bad."

I stand. "All I can do is watch."

Lisa turns to me. "What?"

I shake my head. "Yeah, nothing. I'm here, that's all. I am here. God, I hated sitting around in Woodstock and at least here one of us is out doing something."

Lisa looks nailed to the floor. She doesn't say anything, so I do. "Sorry, Jesus, I don't want to make things worse for you. You know I'm constitutionally made to be available, but there isn't anything I can do for you, except housework and taking care of the kids."

I'm keeping my voice as low as I can manage under the strain I'm feeling, but I turn to see if Keith is listening. Keith's pushing at Ally's feet every time she swings forward and the noise of the metallic cranking of the swing probably obscures anything coming from his parents seven or eight feet away. Keith is fed, dressed, washed and ready to be driven to school.

"And you know how much I really love taking care of the kids. Nothing's more important," I lean toward her and whisper that, hoping she absolutely gets that.

"Can we talk about this later? You haven't said anything about anything for a long time, like about two years. And this suddenly came out."

"I know, sorry."

"No. I want to talk about it. I just have to go. It's hard to explain, but I really promised this guy."

It's after dinner and the kids are in bed. Lisa's reading to Keith and I've done the dishes and cleaned up the kitchen. I want Lisa to sit in the living room. She does sometimes. At times, if Ally's asleep, Lisa sits in a chair in the corner and reads or answers emails or watches old Jamie Oliver cooking shows on her computer. Tonight, I want her to sit in the living room.

I ask her to do that when she comes out of Keith's room, as I pass by her to say goodnight to Keith. She looks a little concerned but nods.

She's waiting for me when I walk in.

"You take your allergy pill tonight?" She watches me sit on the stripped chair diagonally across from her.

"No, I'm stopping. It's dry now. The walls are dry because the heat's on or something. But look, sorry but we have to talk." She's waiting. "I'm never going to get any work. I've done all the standard stuff. I mean, down here, out in the woods. Yeah, it won't work."

She looks mortified. "I know you've been trying."

"Right, yeah, not as much lately. In the last couple of months, I mean, really since we moved here it's been sort of a joke. Right? First there's all the painting and taking care of the kids. But I'm in my late forties and I don't have any contacts and I have an art museum background."

"No, I know. We've known that for a long time. Contacts are all back in Boston."

"Uh, yeah, from years ago. So really, that's it. Woodstock was a sick joke. Here, yeah, even worse. And I've profiled the hell out of myself online and get sympathy back. You know, sad people chat with me and commiserate."

Lisa says, "We need you here to take care of the kids."

I sit upright. "Yeah and Lisa, I'll keep trying to conjure up some consulting work, maybe in grant writing or something. But we know I'm just one of millions of sad sacks in fund raising and small museums don't have any money to hire anyone at all. Sorry. What more can I say? We've known this in the last couple of years."

"Well . . ." she drifts.

"Anyway, Lisa, I have to build something. I'll keep trying to create some income generating consulting work on the computer. But if we borrow the money, I can make the house, you know, ready for resale. It's what I can do while you're doing your awful job. Then if you quit in a year or less, we'll be able to sell."

"Quit? How much money are you talking about borrowing?"

"Thirty thousand."

She pulls her head back. "How are we going to pay *that* back?"

I stand up and face her. "Sorry, but I think we could get this place up to a level that would get us back more than we've put into it."

"What if we don't. If we can't sell?" She's twisting the arm of the sofa with her hand.

"My fear is we won't be able to sell at all, if we don't do this. And look, Lisa, you're not going to be able to do that fucked-up job much longer. I'm sorry. Maybe I could have found more of a standard house somewhere out here, down here . . . down and out here. But this place could be great once we add a bathroom, finish the kitchen and put a small addition on. I think we can make some money when we sell."

She's stuck, staring at me while I'm giving my pitch. She says, "For thirty thousand? Sounds more like a hundred thousand."

"No, not that much. But I know. I know. Thirty thousand is all we can afford for now. Most of the thirty thousand might go into just finishing the bathroom we have and maybe starting to fix up the kitchen. Obviously, you don't think this house could ever be worth a damned thing."

"No, I just worry it's not a good location for ever selling. If we owe a lot of money on it and we can't sell, that would be a nightmare. We'd be stuck here with no jobs. You think we're going to get that bonus. What if we don't? Plus, we need that bonus to pay down the credit cards."

"Yeah, I know. It's a gamble. If we don't do this, I think that's worse."

She gets up from the sofa. "I can't deal with this right now. I think it's a ridiculous risk, but I know you don't and you want something to do. I have to get to bed. Sorry, I'm exhausted."

She's just walking away from me. I have to ignore Lisa thinking I'm a dangerous idiot and just look into what some construction work would cost.

I'm awake pacing downstairs in the living room, having to think. It's three-thirty in the morning. It's the mold. The weather turned just warm enough to soften the frozen ground and moisten the stone and mortar and stucco and turn off the heating system inside. That's tonight's reason. There are nights I just can't sleep now.

There are nights when sleep is all I want and I get dragged out of bed by Ally crying or Keith waking up, wondering where he is. But there are nights I get up from some damned anxiety riddled dream. Then I start thinking and that means I'm awake.

Lisa sleeps. She jokes about how much she loves to sleep. She's always gone to sleep early, often around nine to nine-thirty.

I try to not say it to her too often because she gets embarrassed and Lisa hates getting embarrassed after growing up with Tricia, but the, early to bed, early to rise, habit might add to her beauty. Because Lisa's unbelievably beautiful. Her thin, very fine, very dark walnut hair glows and all she has to do is wash it in the shower, towel dry it and get it cut twice a year. She has that classic Gibson Girl hair, or hair like the women in John Singer Sargent paintings. She's never dyed it and there are some gray strands that just add an elegant accent.

In Boston, at the museum or in Back Bay at the Art Collections Care Center, yeah, people were agape. Lisa wore plain, elegant, expensive, conservative clothes that she bought for a song at secondhand stores in Boston. There's something about her understated, gentle, steadiness that draws people in. Jesus, it draws me in.

But we're off each other now. I'm useless and she's driving a couple of hundred miles a day, trying to connect with Amish men who think she's the female anti-Christ or something. Lisa's under all that Goddamned ridiculous pressure.

Chapter Thirteen

IT'S THE FIRST WEEK OF December so the roads have been slushy in spots and chunky in spots from that snowfall last week. We don't have far to drive, just a few miles, but I'm nervous because it's Friday night and around here guys in pickup trucks get drunk after work and come around corners on the wrong side of the road. There are no streetlights anywhere and the only thing I can see is the narrow white tunnel carved out by my headlights. I'm driving Lisa and kids to the Abramowich's. Her name is Cora and his name is Bruce. I have to practice memorizing names. I've met her a couple of times and only saw him from a distance once, at a PTA meeting. Their son's name is Shawn and he's been over to our house twice to play with Keith. I drove Keith to their house one Saturday. Cora, Bruce and Shawn. Cora, Bruce and Shawn.

We pull down a long driveway crunching less now because the narrow driveway's been plowed well and, after a hundred yards the Jeep Wrangler with the very plow is facing us, a fang-baring metal beast, and then there are three cavities of the wide garage filled with cars. Four other cars are parked to the left of the garage where the black tarred driveway has been widened.

"Why are all the garage doors open?" I mumble.

"To show off the cars?" Lisa mumbles back.

"The garage is bigger than the house."

"I know, but Stuart . . ."

I shut up. The house itself is a colonial style with a facade of tan brick in the front and yellow vinyl clapboards on the side. It's a standard two-story house but it seems dwarfed by the amount of driveway and garage and by the dense woods all around a fairly small lawn.

Someone is driving in behind us and I just park next to the lawn leaving enough space for cars to get by.

Lisa carries Ally and Keith and I walk behind into the huge garage, following a cardboard sign that reads, *BEER THIS WAY.* As Lisa opens the kitchen door, the noise of people talking and music exits, and two adults and a little boy walk into the garage behind us.

"Hey Keith."

"Hey Brendan."

I shake hands with both of Brendan's parents, forgetting their names as I turn to follow Lisa inside the kitchen.

We meet Cora who walks to us near the door saying hello and thanking Lisa for the bottle of wine. Cora then leans over and grabs Bruce's arm, pulling him away from two guys standing near the sink. We all shake hands and Keith scurries away with Shawn and Brendan. I'm thinking that there are a lot of Celtic first names in this place. Cora was telling Bruce that I'm a stay at home father. Bruce is big all around in a solid way, with a shaved head and two-inch-long mustache like Butch Cassidy or Wyatt Earp.

Bruce's face contorts. "I know. You told me. Yeah, lucky guy. How'd you get that gig?" He's smiling, sort of. Yeah, that's fear in his eyes. And Cora laughs loudly to compensate.

"Well, by becoming unemployed," I say. "But it's working out for us so far."

He smiles that unhappy way again and looks away. Maybe he was unemployed once?

"Stuart and Lisa met at an art museum in Boston. You worked there?" Cora says, turning to Lisa, who's wrestling with Ally who wants to get down. Ally probably wants to have a beer and crawl around the house to check it out.

Lisa says, "Yup. Just for two years. Stuart was there much longer."

"Oh, I love Boston. I only went there once and always wanted to go back."

I have to aim us somewhere else. "So Bruce, do you work around here?"

He has a deadpan angry look now and just deadpans me.

"Help yourself to some drinks." Cora points to the refrigerator and then steps to the side to talk with Lisa and I step toward Bruce, just for the hell of it.

Finally, Bruce says, "I run a construction crew, Miller Construction. Out of Kunklestown."

"Great. So do you build houses or commercial stuff?"

"Yeah, both. Excuse me. Hey Bobby!" Bruce takes a couple of steps around me and taps the shoulder of a guy who just walked in the door with his wife and two little boys who are clearly twins. They don't just have the same freckled faces and short dark haircut. They have on the same black nylon jackets with Philadelphia Flyers insignia.

"Stu, grab yourself a beer, out of the fridge," Bruce leans past me as he says this. He's in the way so I can't move. "What do you want? Bud or Coors? There's Yingling. Bobby?"

"Yeah, Yingling would be great," I say to the jammed space I'm wedged into. And I wait, thinking I won't finish whatever he gives me. I don't drink really.

"Coors." Bobby's even bigger than Bruce but it's mostly fat. Bruce has more bulges on his arms than your average construction worker. His wearing a T shirt in the winter is a bit vain, I'm thinking. Maybe even frivolous.

The women are in their own clusters and two other men are talking a few feet away as Bruce, Bobby and I stand there in the middle of the crowded, noisy kitchen. I see Keith and a few other boys open a door and run downstairs into the basement. I'll have to check on Keith in a few minutes.

"Jacky got a muffler on his bike," Bobby says.

"No shit. I don't believe it. Why, the cops finally made him?"

"No, maybe. I don't know. He just told me yesterday, like he was, you know, miserable. Something about the neighbors bitching so much."

"Yeah, no shit." Bruce turns to me. "This guy we know, who works for me, sometimes."

"Yeah, like when he shows up," Bobby says. "Like when he wants to."

"No, I only need him a few times a month."

"But he's a hard worker, like a fucking maniac when he does work," Bobby says.

"Yeah, he's a maniac. Anyway, he's had this old Harley for a long time. It's like, since we've known him. The same one, he fixes all the time and he never gets it right."

"Fucking throws out some fumes," Bobby says.

Bruce shakes his head, amused. "Crazy. The thing's so fucking loud. That thing makes a fucking racket. Cora got pissed a while ago when he showed up here. I told him to keep that thing outta here."

Bobby adds, "Suzzie goes ape shit. She gets so pissed when it's late, or like when he revs it up driving past at like five in the morning. I sleep through anything."

"And so now the cops finally nabbed him? That'll piss him off." Bruce takes a swig from his can of Budweiser.

"Yeah. Fucking cops." Bobby turns his head slowly to me. "So you have a kid here?"

"Yeah. Keith."

"Keith? Keller?"

"No. Macnayer," I say

"Oh, new kid?"

"Yeah. We just moved here a few months ago."

"So you work around here? Where'd you come from?"

"Boston. Yeah, no work yet. I'm looking."

"What do you do?"

"Uh, well, I worked in the arts. Arts administration, I guess is the best way to describe it."

He stares at me like I might not really be there. He's at a loss for words.

Bruce says, "His wife sells engines and chainsaws and blowers."

Bobby looks stunned. "You shitting me?" He's looking at Bruce but half turning his eyes to me, disturbed. I'm disturbing to these guys.

Bruce says, "Cora told me. Four stroke and two stroke engines and that shit, right?"

"Yeah. She's an ace at it," I say and then have nothing to add. In a minute I'll excuse myself and check on Keith or maybe relieve Lisa by holding Ally for a while. My regular guy bonding has hit the skids here and they're looking away. Bruce turns around and starts talking to two guys behind him. Bobby just walks into the dining room to escape. That's that, unsurprisingly.

Lisa seems happy to see me. I take Ally, who's getting heavier as she gets older, and stand there wondering what to do next. Lisa looks lost too.

"Cora seems nice," I say, leaning forward.

"Um." Lisa nods.

I wrinkle my brow at her. She smiles crookedly and shrugs. We walk into the dining room and stand at the table and eat some corn chips and sip from our beer bottles. Bobby's there talking in a loud voice about the Flyers to four people and Keith and his friends run by and go up the stairs. There are shouts from some of the little boys about a video game they were playing in the basement.

"God, I hope it wasn't some psycho-violent video game," Lisa says.

"Keith knows he's not allowed to do that." As the words leave my mouth, I smirk at my naivete.

"We should have gone down there. Maybe we should go upstairs," Lisa says. Ally's wrestling with me, twisting and turning. I let her sit on the floor a minute ago and she started to pull at the leg of the table with all the food on it.

Christ, I'm as bored as Lisa and Ally look. After picking up Ally and handing her to Lisa, I walk through the door to the front hall and leer into the living room, which is empty. Nothing living in it, just modestly priced dark stained decorative furniture and mirrors and photographs of pets and relatives on white drywalls. The floors are a series of shiny narrow, brown stained wooden strips with manufactured, fake grooves in them to simulate grain.

I head upstairs to get Keith. The soft, squishy light green wall to wall carpet folds into the stairs and then continues down the hallway. I turn right following the sounds of electronic voices and shooting and boys squawking. As I open the door a few of the boys turn to see my large adult form suddenly overshadowing their game. The wide screen TV is on the floor to the right and some thug-like males are moving awkwardly as two boys use hand controls to maneuver through the city of darkness and violence. Guns blast with shouts and groans inside the set and the room. It's precisely what we don't want Keith doing.

He's kneeling behind one of the boys with the hand controls, urging him on.

I step into the middle of the room. "Keith." Nothing. "Keith!" He turns and looks at me, and for a second, he wants to block me out and continue in his electronic hunt for whatever they're after. Guns are still blasting, even though most of the boys are too aware of my presence and I feel like the adult at the end of the book, "Lord of the Flies", ending the uncivilized purging. But I'm angry.

"We have to go."

"A few more minutes?"

"No-no, now." I glare at him and then a few others as voices ask for Keith to stay.

He knows. His father's looking at him. His father will look that way at everyone in the room, given any chance to, at all. His father hates violent games, movies, TV, and internet. His mother detests fantasy violence. Daddy brings blame.

Keith walks out of the room looking disappointed but recovers as we reach downstairs. I haven't yelled at him. But I almost never even raise my voice or show anger to little ones. I'll no doubt show some anger toward my kids when they're teenagers, just to maintain authenticity, but that's years away.

Chapter Fourteen

EVERYTHING'S A DRIVE NOW. I'M packing the car while Lisa feeds Keith and Ally in the kitchen. The ancient Pennsylvania Turnpike makes every drive feel like a haul because there are two lanes right next to two oncoming lanes. The narrowness of the view feels claustrophobic after an hour, and this drive to Pittsburgh will take us almost six hours. Merry Christmas.

It's nine-thirty in the morning and we're finally pulling out of the driveway. Keith has his computer and his books and Ally has Keith back there to stare at and kick her little soft feet at, almost. She can't reach him. She tries to reach him with her hands. Keith thinks that's funny.

"Why does she stare at me?" he says, laughing.

"She's a spy. She looks like a baby but she's forty years old and she works for the Russians. Ludmilia. That's her real name. Ludmilia Rostopovich."

"Yeah, Daddy's so funny." Lisa turns to look at the scene in the back seat.

Keith's poking at Ally's arms and knees now, laughing. Ally's gurgling and jumping in her car seat, the way she does when Keith laughs.

"She has funny looking knees there," Keith says.

"Careful. She's waiting until we're not around. Then she'll phone the Russian embassy and tell them you said that."

"Oh, don't say that. *He'll have nightmares.*" Lisa leans back and mouths and whispers the last words.

"Why's she so small if she's a spy."

"They shrank her."

Keith laughs loudly. "They shrank her! How'd they shrink her?"

"Those Russians shrink people. In fact, I don't know. I don't know! I…think…you might be one of their spies!" I reach back and try to grab his leg and get his knee and tickle him. He jerks and laughs and moans and I stop.

Keith keeps saying things about Ally being a spy. He says her food, that looks silly and disgusting to him, is Russian and that she speaks Russian. The winding, narrow roads have ended and finally we get on the nasty highway. Keith's engrossed in his phone that Uncle Ron gave him for Christmas last year, and Ally's fighting sleep. If I angle the rear-view mirror, I can see her blinking and slowly narrowing her eyes. The bright sunlight infusing the whole inside of the car is making her want to close her eyes. If she sleeps now, she won't later.

No one's jaunty by the time we're pulling into 110 Lathrup Road, over six hours later. Like so many drives around Pittsburgh, this involves negotiating hills and the few inches of snow, making me wonder how we'll do. But we make it. Were on the top of one of the many hills surrounding the city. The brick houses are very small at the bottom of the hill, near MacKnight Road, the local strip highway. Winding up toward the top, the houses get larger and 110 is surrounded by three and four-bedroom houses all built in the nineteen fifties and sixties. The trees are large and surround the houses. Everything seems to be red brick or painted brick, or brick combined with clapboard. Nothing exciting, but stolid in some generic way that reminds me of so many of New York's old suburban neighborhoods on Long Island or parts of Westchester. Not beautiful, but far from ugly.

110 is almost a single level house, like a ranch, but then there's a peaked roof second story in the middle. Next door is that Colonial hybrid with the entrance on one side and a nineteen sixties large picture window dominating the front. The semi-modernist glass and steel house across the street has a cedar front porch and old-fashioned shutters on some of the windows. These houses sit on an acre, more or less, and have views of suburban sprawl below.

As we crawl out of the little jammed Jetta, Tricia comes out of her front door, thirty feet back from the road. We all hug her, and exchange small talk and I stay back as they go in so I can unload the car. Most of the trunk is filled with presents for Keith and, even though they're wrapped, I have to get them inside somewhere hidden until Christmas, the day after tomorrow.

It's half an hour until dinner. The smell of Christmas tree pine is mixing with the bubbling sauce smell, the tomato and eggplant with green and red peppers drifting from the kitchen. I'm not going back in there and witnessing the strain between Lisa and Tricia. I've just set the table in the dining room/kitchen and want to stay here in the living room. Tricia's still on her cell phone, walking around the kitchen doing cooking things. I can hear her. I can hear her talking back into the phone and at times saying something to Lisa. Keith is downstairs playing pool and throwing darts and watching,

Medieval Castles of England, a disc Lisa and I bought for him for his birthday. I was down there with him for a while. I have Ally in one arm, on my hip and am trying to put a CD in an old boom box. Ron comes in the front door. He walks straight into the living room in long strides and booms deeply and slowly.

"Hellllllo. Merrrrrry Christmas, Merrrrry Christmas." He likes saying that.

We shake hands vigorously. He looks genuinely excited to see me and I'm thinking, yeah, he really likes holidays like Christmas. He has on a tan hoody over a sweater and jeans.

He shouts hello to the kitchen next to us. Tricia scratches out a hello back. Ally stares and stares. She points at him. She does that lately. It's almost unbearably cute. He grabs her finger and laughs. Then he marches inside the kitchen and Ally and I follow.

Tricia hugs Ron with her one free arm, then Lisa and Ron kiss each other on the cheek.

Ron reaches into the refrigerator and grabs a can of Budweiser. The pop and hiss of the can amazes Ally for a few seconds.

"So you watching the Steelers?" he aims this at Tricia. His voice is twice as loud as anyone else.

"Yeah, I was. Put it on. Ginny says hello. Dinner will be another twenty minutes."

"Hey Ginny." Ron leaves the room as quickly as he entered.

"You need any help here?" I ask, lost between worlds.

"Nope. Go watch the game with Ron. I know you just love the Steelers." Tricia says, half for her phone friend, Ginny. That's about as complete as Tricia's sarcasm ever gets.

Lisa looks tired and I look at her to see if I can help, but she nods at me and I just leave the kitchen.

Ron has the sixty-inch TV on. It's mounted to the living room wall.

"Ohh! God Damn! Threw the ball away. Son of a . . ." He's standing and turns to Ally and me. "Second interception on Grier. And it's the first half."

"How are they doing this year?" I'll make an effort.

"Good. Yeah, they're doing okay. Yeah, they could do better, though." He thin-lips a smile at us then turns back. He sits on the sectional sofa with his arm extended to one side and the beer held on his thigh. This is a guy who exercises a lot and has muscle bulk that's visible through his dark blue cotton sweater and black jeans. I sit to his right in a small wing chair with Ally bouncing on my knee. The noise of the TV gets her focus for a minute, but it's not as interesting to her as Uncle Ron. Her eyes are welded to him, occasionally stopping to put her fingers or part of the little sleeve of her sweater in her mouth. Then she points at him, "Noo. No. Ahbababba. Mamama, mama. Dadadada. Da." She points at me almost straight into my eye. Ron's focus is straight ahead, on the TV. I bounce Ally a bit, kiss the side of her face and then put her on the wall to wall carpet. That intrigues her. She picks at it with her tiny, narrow pink fingers with her barely visible celluloid-thin, perfect little fingernails.

We eat dinner and Ron helps me clear off the table and put the dishes in the dishwasher and wipe everything. Lisa and Tricia are sitting in the living room. Ron and I barely talk. There are a few bits about the Steelers and the weather. Then he yells goodbye and leaves.

It's the 24th and since Tricia took Lisa and Keith shopping around ten this morning, I'm free to relax here with Ally lying on the carpeted floor or walking around looking at bland things on bookshelves. There are rows of self-help books, like, "Feel Good So You Can Do Good" and, "Fatless Around The Clock" and, "The Future Starts With The Number One". Then there's an eight by ten framed photograph of Larry, Lisa's father; silver hair brushed back and the long, pointed nose. That's got me staring. He was always very distant. Lisa always says he was physically there but emotionally detached.

Even in this picture he looks detached. He has a placid, controlled smile in the formal picture and the odd thing is that was how he always smiled. But he wrote Lisa that letter shortly before he died saying how proud he was of her going to a good college and finishing and finding work that she found rewarding and having a family. He said he wished he had finished at Carnegie Mellon and gone into hotel management. As a young guy he wanted to go into hotel management. Lisa breaks up a bit just about any time she mentions that letter. Christ, it's too bad he smoked.

He and I were not exactly close. He didn't give a damn about art museums and I don't care about professional sports and I was a son-in-law. I only had that one intimate conversation with him and that was about how much he liked retirement. I'd heard him say he liked retirement a bunch of times, but that time he said it with emotion. It was in their summer time-share on Sanibel Island, Florida. We'd all been on the beach all day, ate at the restaurant Larry and Tricia loved and he and I were on the deck alone, almost in the dark. The only light was ambient, coming through in curtains and from the translucent blue southern night sky. He had a few drinks in him, and he did drink a lot most nights after dinner.

So he sipped his martini, smoked and talked more to the lush southern air than me. He said he'd become very tired of his job and waited for years to retire. I listened, thinking, yeah, he retired early, at age fifty-seven. He said it felt like the wait took forever. I remember those words. They surprised me, that much angst coming from him. *It felt like the wait took forever.* Nothing else was said, except something about the weather.

I was surprised he confided even that much in me, and his sentiment seemed very understandable since I was doing stimulating, important work and he did crap work for so long. Now, with Lisa working for the same company and me jobless for so long, yeah, now the irony is one hell of a slap in my face.

Ally's actually fallen asleep on the sofa. I'd like to leave her there, but Lisa and Tricia will wake her up when they get back. I very slowly, carefully pick her up. She starts to twist, so I pull her close and hug her just firmly enough, but not too much, as I walk down the hallway.

As I tip toe out of the guest bedroom, leaving an exhausted Ally in an old crib, I hear Lisa and Keith and Tricia come in the front door.

I stop. No crying from Ally. Okay. I step down the hallway and into the living room. Lisa's standing in the kitchen doorway staring at me, or in my direction.

"Have fun? Where's Keith?" I whisper.

"He was bored. Yeah, he's downstairs watching Medieval Castles again."

"Where's your mother?"

"Downstairs wrapping presents. She got Keith a ton of clothes at the Gap. There was a major sale and it was crazy. The place was packed."

"You didn't buy anything?"

"Nope. My mother bought me some shoes."

Lisa smiles with guilty pleasure, kisses me on the cheek and shrugs and walks past me.

We sit down in the living room and look at each other from ten feet away. The air smells stale in this tightly insulated house.

She twists her mouth slightly and folds her arms.

"Maybe we can have our own Christmas next year," she says.

I nod, knowing it's what we say every year.

Chapter Fifteen

THE SLOW ARC OF CHRISTMAS Eve pervades and waiting is all there is to do. Keith's in bed, asleep finally. I saw that while I was getting presents out of the closet down there. Putting the presents under the tree, I'm excited. I'm excited by the ones I've picked out, pretty much the same way I get every year, waiting to give them.

I got Lisa some Chanel Number 19. It's a tiny bottle but still cost a lot and she'd never spring for it herself.

Lisa's downstairs in one of the finished basement rooms wrapping some things. Tricia's been on her phone, chatting to Paul somebody and watching me put some presents under the tree and now I'm sitting here, in the Christmas infested living room across from her. She's off the phone.

"I just love Christmas with the kids. It means so much to me that you could be here." She's sipping some white wine.

"Yeah. It's great for us too." I lie more to Tricia than anyone in the world.

"I know you're working so hard on your house and taking care of the kids."

I half shrug and half nod.

She stares at me. "I thought I'd never have grandchildren and it means so much to me. You must be very glad you have kids. Do you wish you'd had them sooner?"

"Sooner? Uhhhh . . . no, I think I can handle the effort. I do push-ups."

She chuckles. "Oh, Stuart you're so funny. I just meant that so many of us used to have kids right away, right out of college and now, you guys plan things more. It's wonderful."

"Yeah, it's fine for Lisa and me. I guess it doesn't always work. I read an article in the Economist a couple of weeks ago that was sort of down on it. Apparently, some people think there can be a few problems when kids grow up with older parents . . ."

Tricia's nodding off. Her eyes have started to droop. It's something she does. Lisa and I have suggested she see a doctor. She suddenly falls asleep sitting across from people. It, sure as hell, is insulting.

She opens her eyes. "Older parents? What? Oh, sorry, what were you saying?"

"Nothing." I wonder if I poured her glass of wine on her head if that would wake her up. It's a few minutes after eight at night, and she started the Goddamned conversation.

"No, sorry."

"An article in the Economist. It's not important."

"And it was good? The article? What was it?"

"It just talked about, uhh, the ways kids are only in their twenties and thirties and have older parents and then get burdened with taking care of them sooner in life."

Tricia's eyes are closed again. I think she does this with other people, not just Lisa and me.

I just sit and wait for Lisa. We'll go downstairs and read and get to bed early.

Keith and Ally seem to be awake at the same time. It's cold. The old clock radio on the chest of drawers says it's seven-forty-seven. My watch says it's six-forty-one. It's dark out. The clock is on some old daylight savings time.

Keith's standing next to Ally's crib. I'm glad we moved her crib to Keith's room last night so Lisa and I could lie in bed and watch a movie on her laptop.

"I told her it's Christmas and she had to be quiet," Keith says, filled with eight-year-old irony.

"She forgot about Christmas in Moscow last year?" I ask.

No reaction. Keith's in a trance and walking down the stairs with Lisa taking a photo of him with her cell phone.

Sure enough, he slowly approaches the tree and all the presents and stops and looks, same as every year. He doesn't rip into his presents. He waits. We have no idea why. He's savoring things?

Lisa's feeding Ally some cereal and I reach down and give Keith a present. He sits on the floor in his stripped pajamas and unwraps a small pinball game.

"It's old...probably early twentieth century. Mommy and I found it in an antique store in Dolyestown and debated buying it but it was so great looking and still worked. See? No electronics, just five little marbles that get shot up inside the small glassed-in pine box. See? Yeah, and through the little maze of hand painted bullseyes with holes there. And the old clown face with tin eyebrows and a bell for a hat. Yeah, there, get the marble in the clown's mouth or the bulls' eyes and that marble goes back for a free shot. Okay? If your marble goes down the narrow tin shoot you get ten thousand points!"

Keith's staring at it.

I say, "It's old."

Keith's playing with it and after a few minutes, Lisa says, "You can open another present, Keith."

She looks at me. "We can play with that."

I laugh and reach for another present for Keith, helping him get started. This time it's a more normal kid present. It's a battery-operated video game called Road Rally Ace. It has a fourteen by eighteen-inch screen encased in red plastic with a black plastic steering wheel attached and a DVD that displays a bunch of country and town roads the player can steer down. It's plastic and shiny and noisy and cost forty-six dollars and will probably break in two hours. He gets right to it and looks excited and Lisa takes a picture. Ally starts screaming a high-pitched wail because of the noise of Keith's car game. It almost like she's imitating the sound. She does this whenever things get noisy, so we ask Keith to turn down the volume.

Tricia enters in slippers, a robe and a murmur, "Oh, Merry Christmas. Oh, look at all those presents Santa left you, even though I know you don't believe in him anymore." She leans and kisses Keith on the head and then shuffles into the kitchen.

Lisa puts Ally on the floor on top of a small pile of wrapping. Ally looks down and around and pulls at the paper.

Presents get exchanged. Lisa likes her perfume and puts some on. Keith likes his robot. I like my new sweater and put it on.

Tricia's been on her phone, sitting on a stool a few feet behind us talking to Ginny. She has her coffee and looks rumpled. Her usual neat grayish-white hairdo is matted, and she hasn't put on make-up yet.

I can see Lisa's getting pissed-off as the phone voice continues behind us. I hand Tricia the present we picked out for her.

"Oh, Ginny, Stuart just gave me a present. Hold on. I'll put you down for a second."

The little phone sits open on the coffee table. Ally makes a move for it, first by leaning on the table, then reaching and being seriously disappointed when her grandmother grabs it first.

Tricia likes the malachite beads Lisa found for her. They were in the same antique store in Doylestown.

"Oh Ginny I'll have to show you the wonderful necklace Stuart gave me." She's back on the phone.

"No, Lisa picked that out for you," I say.

"Lisa and Stuart, Ginny. Beautiful old round green stones. It's wonderful. Barry what? Oh, I'm being terrible Ginny. My daughter and son-in-law and my grandchildren are here and I'm just ignoring them. I have to get off." Tricia shuffles back to her stool talking to Ginny about some necklace Barry, Ginny's husband, bought her for their wedding anniversary.

I murmur to Lisa, "Merry greetings-seasons."

Ten minutes go by with Keith surrounded by his new toys and Ally finally getting tired of ripping up wrapping paper and Lisa and I get up to get some cereal and coffee. Tricia gets off the phone.

"Oh, let me give you all my presents now. Bring your cereal in here. That big box over there's for you, Keithie."

She knows Lisa hates her calling Keith that. We oblige, get our cereal and coffee and sit back down. Keith sits on the floor and eats some cheerios as Tricia drags a three-foot square wrapped box next to him. He kneels and pulls at the paper.

"Oh, just rip it open! That's part of the fun at Christmas. Oh, maybe mommy and daddy don't want that. Oops." She widens her eyes and puts her hand over her mouth.

We both just shrug. Keith pulls at the paper a bit more aggressively, just not much more, but soon the box is exposed with a picture of a tent.

"Wow. Is that a tent?" I say.

"Yup," Tricia says. "I thought since you live way out in the country, Keithie, you could camp out."

Keith is really excited, and we open the box and look inside and then read the instructions and look at diagrams of a large, dark blue, four room nylon tent.

I'm finishing the breakfast clean-up, standing next to Tricia who just got off the phone with someone named Paul, when the front door opens.

"Merrrrry Christmas! Merrrrry Christmas! Hey, Keith what's that? A robot? Wow!"

Ron makes his way into the kitchen and laughs at all the excitement, half of which he's creating, rolling a big shiny bike.

"I wonder who this is for? I forget. Oh, that's right. It says Keith on the card!" he booms.

I don't know anything about bikes, but it looks like a serious one with lots of gears and shiny dark green metal and stainless-steel spokes. Keith is in shock.

"Wow, Keith," I say.

"Oh, I can't believe it. Oh, Keithie, that's a big bike. Can you ride a bike that big?" Tricia asks.

Keith starts to shake his head.

"Sure. He just had training wheels on in Woodstock, but he was starting to take them off," I say.

Ron says, "Yeah . . . this is a dirt bike. Yeah, an off-road bike. The wheels are thicker. It'll be good on the grass and mud."

Keith's starting to touch the big beautiful bike.

"What a great present. Thanks Uncle Ron." I squeeze Keith's shoulder a bit.

"Thank you," comes out of Keith.

Lisa arrives with Ally in her arms. "Wow, what a beautiful bicycle! Who's that a present for? Daddy?"

Everyone laughs and then Ron leans the bike toward me.

"Here, Keithie, I have to go to my car." Ron leaves.

We roll the bike into the living room and Ron comes scraping through the front door with wrapped presents. The next half hour consists of Ron sitting on the ottoman handing presents to all of us.

Tricia gets a cashmere turtleneck. I get two white shirts from Brooks Brothers. Lisa gives him a Jamie Oliver cookbook. Tricia gives him two golf clubs. He gives Lisa two shirts from Brooks Brothers. He says he has to leave to visit some friends. He offers to ship the bike to our house.

The drive home feels like a slog forever, as always. But the weather's bleak. There's only an icy narrow two-lane highway in front and one old dull gray blanket of snow out the side view. I can't see out the back at all now, with all the presents jammed into every open space. After a few hours of driving Keith and Ally are both asleep, exhausted. Lisa says she doesn't want to sleep.

Keeping her voice low, she says, "I don't know how Ron feels about it, but I just hate the idea of making that our Christmas celebration."

"Yeah, it's a special kind of dull."

"Yeah, well, I feel like I'm dripping with insecurity when I'm in my parent's house nowadays. I might as well be thirteen."

"Did your mother say anything to you? Anything about who can be an owner and who can't?"

"Nope. Nothing, thank God. Why?"

"Lisa?"

"What?"

"How is this not a lawsuit situation?"

Lisa frowns. "What lawsuit?"

"There are laws to protect people from discrimination and isn't this a classic case of sex discrimination?"

Lisa just shakes her head. "I'm not going to sue my family, or the company."

"Why?"

"I just started working for the company. Maybe I'll be made an owner after I've worked for a few years."

"You were told no women could be owners and there are no women owners."

"But Ron did offer me a decent paying job and he could still offer me an ownership position. I think he will after a couple of years."

"Okay." I have to drop it.

Chapter Sixteen

MID-JANUARY IS COLD, AND I have Ally in the car and now I have to get the ice off all the windows. This is going to make me late for picking up Keith at school. I can't find the damned scraper. I just used it yesterday and I always put it on the floor behind the driver's seat. It's not there. It's not under the seat. It's not under the passenger seat. It's not in the trunk. It's not on the floor in front or on the shelf in the back. Ally's being very patient, gurgling at me when I open another door. She seems to think I'm playing peek-a-boo.

The car engine will help defrost some of the front windshield and some of the back, but the ice is an inch thick in places and I'm really late now. I grab a stick from the side of the driveway. It's a sturdy enough, two-inch-thick bit of old branch with a bit of an edge that might work. But it doesn't. It does next to nothing, except carve a few narrow lines where I've rubbed especially hard for too long. I grab a rock. It has an edge and it works. I get enough snow and ice off of the front, back and side windows so that I can get a move on.

The windshield wipers start to do their jobs, front and back as Ally and I drive down Knight Road. I notice lines and spray wiper fluid and turn the wiper to full speed. The lines are still there. All of them. They're on the back window and, in fact, they're all over the side windows.

The glass is scratched all over? All the windows are scratched? As the ice melts and we enter the school pick-up line, it's obvious that I've scratched the hell out of all the car windows with a rock.

I'm on my way out the door to Phil's sad convenience store for some milk, but I'm stopped, holding a letter that just arrived in the mail. Lisa walks into the kitchen holding Ally and asks me what it is. I wave it.

"The check from the insurance company to cover the car windows."

She puts Ally down and I hand it to her and the form letter with it.

I say, "Read the technical term for what I did."

"Yeah?"

I walk to the door, taking Ally with me. I say, "Self-vandalism."

Lisa's repeating, "self-vandalism," loudly, gleefully, as I close the door and head for the car.

Standing in Phil's Convenience Store, I'm facing the same middle-aged angry sphinx who seems to always run the cash register. She probably hasn't smiled once in her life. She's stocky and looks like she cuts her own hair, hacking it very short for convenience. I see a business card on the glassed-in counter: *Ian Hays, General Contractor – Carpentry. Lowest Prices With Highest Quality. Westtown, PA.* I've seen it here before.

"Do you know this Ian Hays?" I'm pointing at the card.

She shakes her head. She has earphones in. She yells, "Don't know most of those people. Just let them put their cards there."

I take my milk and leave whispering the name and telephone number to Ally. We pull in the driveway and I phone the guy.

He's able to come to the house on Monday, two days away, which should ring alarm bells, but it's just an appointment.

Maybe it's the name Ian that made me hesitate calling him sooner? But I shouldn't be stupid. And now I'm holding Ally, watching a small pick-up truck pull into the driveway. The guy who gets out is tall and slim and has on an old tan waxed jacket that's open, despite the frigid wind, and a tan wool cardigan over a red and blue tartan flannel shirt and faded jeans. He's mostly bald and looks like he's just a few years younger than I am. There's a slightly refined tone to the guy, more than any of the carpenters or handymen I've ever seen. We shake hands and he aims his smile at Ally who points at him and that makes him laugh.

"Hey, I have a daughter named Betsy but she's too big to play with you." He squeezes her finger and coos at her.

He looks at me. "Yeah, I remember Betsy being a baby. She's my oldest and she's in her first year of high school now and I miss this baby stage. You have any more kids?" Frost clouds come out of his mouth in bursts.

"One. A son, Keith. He just turned eight a couple of months ago."

"The same age as my son, Gabe. So you decided to wait to have kids. Yeah, I'm just hoping I have some grandchildren before gravity pulls me down."

"Gravity pulls you down?" I smile but want to get on with business.

"Yup. We all lose enough strength to fight it and then we crumble down."

I shuffle around, wanting to chuckle but it's too cold and I'm bouncing Ally to keep her warm.

He looks around us. "I saw your Connecticut plates. Did you just move here?"

I nod and tell him we should get inside out of the twenty-degree wind.

Standing in the kitchen I tell him briefly where we moved from and why.

"Wow. Sounds like a radical shift. How's that going?"

It seems kind of personal and off the tracks, so I lie and tell him I'm doing fine and so is Lisa and that I love old farmhouses, especially stone ones. He's smiling, approvingly, so I end it with, "You can't beat thick stone walls and old plank floors."

"Damn. Ain't it the truth?" he says smiling broadly, looking around.

I shuffle a bit nervously, taking off Ally's winter play suit.

He takes in a big breath. "Okay, so tell me about what you want to do here. You got yourself a fantastic property and a great, solid old farmhouse. Looks like some of the Moravian or Quaker ones up here . . . yeah . . . ." He's gazing around, standing across the kitchen from me and Ally. I'm a little halted by the exaggerated compliment. I begin telling him about the kitchen issues as we walk around the room. He looks at the cabinets and the ceiling.

We're going up to the attic, Ally on my hip, and Ian gets very excited about the post and beam construction. We head back down and look outside the side door at the cement foundation and I tell him about the long-term ambition for a small addition. He listens, nodding and grabbing Ally's finger occasionally. That pleases Ally. Then I ask him what he thinks.

"Yeah. Well congratulations on getting such an old gem, first of all. Damn, so many of these old houses have been gutted and sanitized inside and out. You know? We live in an old farmhouse too but don't own it. And Molly, my wife, says I'm a sucker to do all the work I do on the house, but I love old houses like this."

I shake my head. "Molly and Ian and Betsy and Gabe. Your names are really different from all the German names around here."

"Yeah, right. We're in old Quaker land down there. I guess our names are different from up here."

"Really? So is it as Quaker as Lancaster is Amish?" I'm half sorry I'm engaging so much.

"Uhh, well, yes and no, I guess. Molly and I are. We grew up with it. There are plenty of non-Quakers around us. We don't compare ourselves with Amish much."

"No, right."

He looks around again. "But anyway, your place here, yeah, the attic's not a big deal, if you can help. The two of us, with materials, I'd say we could do that for a couple of thousand. The kitchen, yeah, I have an idea here that you can veto, but here it is. What about getting Home Depot or IKEA cabinets for the peninsula you want to add, and I put doors on the ones you have?"

"Really?"

"Sure, if you want. You can get great sales at some place like IKEA and get some cabinets for a few hundred and I could do a countertop out of Pennsylvania Blue stone. I have the stone in my backyard. I have to get rid of the stuff anyway, so that's free. But here's what I'd recommend. I do carpentry. That's what I do and I can make you a nice mahogany top for the peninsula you want to put in there . . . for about . . . eight hundred dollars. It'll sit on top of the cheap cabinets and it'll all look good. I mean, you said you can't afford the high prices of custom cabinets and they'd probably be about half as good as mine. The cabinets I build are my pride and joy, but I have to charge a lot for them. This will work, look good and I'm guessing the whole kitchen would cost…under five thousand, if you put the cheap cabinets in yourself. Is that in your ballpark?"

"I guess." I'm thrown by this guy.

"No, I don't want to rush you. I'll write it down and you can think about it."

"Okay. And what about the addition?"

He swivels around and sticks his chin out, rubbing it with his hand, thinking. "Yeah. Well, again, a lot depends on what you can do to help me. Otherwise, I have a guy who works with me when I need him for framing jobs or drywall, but that means more money. There are the windows and doors. And then there's the electrical and plumbing. That's where it gets priccy."

"If I can help you with the framing, meaning I can hold the piece that you've measured and cut and we nail it in place. Would that work?"

"So grunt labor? I do all the skilled stuff and you show up drunk and late?"

"Yup."

"Right. That's the way to keep costs down. I'd have to measure things and we'd have to get it down on paper."

"So, but the ballpark? Sorry, I'm just curious."

"Uhhh, maybe between thirty and forty thousand. It depends on how finished you want things. Again, plumbing can be expensive. Let me think about that."

Chapter Seventeen

IT'S THREE IN THE MORNING and I'm down in the living room awake and poking at my computer. Ian Hayes. He might be a loon. He really might be, or he might be a way to get some things started. His verbal estimate was incredible. It was less than half what other estimates have been. Lisa and I could get some real building done, if the guy's legit. But that's what has me awake. It has to be too good to be true. I had the feeling he wanted to see if he should do this work for me at first, to see if I was someone he wanted to work with. Then, his prices were so damned low. Usually guys want to avoid the complication and loss of income of working with a client. Is it Quaker stuff? The Amish build houses and barns together that way, so maybe Quakers do too. Except, I'm not Quaker.

When I put Westtown on Google search, I get, *Westtown School, established 1799, a Quaker day and boarding school, forty-five minutes west of Philadelphia.* It probably wouldn't have anything to do with Ian and Molly and Betsy and Gabe. As I'm reading about Westtown School, I remember hearing the name before. It's a famous old school. Where did I hear about it? I sit back and get nowhere. I remember a book that we were assigned in an American History course in college. I still have it because I liked it so much: *Puritan Boston and Quaker Philadelphia,* by Digby Baltzell. The author's last name being the same as Lucy, my fleeting college wife, seemed interesting, in a perverse way. Lucy said they weren't related as far as she knew.

I'm in the attic being as quiet as I can, opening some cardboard boxes filled with books and, after four boxes, I find it.

Downstairs again, I page through the book. I remember the author compared the big Puritan and Quaker influences on American culture for our first few hundred years, but it's the middle of the night and I have to get back to bed. I go to the back of the book and look up, *Westtown School* in the index. There are a bunch of pages devoted to it. I'll read about it some other time. I'm walking slowly, quietly up the old stairs that creak no matter what. The temptation to get some building done cheaply and quickly might be dangerous. I don't want it to be Ian Hayes or nothing and we don't want to get involved with another religious sect. Bad enough Lisa's up to her eyebrows

Lisa's looking like I've never seen her, with her face tight and her eyes burning, and she wants to say something or yell something and it's clearly at me. She had nothing to say to me at dinner and turned away anytime I aimed myself at her at all and now she's aimed at me in the bedroom, with her head down but her body pointed straight at me from a standing position ten feet away. I've never seen her this way.

"What's wrong?" I ask in a low voice not wanting to wake up Ally.

She shakes her head and starts changing into her pajamas. I wait. I know she hates confrontation and that she needs to wind down somehow.

She shakes her head some more.

I wait as she walks around the room, putting clothes in her chest of drawers, then slamming the drawer shut. Ally turns but stays asleep.

"We can't afford any of this stuff."

I wait, then say, "The attic and kitchen?"

"We can't afford any of it. I don't know what to say to you." She walks past me to the bed. "We don't have any money and you're just going ahead and we're going to borrow so much money that we can't pay back. It's making me sick. I can't stand it. Really. I can't work all day doing this awful job, not knowing how I'm going to keep doing it and worry that we'll owe so much money that we'll have huge debts and not be able to pay them off. I haven't said anything while you talked to these guys thinking you'd find out it's all too much money."

"Ian's a lot less and we don't have to do more than the attic and maybe the kitchen."

She just shakes her head and tears start to stream down her face and my gut wrenches and I stand still sinking into the darkness between us.

I wait, then say, "Okay, I'll call it off. Sorry. I'll call it off."

I walk to her and put my hand on her shoulder. She looks away, fighting the tears.

"It's okay, I'll call Ian tomorrow. It's okay."

"No, it's not. I hate it. I don't want to be some screaming bitch because we can't do this. I just need some sleep. I have to get up early tomorrow."

There's nothing I can say or do, so I leave and go down to the living room. Pacing gets me nowhere, so I sit. I can't get any air inside me, so I stand up and go to the cheap, ugly temporary coat stand in the kitchen, put on a scarf and winter jacket and gloves and a knit hat and go outside. I walk quickly around the front yard, taking long, slow strides to make as little noise on the crunching snow as possible, until I get farther away.

After walking diagonally to the farthest corner of the road and our property line where the tall birch tree stands next to several acres of Gord's wild red cedars, I walk back across to the other side where the dark driveway loops around seven big, old yews. Then, I walk back where I just was next to the birch. Eventually I wear down some of my frustration.

I'm standing facing the small white stone house. My breath is frosting in front of me and I'm anchored in place, hating the sensation. From the rise of the front yard I'm about even with the second floor and seventy-five feet back. The white stucco blends with the snow all around, all that held down to earth by the endless black frigid sky. The windows project their own small indoor spaces, four on top, two below, each one glowing different yellow hues. I can see Lisa's head lying sideways on her pillow. She sleeps with lights on, or off. When she can't do the job anymore, we won't be able to sell the Goddamned house. Double the pain.

There's my family. And I'm here. I want to yell and rant at the endless night sky, but I can't. Some instinct tells me I can't. I have no idea what else my instinct's telling me except to drag myself around the yard some more.

Two days later and Lisa's a nervous wreck around me. She's walking around the house sounding cheerful. I've been trying to be cheerful back just to defuse the pent-up guilt she seems to be feeling. It's making me feel guilty. We've always been pretty upright-forthright with each other and now our behavior is undermining my sense of well-being.

She's in the kitchen cooking. I walk in holding Ally's hands as Ally tries to walk. She can't. She sticks one leg out toe first and slowly jerks the other one out so that she's in position to sit down. I let her try again.

Lisa says, "Oh, Ally wants to walk. Daddy's helping Ally be a big girl."

"It'll be a while longer," I say. "What can I do in here?" I let Ally crawl.

"Hm?"

"With dinner."

"No, I'm all set. I don't need any help."

"Really?"

"Yeah, I'm fine."

"Jesus, Lisa?"

"What?"

"It's okay. You're going to drive yourself nuts. Forget about the attic and stuff."

"What do you mean?"

I lower my head and just stare at her.

She says, "I've been thinking about it. Did you call Ian?"

"Yeah. No problem. We're all set."

"Oh, I was going to say to forget what I said. You were just freaking me out. Money freaks me out. You know that. And you never care about it. It's just numbers to you. You're just out of control and crazy and scare me sometimes."

Now I'm staring for real. I wait. "Okay," I say. "You want me to roll around on the floor and pound my head and chew on my arm."

"No, sorry. Really, you think this Ian's going to be all right? Why's he so cheap?"

"I have no idea."

"But you think this is a good idea? You can design something good?"

"Lisa, yeah, it's just something I can do. Or, I don't know, try to."

She stands still, no longer stirring the potato, leek and carrot soup. She just looks at me and then picks up Ally and puts her in her metal swinging-cranking machine.

I half want to grab Lisa and half want to go for a long run in the snow in the woods, barefoot.

"Let's just think about it," I say. "I don't want to get us in too much trouble . . . even more than we're in. You weren't exaggerating the other day."

"No. Really, I don't think we can afford anything this year. But, try him out, I guess. See if this Ian's for real at all."

Part Three

Chapter Eighteen

My cell phone rings, and I tap the button on my steering wheel for my Bluetooth.

"Hi, Lisa, it's Janet. Some guy from Lancaster's called twice and he's like, 'Are you serving a hot meal at the meeting this year?' Oh my God! It's like these guys call every year and ask this stupid shit. I'm so sick of it. Can you call him and calm him the heck down? Marvin Zimmerman? Fuck."

Janet's the one who should calm down. I won't tell her that.

"Yeah, thanks Janet. Sorry. I'll call Marvin back."

I drive on, thinking. Just having to talk to her on the phone brings up images of the sad mass of people in the Pittsburgh office. So I'm trying to memorize the office staff. Janet's another bitter female sibling of another owner, Mike. Wow, Mike's a load. Of all the gray, sad-assed people in the office, he could be the grimmest. Of course, Mike does something with accounting. He sits in that office with no windows. His brother, Mat, sits jammed in there with him doing bookkeeping.

I have more and more of these images to live with daily now. Murray's coming to the update meeting. He's another male owner who does some sort of administrative work in the office with windows and Ron has an office, with a window.

I call Marvin and leave a message asking him to call me. His phone's on a table in the middle of a stable filled with horses and bales of hay. I saw it once when Ester Mae gave me a tour of their farm. I imagine the ringing phone and then me leaving a message to the horses.

I've just spent two weeks setting-up the OhPa update school. I'll have to do this once a year? Ron and Murray and the Bears travel around to different parts of OhPa's territory to tell dealers about the latest products and do repair classes and whatever. It's in my territory this month. I have to organize it. I've been pretty surprised how excited my dealers get about it. They don't get out much.

Marvin phones me back in less than ten minutes.

"Hi Marvin."

"Yah, hello Lisa. Yah, I did phone OhPa. Is there going to be hot food this year for the dinner? Last year it was cold and not so good."

"Turkey, Marvin. Hot turkey, mashed potatoes, corn, gravy, stewed tomatoes, a salad and cherry pie and tea or coffee. And, as I told you last month, it's at Gaebler's Table." I think that's a favorite restaurant for old fashioned food.

"Oh. That's good. Yah, okay. Thank you, Lisa. And I send my money to OhPa in Pittsburgh?"

"You can give it to me there. I won't tell anyone it's late. I just need to have the right number for the restaurant cooks."

"Yah, Silas will come there too."

"Any other relatives, Marvin?"

"What? No."

"Just teasing Marvin."

"Oh." He laughs. "Ron tells good jokes there too."

I'm confused. "You mean at the update schools?"

"Yah."

I can tell Marvin's excited. We say goodbye.

He's really late. The lunch and update school are in two days. Thank God the weather's starting to be springish, even though it's early March. But we have to do this before the guys get really busy with spring and summer sales.

I call Gaebler's Table in Mount Joy to add two more for dinner, or what we English call lunch.

Waiting for Ron in this remote farmland version of a banquet hall has me jittery. It's almost seven-thirty and the woman who let me in hinted that, since the place didn't open until eight-thirty, maybe I could just wait inside by the door. It's raining out.

My phone dings. I have a text.

Lisa. I'm on my way. Ron and Murray are in a separate car. Will meet at Gaebler's at around seven-thirty. The Bear.

I start to answer him but see Ron and Murray walking across the parking lot toward the doors I'm behind. I push a door open.

"Hi."

"Hellllo." Ron grabs the door and pulls it back for Murray, who hesitates but then, bent forward in the rain, walks in. They both have large, dark blue canvas laptop cases with straps over their shoulders.

We all say hello again.

"Talk to anyone here?" Ron asks me.

"Not yet. They weren't open, but I see some lights on in the back rooms now."

"Yeah, we can just start."

"The Bear's on his way." I say as I follow Ron and Murray around and between the restaurant tables in this large front dining area. There must be thirty to forty tables in this darkened room with their chairs sitting upside down on top of them. This is the public restaurant.

Murray twists his head halfway, still walking quickly and says, "The Bear's always late. He'll be ten minutes late at least."

"No problem. No worries," Ron says in his slow baritone.

"It is what it is," Murray says.

"It is what it is," Ron repeats, slowly, to the air in front of him.

Murray, wrapped in some sort of black nylon running jacket and pants, is stooped over as he's walking, but I'm guessing he's about six feet tall. Ron's about an inch shorter, but he always remains very erect and athletic looking. I'm looking at their backs. Ron has on a tan fleece pullover and black runner's pants that swish just a bit as he walks. His shoes look European.; some sort of sleek, black running shoe. I have no idea what men wear. Stuart still wears leather shoes and brags that he likes nineteenth century fashion. Stuart refuses to wear any clothing with writing on it and never wears shorts or T-shirts, except at the beach. My husband, the hostile Romantic.

Jesus. I'm the only woman in a room filled with about a hundred Old World men. Ron is sitting at the other end of the hall and the Bears and Murray are around him. I sit down at the end of the nearest table, not wanting to be unfriendly to Ron but not wanting to be even more on display. I sit down at the closest table. I'm not inconspicuous. There are glances, lots of them.

There's a prayer and we all lower our eyes.

Prayers over, these guys are devouring this food and there's more noise from knives and forks on plates than from chatter.

After a few minutes of eating and nodding at dealers I recognize, I turn to Raymond Nolt sitting next to me.

"Did you get a ride here?"

"No. I rode my bicycle."

I have to take that in. Raymond is Horse and Buggy Mennonite and in his late sixties.

"But, really? All the way? Isn't it, what, about ten miles?"

"Yah, twelve or so and I got an early start."

"Oh." I think for a minute. "How early?"

"Oh, four-thirty. But I milk the cows every morning then. This morning I had to change my clothes."

I nod and smile. He has on a black wool suit. I saw guys riding their bikes on the roads when I drove in this morning. It was raining and they all had on black wool suits and black brimmed hats. Some arrived in crowded buggies.

"In the rain? In the dark?" I ask.

He nods, forking potatoes and turkey into his mouth. He chews and I go back to doing the same, trying not to look too demure.

"Not much rain," he says.

The meal finally comes to a close. It tasted really good. It was real potatoes and local turkey and even the carrots were good. Raymond sure as hell liked it. He rubbed his stomach before and after the cherry pie and smiled at me. I gave him the rest of my pie after just one bite.

We all move on and I'm hanging around.

Ron's speaking. His Power Point show is on warranty issues. I stand still and watch when he shows a picture of a dirty, abused looking old engine sitting on a work bench. The crowd grumbles.

"So, your worst customer brings this in."

Lots of laughs.

"His name is John Smith. Or maybe, it's Aaron Zimmerman." He shows a picture of an overweight man in shorts and a Penn State Sweatshirt and hat holding the engine, looking sad.

That gets a roar. I notice Elam and Aaron laughing, then I look over at Marvin and he's leaning back, roaring.

"John Aaron Smith Zimmerman says his engine won't start and he says that it's the new Z Rite engine and he has the receipt. He bought it two months ago. It's new."

Now the place is in an uproar. This is like Vegas for these guys.

Ron waits until the laughing dies down.

"What's the first thing you do?" He leans forward and places his hand behind his ear.

Disparate shouts of, "Check the oil," come from the crowd.

Ron nods and shows a close-up of a mechanic and of the doleful customer looking at a dry dipstick.

They all roar.

"You guys have experience with this?"

More laughs.

"Mr. Smith-Zimmerman bought his engine at a big box store, for cheap!" There's a picture of the beaming man leaving a large store with a huge box in a shopping cart.

More laughs.

"And he didn't know that they didn't put any oil in for him. It was written on the box, but . . ." Now the picture's of the man trying to start the engine in his backyard.

Lots of laughs.

"You know the warranty doesn't cover Mr. Smith-Zimmerman. And you see plenty of burned-out engines from owners not checking the oil. But some of the newer engines can handle synthetic oil for longer periods of time and there's a new Foster and Knolls warranty covering that issue."

I walk along not hearing the rest. The laughing has died down but continues at times. Ron is a charmer with strangers and my mother and father were always that way too. Maybe I am too. A family of salespeople. But these guys are as strange to him, and him to them, as it gets, so he's in heaven and so are they. No shunning necessary.

I sit on a foldout chair in the back and plan the exit strategy for four o'clock. There's a large double door in the back of the hall with an exit sign above it so I get up and walk to it. I don't open it because it'll make too much noise, but I lean against it for a while and hear nothing coming from the other side. When I parked my car, I was behind this part of the building, so this is the back exit.

Back in my chair, I try to listen to Murray giving a PowerPoint talk on the two new Foster and Knolls engines coming out in the fall. At the end of that I make a bee line to the back doors. I point to them and the guys begin to follow me. As I push open the two doors, looking down at first to see where I can hold them open, I see another hall, filled with people. It's another conference, just quiet. They're making grumbling noises. They're all turning now, looking at me and the stream of Old Order men entering their space. The grumbling noises mix with gesturing. I see the whole room gesturing. Sign language. They're deaf. It's a large conference of deaf people.

I stop and stare and try to think, but the men following me keep coming and coming. The deaf people begin to stand up and, after looking astonished at the growing number of Amish and Mennonite men in their midst, they gesture for them to walk through. The Old Order men are clearly astonished and stop and stare, mumbling in German. They stream through. Everyone's startled and everyone's extremely well behaved.

Chapter Nineteen

THROUGH THE KITCHEN WINDOW, EACH day it's March windy and cold, then warm and then cold again, in one long shifty gray day after another. These are days of me inventing things to do, places to go, on and on and on behind the steering wheel. Today I have to drive to Mount Zion Lawn Care to see Lonny Huss, to see what's up with his spring order. He's been putting it off and he's really late. All the other dealers have their new engines and chain saws and weed whackers that they've been selling for weeks. This will only be the third time I've been to Lonny's.

Lonny didn't hit on me the second time I went there, so maybe he'll control himself today.

Stuart's anxious for me to leave. He wants to get to the attic project and Ian's coming over to help him finish it. The insulation's in the ceiling and most of the sheet rock is nailed in place and I don't want to be here and in the way. Ally's waddling around the kitchen.

"Ally, what are you going to do today?"

"She's going to watch some old reruns of Barney. While Daddy and Mr. Hays make a ceiling in the attic," Stuart says.

Ally turns in circles, then waddles to me. "Barney."

Keith walks into the kitchen and Ally runs to him and throws her short arms around his waist.

"Whoa," Keith says.

Ally whines a bit and holds on and Keith waits. It's a morning routine now. She cries when Stuart takes Keith to school. Apparently, she cries when Keith gets out of the car and walks into the building. She misses Keith, but she also seems to want to go to school.

"Barney's a little lame," I whisper to Stuart.

He leans toward me, exaggerating the posture. "Not for a fourteen-month-old. We can tell her she graduated from Barney in a few months."

"Well, she told me she thinks the show's obsequious," I say.

I grab Ally and pick her up and hug her and kiss her pudgy little face. I put her down and grab Keith.

"Whoa." He resists a bit but lets me kiss him on his cheek a few times.

"Oh, I want to pick you up but I can't."

I leave after a few exhortations from and to everyone about having a good day.

I'm a little anxious to see the sign I managed to get Lonny to buy. It's a huge, four by eight foot, double-sided, lighted Foster and Knolls sign. Lonny paid half and Foster and Knolls paid the other half and God knows why Lonny went for it, except that I found out that OhPa had a sign that had been sitting in the warehouse in Pittsburgh for years and talked the Bear into selling it for half the usual price.

So the wind is trying to blow me off the road and my silver van stinks, even with the back window open, so maybe I can flog some of those damned chain saws sitting back there and be rid of them. I won't put gas in the next ones I get. Dale and the Bears do that to demonstrate the things. I just leave them with guys for a couple of weeks and let them play with them. It seems to work. The demo models get all banged up and the dealers use them at home or around the shop, but I think they feel gratified and obliged. Because it's worked every time and I get all sorts of orders…orders for OhPa, not for me, but I feel compelled to sell this crap. Why?

I'm driving up the steep slope of the highway where Lonny's tall sign comes into view. There it is!

On the two long metal poles holding his original sign, *Mount Zion Lawn Care*, now there's also, *Foster and Knolls*, right below.

I sigh and laugh. It took too much persuasion to get him to do that.

Lonny sits on his stool behind the counter looking grim as I exclaim on the thematic effect of seeing the signs from the highway.

"I know. Yep. Sure as shit, I've got all these guys coming in now saying, 'You sell Foster and Knolls engines? I didn't know you sold that stuff.' And I'm like, 'Who the freakin hell doesn't sell Foster and Knolls?' All outdoor power dealers sell that shit. And I mean we've been here selling the stuff and repairing it for like fifty years. Man, how f-in stupid can people be?"

"Okay, but that's good right? You're getting more business."

Lonny's face darkens. "Shit no. Yeah, sure some more, but not much. Most of these douche bags buy the stuff at the big box stores and bring it here to get fixed. And still the damned Amish dealers sell their stuff so cheap, guys like me can't compete. I don't know what the hell they charge per hour for repairs, but not much."

"I know. The Amish and Mennonite dealers are small, though and do a limited business in their own areas. I know you know that."

"I just can't sell all the stuff I have, that freakin Dale had me buying last year and I'm paying interest on it now."

I stand still and reverberate. If his life sucks, there's almost nothing I can do to change that. Meanwhile, am I hearing organ music coming out of the back room?

"Lonny, then don't buy anything more until your inventory's down. There aren't any new models coming out this year that I know of. Concentrate on the repair side of your business for a while. That's the edge you have over Home Depot and Lowes."

"You're not on commission, are you?"

"What? No."

"Um." He brightens up a little, but he seems to be peering at me a bit intensely, so I step to the side.

"Who's playing that? Is that Bach?" The sound is fairly distant and quiet but definitely some organ fugue.

"Yeah, that's Luke. He loves his damned old CD's. I tell him to turn the shit off but let him listen to it sometimes."

I'm not able to respond except to narrow my eyes.

Lonny's watching me. "Yeah, he collects the shit. Tons of recordings. He has a whole house filled with organs. I saw them once, after his father, Merle, died. He was taking care of his father and working here and stuff and the old man let him put in them organs, I guess and play them, I guess. That's what he said."

I try to remember the short, shabby guy I saw back there repairing little gas engines.

"Hey Luke! Luke!" Lonny's shouting as loudly as he can, turned to one of the back doors.

I say, "No. That's okay."

"No, he'd love to tell you about that shit." Lonny's looking benevolent, smiling, probably because I actually haven't tried to get him to buy more things.

Luke can't hear Lonny's shouts, so Lonny has to walk back and lean in and shout again a few times. The organ music has stopped, and Luke appears and walks with Lonny to the counter. Luke's the same middle aged, thin, gray-faced, raggedly dressed guy I remember. He tries to hide his dark, tobacco stained teeth by not smiling.

I say, "So, Lonny says you collect organs. And, so do you like other kinds of music?"

"No, he hates the stuff I wanna play," Lonny says loudly.

Luke shakes his head, "You mean other instruments? Like violin or piano?"

I nod.

"Yeah, some. I like the organ because I play it in some churches and did when I was a kid with my dad. My mom sang with my sister and brother in the choir. Yeah."

I need to know more. I wait a second as Luke stares shyly.

"Yeah, he plays organs all over the place," Lonny shouts. Lonny seems to feel the need to compensate for his dirty little worker this way.

"Do you?" I ask.

"Yeah. Mostly in Pennsylvania, but in Maryland some. Ohio some. I go up to Bethlehem for the Bach Festival every year."

"You should see his house. It's jammed with huge damned organs," Lonny says.

"Yeah, I bought a few. Fixed them."

"Neighbors gotta love you!" Lonny belts out and laughs and I join in but notice Luke doesn't, so I stop laughing. I'm wondering if he cleans himself up for these organ recitals. I'm trying to take it all in.

"You listen to classical stuff?" Lonny asks me.

"I do, sometimes in the car while I'm driving," I say, still looking at Luke.

"Bach's not Classical. You like Bach?" Luke asks.

"Sometimes. Yo-Yo Ma."

"Yeah, cello." He looks a little disappointed. "I think he rushes it too much. Try listening to Pablo Casals or Ralph Kirshbaum play Bach on cello."

He's staring at me and I'm nodding but speechless. I'm fascinated by his artistic inner self, but I don't want to go to his house to see his organs. He might be a great person. He might be a genius. Or he could have his family stuffed and sitting in armchairs.

No organ viewing today. I leave saying I'm late for an appointment, not saying I have to get away to phone Stuart to tell him about Luke.

March is blustering on outside the little bathroom window. I'm brushing my teeth and getting ready for another day of outside sales in the Old World.

Downstairs eating some cereal, I'm looking around the room. Stuart and Ian worked on the kitchen. Ian is definitely odd. He doesn't look like a guy who would want to do this work. Or, he looks like a nineteen fifties Hollywood musical version of a carpenter. Slightly chic shabby with heavy jean shirts over beautiful flannel plaid shirts, clean jeans and handsome work boots. Add Stuart, in his old, worn white shirts and tan khakis to the picture and nothing makes any sense anymore.

But Ian's a stranger and yet he's doing all this work with Stuart for a fraction of what it would cost normally. So now we have a new ceiling in the kitchen, with new cabinet doors and a counter of slate fixed in cement and framed in wood. It's rustic and unusual but the house is, so what the hell, I guess. As long as it will sell, if we have to.

Now they want to put in a new tile floor and a peninsula from the stone wall out. That'll be another twelve hundred dollars. It's a super bargain, according to Stuart.

I'm kissing Ally and Stuart and I'm leaving. Ian makes me very nervous because Stuart wants to keep spending money because Ian's a Godsend. Stuart's a nonbeliever, but maybe Stuart's becoming Quaker anyway. I'm not becoming Amish. I have to see Aaron Stoltfus today and I'm driving out the driveway just as Ian is pulling in. We're waving.

This Route 322 is very familiar to me. No more panic attacks. I blink and see the pastoral scene around me, then don't and drive and drive and drive and drive. I have a back support attached to the seat and that's helping. My back's been bothering me lately.

Pastoral bliss is an act of will. It's Aaron's farm and that's familiar. The Old World is familiar at this point. I drive down the long gravel and grass driveway with Aaron's beautiful white stucco over stone house to my left and the large, half stone, half wooden bank barn. My car door's closing sound emptying into vast insulated, blank space all around feels like an old familiar bad dream. Aaron's two sons are probably out there somewhere on the sixty acres of alfalfa and corn, but I can't see them. I don't hear anything but a breeze and a far-off crow. I'm heading inside the workshop where Aaron and his son-in-law manage their business. They do some of the farm work too. I see a wagon parked near the house. It's bigger than a buggy. So they must be having church here this Sunday. I've seen wagons like that before and know they're for folding chairs that get moved from house to house. Can't skip out on much when you're part of a community, I'd guess, me being a lost drifter.

The butane torches are going strong but it's ten in the morning and still cool and damp and the torches try to dry out the inside air. Aaron or Hubert will turn them off in an hour or two. That's what they've done the last few times I've been here. Aaron and Hubert detached the metal grates in the center of the sky lights and some additional sunlight entered their workspace. But that will be later.

Hubert tells me Aaron will be down from the house soon.

Hubert's always shy.

"What for a car do you drive?" he says in his version of English.

"A Chrysler minivan."

He nods, probably not knowing much about cars.

"Yeah, it's cheap and holds a lot. It's not bad." I say.

He walks to the PVC pipe and shouts into it and then leans over and holds his ear against it. He waits. Finally, a little voice scratches back into his ear. He shouts into it again, "Yah. Okay."

Sure enough, Aaron comes down the yard on his scooter and walks inside.

"Yah, sorry, Lisa but I was eating some food because I was up all night with a colt."

I'm not sure if he has a cold or a young horse.

"Oh, sorry Aaron. Please go back and finish eating. You look tired. I just came in to give you these."

I hand him a three-page glossy brochure listing promotions for spring and summer.

"I finished." He's thumbing through the brochure and I feel bad that he's probably just being polite.

"Basically, the deal is, twenty percent off on those models if you buy them before May first."

He's just nodding at the brochure and I wait, knowing, like a lot of the Amish, he likes to be very deliberate and not rush. I try to remind myself constantly that it doesn't matter if I'm just standing around, seemingly accomplishing nothing.

Still, after a minute, him breaching my inner yuppy time limit, I say, "There is a new Foster and Knolls engine on the first page. I just found out about it myself. It's a three cycle, liquid cooled engine that's supposed to be more powerful and produces fewer emissions."

He looks at the picture and I wait again.

"So, any questions about anything?"

"No. Yah, we did have a problem a few days ago with an engine that Samuel. Well that someone brought to us here. He bought it two years ago from us. It is a Z-Rite Foster and Knolls engine and it wouldn't start for him. He tried and tried, and we did that too and looked at it. I wondered if this is a problem these engines have sometimes?"

Aaron knows a lot more about engines than I do, and I get the feeling sometimes that, even more than most Amish, Aaron likes to push for a deal. Like, maybe his friend, Samuel could get OhPa to replace his old engine?

I ask, "Did it have gas in it when he brought it in?"

Aaron gets a glimmer in his otherwise tired eyes. "Yah, it did."

"Any chance it was stale? I know people leave old gas in engines over the winter sometimes."

"Yah, Hubert and I said so to him. That might have been it. He doesn't keep his engines so clean."

"He could just clean it up and try it again," I say and step back and look around. "What's Hubert working on? I like to ask questions so I can learn."

Hubert looks up. "This is old. Ten years old, I think. It has a leak, but it was outside."

"Outside?"

"For a clothes washer," Hubert says.

I've seen those washer and driers sitting outside houses, usually enclosed in something. In some ways their lives are more complicated than my life.

"Foster and Knolls engines run the appliances and nature vents them," I mumble.

"So, Lisa, is that covered under a warranty? Samuel told us it was covered for ten years," Aaron says.

I'm stopped. How could that old engine be covered under warranty for ten years? Aaron's smiling broadly.

"It was covered out there, with a tarp," he says.

"Oh, this is a joke." I smile. "I won't ever get your jokes Aaron. Does Hubert?"

Hubert looks embarrassed.

Aaron says, "Yah, Hubert is not English. If you spend more time with us, you will tell us the same jokes."

I tell him I look forward to that or at least telling him some good old English jokes. I answer a real warranty question by texting the Bear as Aaron and Hubert wait. Then I leave. As I'm driving away, I phone Stuart to tell him Aaron's joke.

Stuart says Aaron should do stand-up.

Chapter Twenty

Driving home after another day of work, ambling, I decide to phone Mom. I can't put it off any longer. What's it been? Three weeks since I've talked to her? I've been busy on Sundays when she usually calls...me slightly trumped-up-busy going with Stuart and the kids to Doylestown, half an hour away, or to a park somewhere.

I'm tired, but I just push my thumb on her number.

"Hi Mom."

"Hello."

"I had a break here. I'm just driving and wanted to call you."

"Wonderful. Everything all right?"

"Yeah, fine. Is this a good time?"

"Well, I'm watching old Oprah's on my laptop, but I can watch them any time. How is everyone? Stuart and the kids?"

"Fine."

"You sound tired. Is the job too much?"

"No. No, the job's fine, Mom."

"Good. As you know, I worried it would be too much for you. And Stuart? He isn't unhappy just being stuck in the house all day?"

"Well, maybe that depends on your definition of stuck, and house. I think he's building things out of sticks and stones while I'm creating a job out of hot air, or tepid air. Maybe. Maybe I've been trading my secular, consumer soul for a few kind words from the Old World. I don't know, Mom."

That's testing the depths of some weird psychological waters with my mother. I can't resist sometimes.

"Is he building a lot? I didn't realize he was doing that much."

I've relayed all of what Stuart does time after time but have to try harder to ignore Tricia's occasional lapse.

"He's building within a strict budget, yeah. Stuart just does what he can, Mom. But, yeah, at least the kitchen's done. Yup, Stuart put in IKEA cabinets and then his friend Ian put that two-inch-thick hunk of mahogany on top of them to create the peninsula I told you about. Two and a half feet wide and four feet long. The kitchen's gone from supremely ugly to approaching gorgeous in some rustic, odd way."

"Wonderful. I'll have to see it. Send some pictures. You work so hard. How do you have time for all that? And after working all day you have to tend to two little ones. I don't know how you do it. I was just telling Ginny about it again. I always brag about you and Stuart. I told her again about the design work Stuart did in your apartment in Boston and she just thought it was a waste of money to do that when you don't own. And I said Stuart does it because he's an artist. He isn't bogged down by practical, everyday boring things. It's wonderful. He's just so artistic."

I'm sort of tired and the country roads are lulling me into some sort of stupor.

"Well tell Gasbag Ginny we own this."

"Ginny doesn't mean any harm. She admires you and Stuart. Send me pictures so I can show her. It'll give me a chance to show off. Now, I know restoring an old house like that has to cost a lot and I know how much you both want it to be more finished for you and the kids, so do you need me to send you any money?"

"No, Mom. Thanks. We've been very careful. No, believe it or not, we've spent a little over ten thousand dollars. And we can handle that. We're fine."

"Are you sure? Because I don't have a lot of money, but I don't have the expenses you have, and I remember how much it costs to raise kids. And, Lisa, I won't have this money much longer, this bit of extra I've been used to. I have to talk to Ray Struthers soon. I'm afraid I'm eating into the principle too much and I won't have enough in a few years. I'll see what he says. So I'm better off giving you and Stuart some money now, because, what I'm saying is, it will just go. Live for now, Lisa. Money doesn't last."

"Not have enough in a few years? I thought Daddy's will set up things so that you'd live off of the interest on some investments?"

"Oh, those investments go up and down in value. I don't know why or how. I don't think anyone does. If they aren't worth what your father thought they were, we're all in trouble."

"But I thought half of what he set up were annuities, so you'd have some guaranteed income."

"Oh, who knows, Lisa. It's so complicated, I just leave it to Ray Struthers. I just hope your father did the right things, but from what I've seen on the web page for my accounts, it doesn't look good at all. But, oh, well, life goes on. I don't worry about things. It's important to live life while you can. That's why I want to help you and Stuart and the kids now, while I'm alive and while I still have an extra few thousand dollars. I really don't expect to have anything left when I die, Lisa. Medical bills so often wipe people out. I wish I could leave you something, but I seriously doubt there will be anything."

"Okay, Mom, you're getting a bit morbid. No one's dying. I hope. You said all this two years ago and Ray told you everything was fine."

"Um, I'm not so sure he said everything was fine. But, Lisa, Lisa, honey, I'm sorry. I didn't mean to worry you. I shouldn't have brought it up. You have enough to worry about. I'll be fine. I really will, I know it. I have enough money, but you have a family to support, a young family. That's what counts. Children are all that matter."

She's the one dragging me out farther into the weird psychological waters. It's like she has me in a lifeguard grip, but we're headed away from land.

I'm too dazed and exhausted to say anything, so she does.

"You just tell me when you need money, okay?"

"Okay. I have to go, Mom. I'm at a gas pump. I'll talk to you soon."

"Oh, okay."

Jesus, I had to just end that conversation. It was going to leave me screaming for help. How does she twist things around to me feeling desperate about money and worried about her? She keeps saying she's running out of money, no matter how many times she gets shown she isn't. She doesn't have a mortgage and she has at least two million in mutual funds.

I turn on some news and, sure enough, it's so abysmal, it wipes out the desperate mother-daughter phone call. But I turn it off after ten minutes. I am worried about Stuart. I'll be home in twenty minutes. Stuart wants to have a talk and I know him. I know what he wants. He wants to build more.

And he'll want to talk tonight. Stuart likes to get to things and finish them and he plans for contingencies, like getting the house finished while we have Ian helping us. I hate the idea of spending all our money. I want to wait until I either get or don't get that bonus. I'm actually worried Stuart's just flipping out, that he's banging away at building things to make up for not having a job, or a career at this point.

As I pull into the driveway, I can see the products of Stuart's struggles in front of me. For a couple of months now he's been digging cedars out of our back field and planting them along the road in front to make a long, tall hedge for privacy. He's planted about twenty so far and he's only halfway done. The yews along our gravel driveway are getting too big. Stuart has to trim them. The fields out back look healthy. We have to get a local farmer to cut them in a month or two. All this damned land is just high maintenance.

We're sitting on the front porch after dinner. The light's fading more slowly these days and even though it's behind the tall trees across the street, the glow's powerful enough to infuse our green yard and white porch. Ally's asleep upstairs and Keith was up in the magnolia tree, but now he's running around the front yard trying to get Finnegan to chase him.

"Cats don't do that unless they're angry or hungry," Stuart says to Keith.

Keith laughs. "Good thing he's not a cheetah or a panther. I wouldn't want to get him angry. Cheetahs would catch you in about one . . . no, two seconds."

"He's a tiny little cheetah." Stuart's trying to not yell and wake up Ally. Keith's running around laughing about Finnegan being a teeny-tiny killer cat, now. Stuart leans forward on his knees and turns to me. "So, Lisa. Money."

"Umm."

"I know I seem like I'm rampaging out of control."

"A smidgen."

"But it's a deal. Ian's been great and we can get a lot done. You've seen the results and I think we should keep going and do the addition."

I just look at him, waiting.

"Ian's not busy until June. If we do this, we can finish some things next year. We can frame it and do the exterior and interior walls, now and even finish the electrical stuff for twenty thousand."

"But that's all the money in the line of credit."

"Yup. And we'd be way ahead of the game."

"Game? I know this is what you want to do. You're right, the place is starting to look better."

"What? Sorry, what?"

"Yeah, shut up. It makes me very nervous, for good reason. We don't know if we're going to get a bonus. Your car's getting old. We owe too much still on the credit cards. I know it's a great deal in a way. I don't want to keep you from building this."

Stuart listens and remains still, pausing in his pitch-giving. He doesn't ask for much. He never spends any money on himself. But when he wants something, he's relentless.

"I think you're from the Highlands. I decided that today," I say. "You actually fit right in here in the distant, foreign wilderness. You're not a city boy at all."

He frowns and then stares at me with a hint of a smile in his eyes.

I say, "Yeah, go ahead. Pretend we're rich. What do we care?"

"Lisa, here's the thing. If we get the addition up, we can have a bedroom for Keith and Ally can go into Keith's little room."

"So what's the attic for? The three-thousand-dollar attic. It's not safe as a bedroom in case there's a fire."

"It's for all of us. I haven't figured out what it's for yet. Space, stupid square footage for resale."

Chapter Twenty-One

SOMEHOW, I KNOW IT'S MONDAY morning even before Stuart wakes me up jumping out of bed and walking quickly to the other side of our room, past Ally's crib. There are hundreds of small insects crawling all over our bedroom ceiling and walls. Stuart's mumbling.

"What are they?" I ask.

"Lady bugs."

The things are flopping from wall to wall. Some are flopping all over the windows in the back of the room. I pick up Allison while Stuart runs downstairs to get a dustpan and broom. I check and there are some in Keith's room, but only a few in comparison, maybe a couple of dozen.

I take Ally downstairs while Stuart brushes the bugs out the window.

An hour later I'm off, with my hated phone sitting next to me. I'm a little anxious about taking Marvin and Ester Mae out to lunch. I'm not sorry I made that deal with my dealers, that, if they bought the new engine displays, I'd buy them lunch. The displays are a serious foot in the door and offer a much better chance of getting Foster and Knolls products sold. Marvin already sells more than enough, so the deal is aimed at other dealers and it is catching on. I've sold seven displays in the last three weeks. Marvin just always seems to be the first to do things.

It's just that, lunch with awkward Marvin and Ester Mae?

Marvin has on a short sleeved white, button-down collared shirt with suspenders and tan chinos and big white running shoes. He has on a small brimmed black hat and he's ready to go. Ester Mae is cleaned up and ready to go too. It's eleven-thirty. She's wearing a pale blue cotton dress and has a thin white apron over it and a thin white head scarf tied at her chin. And she has on the same big running shoes, except hers are blue.

We walk out to my car and Ester-Mae gets in the passenger seat and Marvin's in the back.

"I cleaned up this car just for you. It's hard to keep it clean with all the things I have to tote around."

They both jostle and smile, looking around.

Marvin says, "Yah, it's the same in our business. There are so many boxes that we get, and we don't know what to do with them if we can't use them."

We're rumbling down the road.

"So, Lisa, has your husband found work?" Marvin asks.

I'm already in trouble here. "No. Not yet."

I'm feeling fairly lost and they're both looking at me.

"Right now, Stuart is fixing an old house, our house, and taking care of our children. If he gets a job, we might change that. I mean, we want one of us to be at home with our children."

"So that's good for everyone. For now," Marvin says. Ester Mae looks over at me and smiles a sad smile. I draw in some air and force a strained smile back.

I'm starting to really, really hate the stay-at-home Stuart question. To fill time and space I tell them about my house and where it's located. Marvin ponders. He knew someone from Becker's Hill when he was younger. Ester Mae just sits quietly and smiles politely. Yeah, I'll avoid telling them about Stuart's design techniques and his background in the arts in Boston. Might be wise to not tell them how hip-cool old farmhouses are.

"Someone said it was a Quaker house, maybe. Are there Quakers around here?" This drools out of me like I'm drunk or hypnotized by my mother. And I'm sorry right away. Ester Mae just looks at me, confused, and then away.

Marvin says, "Yah, Quakers? I think some are Quakers in Lancaster. Yah, not so many."

After a rigid silence Ester-Mae says, "You are? You are Quaker?"

"No. No. I'm Lutheran."

"Oh, yah." Marvin says, as if this makes sense and Ester-Mae nods, smiling and my heart sinks like a little stone off a huge cliff. I'm trying to tell them I'm religious? I'm almost like them? Except it's a grotesque lie? Am I nuts?

I try to stay silent, noticing they don't seem to have a problem keeping quiet. It turns out I'm the one who's awkward.

"There's a man helping my husband, who's Quaker. He's from Westtown?" I say finally, realizing I have no idea if Ian's any more a practicing Quaker than I am a Lutheran.

Ester Mae squints and shrugs slowly, then shakes her head. Meanwhile Marvin's making guttural noises, thinking noises.

He says, "Westtown. Yah. Yah, I have heard of it. Your friend lives there?"

"Yes," I say.

After a minute Ester Mae turns to me. "Does he dress like us? Plain? The man who is helping your husband?"

"Not really. Some might, sort of," I mumble.

"Good people, I think," Marvin says.

I want the drive to end. Ester-Mae pauses, clearly thinking about something.

Fortunately, we're pulling into the parking lot of Gaebler's Table and I can get myself to stop talking about religion. It's almost making me sick.

I'm seeing the building more clearly on this sunny day. I'm lifting my head and looking. It looks like a very large, solid wooden garage or a small airplane hangar with reproduction colonial tables and chairs spread onto the open space of a painted wooden floor and then steel girders or beams above. The electric lights are helped by skylights throughout the corrugated, metal ceiling. There are three areas where the wood burning stoves sit, cold now that it's spring. The additions all mimic this style. I wonder if there are any interesting conferences going on today. As we walk in people gaze at us from a couple of other tables. They know Marvin and Ester Mae are Mennonite but stare at the English woman with them. We're far enough away from the tourist hordes to make them wonder.

I opt out of the buffet and get pea soup, half an egg salad sandwich, salad and iced tea. My meal will cost me less than six dollars. Actually, it will cost OhPa that. Marvin and Ester Mae have filled their plates with ham and boiled potatoes and peas. The buffet costs nine dollars a person, for all you can eat.

The place is busy, and more than two-thirds of the customers are pretty clearly Amish or Mennonite. I try not to look around much because we're still being looked at by a few people. I sense that they're trying to figure out what I am. I don't look Amish or Mennonite, maybe, but maybe I don't look like the tourists they see. My hair's plain and so are my clothes, I think. I don't wear homemade dresses but, even if my white cotton shirt and narrow chinos are well tailored, that's it. Streamlined, but no bling.

Marvin says, "We like to eat a lot for dinner because we get up early in the morning and so we've been working for over seven hours by the middle of the day."

"How do you manage running a farm and a business?" I ask.

They both raise their eyebrows. Ester Mae says, "Our children help with all the work."

Marvin says, "Yah, my father and my sons help with the farm. The girls help Ester Mae. And we have one and a half dozen kids, so we get lots of help."

I'm repeating the words, *one and a half dozen,* in my head and see Ester Mae smiling and shaking her head and Marvin's beaming.

"Oh, one, and a half-dozen. Yeah, seven. Very funny," I say, grinning, thinking this is humor from two hundred years ago. I chew.

"How big is your farm? Sorry, I shouldn't be so nosy."

"No." They both shake their heads and tell me about their forty acres that was a wedding present from Marvin's family. It's a small dairy farm. They tell me both their families had bigger farms, but that land got to be too expensive and that was why Marvin started the business. We eat.

"So, would you rather just farm?"

"Yah, yah, sure we would." Marvin looks at Ester Mae. She nods solemnly.

She says, "Our families all farmed, always. Since we came to this country. And before."

I eat, pondering that, and let them eat. Ester Mae wants to say more. "It's the land that really gave us our lives. Businesses are good and we are happy to have some money, but..." She drops off and we stare at each other.

She says, "Did your family farm ever?"

"No. My grandfather started this business."

"Never?" She looks disturbed.

"Oh, I have to think . . . yeah, maybe back a bit. Actually, I guess most people did back before . . . like in the nineteenth century or before. I guess I don't know much about distant relatives."

They don't want to hear that, and both have expressions of pity for me and I want to steer things in a new direction.

"It is terrific to have your children helping you with your farm and your business."

They nod politely.

I add, "So some of your children can farm when they get older and some work at the business?"

"Yah." Marvin raises his head, alerted. "The farm is too small for much. We will see. Land gets too expensive and then some people move to Ohio or even farther."

"We don't want that. We would have to all move and we don't want that." Ester Mae's eyes bulge a bit.

"No. No," Marvin says, agreeing with her. "But we have to do what we can to stay together. Our business is good, for now."

"Yah, business is too good for some in our community," she says. "That is not the reason for our community. Farming the land is better."

A dark, anxious silence shrouds our little table.

Trying to ease up, Ester Mae says, "Our daughter, Sally, is seventeen, so courting age. She is very excited and has her courting room all filled."

I'm baffled. I wait, then ask what a courting room is. Now Ester Mae raises her head, thinking of the words.

"It's the room Marvin's great-great-grandparents built onto our house. Sally can decorate it any way she likes. The young man can visit her, and they have some privacy. When she marries it is all her furniture, then."

Okay, Ester Mae's not setting up a make-out parlor or something. Clearly Sally gets watched fairly carefully. Still, it sounds oddly like trouble to me. So I say nothing.

"We can show you. Sally likes you very much and she's so proud of her decorations."

That's sweet. Wow. I thank her, but I'm thinking seventeen sounds really young for getting married. But, if you're going to have eight or nine kids, maybe not. I'm managing to just smile and nod and keep my mouth closed. And they're off getting pie with ice cream. I'm still not looking around. I don't eat deserts very often, because I want to eat less sugar. So maybe these people are wondering if I might be some uppity little English wench. I came in from wandering their countryside and am eating at their table, on some bitchy little diet.

Chapter Twenty-Two

STUART WANTS TO WALK THROUGH the woods out back. He's on some sort of mini mission. He wants to encourage the kids to play out here, to use this land. It's a stunning day and it's Sunday and we're all needing to get out of the house and do something, and the middle of April seems to mean nature has erupted. That Pennsylvania golden light from the sky is feeding green everywhere below, and then feeding it and feeding it. Yesterday, Stuart cut a path straight back from our yard through the seven or eight inches of wild grasses and weeds and flowers in the field, to the edge of the woods in the back. He was in a hurry he said because in a week the field would be too high and thick even for our heavy-duty Wright Stander to get through.

"So there were more fields here before, I guess. These trees are about twenty to twenty-five feet tall." He's holding Ally in front of him now and, sure enough we can walk straight ahead on the path.

He goes on, "The people before us must have cut through here, but the trees have grown in. We can cut it back."

"Foray on! Foray forth where our fierce fore-bearers feared to foray!" I'm spitting half of this.

Keith laughs as Stuart turns and comes for me. I scream and Ally starts to laugh, and Stuart half starts to grab me, and half tries to not grab me and hug Ally.

"Help, Keith! Help! A pioneer is attacking me!"

The three of us are a writhing circle, grabbing and pulling and pushing. Stuart's squeezing and bouncing Ally to keep her into the spirit of this melee. Keith is grabbing his father around the waist and pulling at him. I'm digging my fingers into his ribs as he moans and flinches and laughs and has to get away. We stop because Ally was laughing but now, she's crying and has no way of grasping that this isn't her world falling apart. She quickly settles down when we do. Pointing, mumbling, she seems to like this walk.

We weave on, stepping over rocks and roots at times. Then the overgrown path bears right, and we follow it. After ten minutes it ends at our neighbor's field.

"Our neighbor keeps his field trim. He's a good steward of his land." Stuart makes his voice low and sticks his chest out, clenched fists on his hips.

Wondering if Stuart's reacting to my stories about the Old-World people in my life, I say with a grin, "He has a huge farm tractor. The thing probably cost fifty thousand dollars"

We backtrack to our field again and there's our small stone house off in the distance.

"You can play back here, Keith. Just tell us and keep your cell phone with you," Stuart says.

Keith's looking unexcited. He seems like a kid who likes cities or towns. He claims he likes Boston.

We get back into the house and settle into our Sunday afternoon exercises in relaxation. As soon as Ally's napping, I'm sitting in the living room reading the novel Stuart bought me for my birthday. I'm aware that Keith's up in his magnolia tree and running around the yard and Stuart's digging a ditch where our yard meets our field in the back. Keith helps him for a while.

Now most of the day has past and I'm staring out the front window in the living room at the beautiful view. There's a thin, distant sunset, a dim haze behind the trees in front at eight-thirty when Keith's brushing his teeth for bed. I hear him creaking down the stairs.

"Mom. I think there's something on my eye."

Stuart's in the kitchen cleaning up. I lean down to look at Keith. "Oh! It's a tick!"

I stand up straight, half panicking, then lean down again, holding Keith's head in my hands. I'm trying to remain calm, but the sight of a big black tick on my son's eyelid has me jumping inside.

"I'll try to get it off. Close your eyes."

Poor little Keith is standing timidly, flinching a bit but not objecting, just waiting for some adult assistance. He has a way of quietly cooperating that makes Stuart and me shake our heads in wonder at times. I flick at it and then pinch, and it's gone. It isn't lodged in yet.

"Good. Got it. Okay?"

Keith nods. We head into the kitchen, me revolted but squeezing my thumb and index finger with all my might, thinking about not wanting it to fall onto the floor and dig itself into our skin during the night.

I tell Stuart and he quickly fills a glass with hot water. I stick my fingers in and there it is, still alive.

"At least it was big. The little ones are the problem," Stuart says, referring to Lyme disease.

"Great. Thanks. The little ones that we can't see!?" I whisper at Stuart as I aim Keith away, back to teeth brushing and bed. Stuart's pouring bleach into the glass with that damned tick as we leave.

Okay, I have to go see Rory because it's April 24th and he hasn't ordered as much as years past and the selling season's supposed to be well underway. It's almost ten o'clock in the morning by the time I'm getting to Lavelle, way up in Berk's County. I did get a late, reluctant start. I can't see what sources of income there could be around here. There are damned few farms and coal or shale is north east of here. The pole building has rolling hills behind it and he probably, *got it for cheap.*

It looks like rain and the wind is sweeping gray grit from the side of the road into mini cyclones. I enter slowly, not wanting to disturb Fred or Buster.

"Hi, it's Lisa from OhPa," I shout to announce myself to Rory and his beasts.

Rory has on jeans with a relatively minor gut bulge and black and yellow sweatshirt that matches his Pittsburgh Steelers' cap.

"Yeah? Hi there." He has a Pennsylvania Dutch accent.

"How are you?"

His jeweler's glasses are on top of his head. They're only effective for close-up work. So, bare eyed he can't really see more than a blur talking to him, I'm guessing. Buster, his seeing eye Rotweiller is already licking my shoes, same as the last time. And there's his parrot Fred, perched behind Rory's desk on what's left of an old cage with no cover.

"Okay. Still not much business. Not much. The new strip down in Bloomsburgh is taking all the business, I guess."

He complained about the big box stores the last time.

"That's why I'm here. You repower lawnmowers and sell them, right?"

"Yeah?"

"Yeah, sorry. I'm still new to this. Marvin Zimmerman, down in Lancaster showed me what he does. He stood on the deck of an Ensling Mower and then raised the deck and exposed the engine and he said the deck was old but solid and good for a long time. But with the new engine he could sell the mower for a fair amount less than a new one and make a nice profit."

"Yep. Repowering. Some do it. The Amish do it and they have all them relatives in the back and working for cheap. But that's okay. But I'm alone now. I can't do it alone."

Meanwhile Fred is looking angry. His head is turned and he's keeping one eye on me, stepping back and forth on his wooden bar. One eye at a time. The last visit he suddenly screeched at me and it was so loud I pretty much screeched back. Rory told me that time not to worry, that Fred hates strangers and bites them sometimes, but only when people threaten him. Buster's lapping at my shoes and they're wet. It's so disgusting I could vomit.

"Yeah, so Rory, I came here today to see how things are going and to tell you I met a guy in Bursonville who's looking for a job fixing engines. He did it for Bobby Knox down there and Bobby's retiring and selling his business."

"Never heard that. Bobby's retiring? Who's that you're talkin about?" His eyes are faced upward.

"Paul Drexel. He worked for Bobby for almost ten years and he's just turned thirty and Bobby says he's really good."

"Yeah, might want too much. I don't know Bobby much, cause, you know I don't get around a lot."

"Well you can think about it." I'm assuming Paul would be a major plus for Rory, but who knows?

Suddenly Fred screeches like a blast from a fire engine and I jump two feet and yell and then shudder for a minute.

"Settle down, Fred. Okay. Okay."

I try to relax but Fred looks worked up. "Well gotta go. Just wanted to pass that on. It's hard to find good, trained mechanics."

"Yep. Hey, Lisa, appreciate it. Can he work a computer?"

"Uh, I don't know. I mean yeah, he was up front when I was there. He was helping customers at one point and looking things up. And he can rework engines."

"Yep, yep."

"I'll tell him to phone you. I'll warn him about Fred, though."

"Oh, Fred's a good old bird. Fred, Fred."

Fred flies onto Rory's shoulder screeching so loudly I almost scream but just have to get out of here.

I'm shaking and my cheap old shoes are wet, and I take them off in the car and sit back and try to relax. I put on my clean shoes and put the old shoes in a small plastic bag, and I'll throw them out as soon as I see a trash can. I'll still smell like Rottweiler drool until I get home and take a shower.

Chapter Twenty-Three

I've just been told I have the best sales record in OhPa. The Bear's email was worth reading. That was nice. Yeah, that makes going to old Elam's less annoying.

But it is the first week in May and this spring selling season is humming. So I have to do this drive to Elam Breuner's to drop off two chain saws Elam needs, "right away". He has buyers and he doesn't have enough stock, because old Elam watches every penny and plays every angle.

I shouldn't read emails while I'm driving but I like to head off any problems that come up, like Elam needing two chain saws.

I'm calling Stuart to release some pent-up energy.

"Can you talk? Where's Ally?"

"Nap time. You called at the right time."

"I was just thinking about how I do like sales, but the main reason my sales are so high is these Old-World shops are amazingly efficient and productive."

"Good."

"No, I know they're not easy to talk to. I was just thinking about this. For work they are easy to talk to. And the large families working long hours looked miserable to me at first. But then I began to notice that they didn't exactly rush around. Right? They look placid and slow moving compared with everyone we knew in Boston or even Pittsburgh. They even speak more slowly. It makes me feel twitchy and neurotic sometimes."

Stuart laughs. "You're not close to being neurotic or twitchy. Want to visit some relatives of mine? Want to drive to New York this weekend?"

"No, I know. But, like the Zimmermans. It's funny." I stretch. "I've seen Sally working there behind the counter, then leaving to do something in the house and Phyllis her younger sister is right there to fill in. They don't go to school past eighth grade. They don't have computers or phones. They work. If possible, they work the land because that's nature's and God's work, but if that's not possible they do some other work. But, I mean, there's no sitting around perusing the internet but there's also no running around and no yelling. You know? It's interesting. So, there's what? No time for any, something . . ."

"Foreplay? Endless self-indulgence?" Stuart says.

"You know I'm not aiming anything at you?"

"Christ, I guess I do. I know you're bored and lonely want to talk to anyone who'll listen."

"No, Stuart, not even close. We're a team. A wretched, mutilated, mutated team. But in sync. You find us places and fix them up. You take care of the kids."

"Yeah, thank you, thank you. I'm good at spending your money."

"You are!"

Stuart grumbles a laugh. "Wow, you're really in a happy, manic mood."

"Yeah. I have to get out of the car and see my next dealer. I'll see you later."

Stuart utters, "Drive carefully."

I'll tell him about my sales record later.

Chapter Twenty-Four

AFTER ANOTHER MAY DAY ON the road tootling along, I'm finally home and Stuart and Ian are still at work nailing or drilling something. I can hear the banging as soon as I turn off my car. Stuart said this morning they'd be screwing drywall onto the addition walls. We only have a few thousand dollars left in our line of credit and I can only pray that we can pay for all of this.

I'm sitting in my car looking at the house. When the framing was done two weeks ago it looked big. First Ian, Stuart and some guy Ian works with, named Jerry, ripped off the kitchen roof, and then they built a frame around the cement slab. It looks like it's doubled the size of our little house. But the addition's still only a shell.

I get out and head to the noise as Keith runs to me from inside and I see Stuart at the back of the room holding Ally with one arm and a piece of drywall with the other. Ian's standing there too, electric drill ready to go. I'm about to make a joke about, *action-packed dudes*, but stop.

"God, I hope she's all right," I say to Stuart.

"I put cotton in her ears."

I move my head to see.

"No, she just pulled them out," he says.

"We've been pretty quiet, and she hasn't complained," Ian says, then takes a step back.

"Come away from the bad people, Ally."

Ally's reaching for me, anyway.

There aren't any windows or doors or finished floors, but I can walk around in it and so I'm doing that with Ally and Keith.

"Um, there are nails everywhere." I'm holding fast to Ally who starts wrestling to get away. "Keith, would you take Ally down to the swing?"

Keith objects, but does it after a minute of persuasion from me and from Stuart.

"So, what do you think?" Ian asks, walking toward me tentatively.

"It's great."

"Yeah? It will look a lot better when you get around to finishing it. But it can stay like this for a long time. You have to stucco the outside, but the walls are in and roof's on and we can put plastic over the windows, and it'll be watertight enough."

"No stairs?"

"No, we'll pull the ladder down so the kids don't get hurt on it. The stairs will have to wait," Ian says.

Stuart's brushing dust off his pants near the back door that has plywood across it. All three new walls are dominated by large holes for windows. It's one large room down here with a small area beneath the stairs for a closet and a half-bath. Above will be two bedrooms and a full bath. An attic will top it off, some day.

Stuart says, "So, some day French doors through the wall into the kitchen and we're in business."

"Or bankrupt," I say.

"Oh!" Ian says, stepping backward. "I hope not."

"No. Sorry. I just had a boring day. It's my bizarre job."

Stuart turns red.

I add, "No. No, it's beautiful."

Jesus. I'm complaining and this Ian's so cheap and clearly an extremely nice guy and surprisingly civilized.

"Well, yeah, it will be. I think," Ian says. "It's hard to imagine at this stage but Stuart did great drawings and you can take your time finishing it. Listen, Molly and I want to invite you guys to dinner."

Retrenched, Stuart and I just nod.

"Betsy, our fourteen-year-old, can look after Ally, and Keith and Gabe can run around in our yard. Saturday, say at five? Does that work for you? That way you can leave at ten, if you want. Because of Ally."

Stuart and I manage to say yes to it all and wave goodbye from the wooden shell covering our cement slab. My anxiety about money needs a walk around the yard. Stuart needs to get away from me for a few minutes.

Chapter Twenty-Five

IT HAS RAINED A LOT in the last week and now the sun's out and it's Saturday and we're driving in Stuart's car down Route 100 toward West Chester and a bit south of there to Westtown. Wikipedia told me some stuff about the old Quaker culture in this area. The University of Pennsylvania and Swarthmore and Haverford and Bryn Mawr colleges were all started by Quakers.

I mention that to Stuart who seems preoccupied with the GPS. I have to ask, "So are Molly and Ian practicing Quakers?"

Stuart's still looking at the small map on the GPS screen, and looks at me and shrugs. "Don't know. Let's ask them."

"What are Quakers?" Keith says from the backseat.

Stuart says, "Uh, well, they're pacifists who came to America from England a few of hundred years ago. A lot of them settled around Philadelphia. Pacifist means they don't believe in fighting in wars. Right?" Stuart turns to look at Keith, then turns back.

Keith's poking at his phone.

Stuart looks in the rear-view mirror. "Keith? Listening?"

Keith looks up.

Stuart continues, "Quakers, yeah, they're basically just very accepting of other cultures and teach tolerance. They say, there's the light of God in all of us." Stuart looks over at me to murmur that last bit, and I'm looking at him. He says, "I read that somewhere online." Again, he looks in the rear-view mirror at Keith.

Keith's not even half listening. He's back to poking at his phone. I'm about to tell Keith to listen but I'm not going to bother.

It's getting leafier as we bend and sway past relatively boring suburban houses and into woods on Westtown Road. There are more and more old stone houses and the dame on the GPS is getting excited because we're getting close to Ian and Molly's house.

We pull in the driveway over gray gravel and patches of grass. The house looks like ours would, maybe if we had a finished addition with windows and doors. It's a white, stucco over stone two story colonial farmhouse with a small yard, tucked into the woods, a hundred feet back from the road.

Molly comes to the door just as I begin to knock. We all introduce ourselves one at a time as she swivels backward, smiling and points us inward. I notice her hair's damp like she just got out of the shower, so it's hard to tell, but it looks like she has very thin, straight blond hair. It's sort of flat against her head on top with a few damp strings just to her shoulders. Her face is hard boned and gently pointed with very pale, just barely opaque skin and very pale blue eyes.

Ian greets us, standing in the living room with his hand on the shoulder of Gabe who's told to say hello to Keith. As the two of them slowly, shyly walk outside through old French doors into a small back yard, Ally tries to pull away from my hand.

"Oh, Ally wants to go with the big kids," I murmur. But as I let go, she walks to Ian and places her hand in his and just looks out at the back yard.

"Wow." I raise my shoulders and look at Stuart. He shrugs and smiles.

"Ian and kids." Molly shakes her head. "Kids love Ian."

"Ally's usually sort of shy, in a determined sort of way," Stuart murmurs to the group, and I laugh, and we watch as Ally still holds onto Ian's hand, somehow losing herself in the space around her.

Molly points to some chairs and we sit down while Ian leaves to get Stuart and Molly some hard cider and me a beer. I can see Ian in the kitchen from my chair here. He has on pretty much what I've seen before, tan chinos and a soft blue, slightly wrinkled and thin cotton shirt. The shirt's dressier. Otherwise he looks the same, which is pretty good in a calm, steady way.

Molly stops playing with Ally and says, "By the way, we're really sorry but Betsy got a babysitting job last minute and we said she could opt out. She's been studying for exams and so we're being a little indulgent just now. Ally can be with us. We'd love to have her be with us. We don't mind, if you don't."

Stuart and I say that'll be fine, although I'm wondering how bored Ally will get. Ally's sitting on the floor in front of some books Molly's arranged and now, Molly turns to me to answer my question about how long they've lived in the house.

"About fourteen years. Yeah, we love it, but we don't own it. The school does, so that's kind of great and not so great."

I must look confused, so she elaborates, telling us that she teaches at Westtown School and gets to live in faculty housing.

"And walk to work," Ian says this handing me my glass of beer.

Stuart asks, "Walk? So it's near here?"

"Right around the bend, past the lake." Ian says.

"What do you teach?" Stuart asks Molly.

"Chemistry in the Upper School."

We all nod. Stuart's looking charmed by all this. And Stuart must have known something about this school they're talking about. Meanwhile, it is easy to get impressed with Molly and Ian. Molly's starting to glow over there. Her flaxen hair is fuller and flowing now, erupting more and more as it dries and as she warms up, crossing and uncrossing her shaven thin legs in that dark blue cotton skirt and soft tan cotton blouse. And no shoes. Yeah, she's Mother Nature's child in some refined way, and I'm starting to gaze at Stuart to see his reaction. He's smiling a lot.

The sun's coming into their living room through the French doors. Their exposed beams are whitewashed like ours and the walls are pure white, thick rippling plaster just like ours. The long wall behind us is lined with books but there's an obvious lack of anything on most of the wall space, and the place is as far from stuffy as a house can be. The plain white plaster walls and the large old multi-mullioned sash widows give it an open, quiet, harmonic glow, not like ours. Ours is a small jumble. And there is something unusual about the furniture here. The old wooden armchair I'm in has a different arm on each side and actually, different legs. The oak coffee table has an irregular piece of maple or something fitted into the center and there's the cutest hand wrought iron Arts and Crafts floor lamp I've ever seen.

They're all chatting about the weather, the kids and the house that Ian and Stuart are building.

"No, Ian's the builder. I just try to help sometimes," Stuart says. Molly uncrosses her legs and smiles warmly at Stuart's virtuous, manly humility. She wants to have his baby.

"Ian, what about you? You do special carpentry, like the top of our gorgeous mahogany peninsula?" I ask.

"Yeah, when I get to it. I've done some built-ins and cabinets."

"Ian designs furniture. He also teaches woodworking at the school part-time," Molly says.

We all wag our heads and mumble at that. Stuart and I both ask him to describe his furniture.

"I go to salvage yards and find old bits and pieces of broken furniture and then I reconfigure or recreate them. Yeah, I'll show you sometime."

Molly points to the coffee table and my chair.

Ian says, "Yeah I did those when we first got married. No, we don't have much here right now because I just sold some. But Lisa tell us about your job? Stuart talks about how you used to work with small museums in New England but now you work with Amish farmers?"

"I sell them engines and a few other things. Yeah, I guess it's been a transition of some kind." I stop talking or thinking.

Stuart says, "Yup. We knew a Russian art conservator, new to English, who used used to say, 'life is a psychophrenic transition,'" He says it with a quasi-Russian accent.

We're all charmed and they're all laughing and repeating the phrase and I'm sort of joining in but I'm feeling less sure than I'd like to feel. Who are these people? And where are we?

Stuart's trying to help by exclaiming what a wiz I am at business and at sales.

I say, "Well, I'm making some money and it's fine for now. We can eat." I shudder at that and need to turn it around. "Anyway, Ian, do you have a website or anything?"

"I did. I'm in the middle of updating it."

Molly says, "He's modest. That's why he doesn't sell more. He went to the Rhode Island School of Design and he's been designing furniture for years and people love his furniture." Molly pauses. "I have to brag for him, because he never will."

We all sit back and smile and Ian asks Stuart about college and majors and all that information gets passed along.

Molly went to the University of London. Stuart asked her.

"Really?" I say.

"Yeah, King's College, University of London. I seriously have no idea how I got in, but I loved it."

She looks around the room blushing as she says this, and then looks at Stuart and then me and asks about our time at the Boston Museum of Fine Arts. Stuart answers but soon gets her to describe where King's College is in London and we all find out that it's smack in the middle of town and that she got to live in Russell Square her first year.

"Did you stay in London after graduating?" Stuart says.

Molly holds her knees with folded hands, arches her back and looks wistfully at the plain white plaster wall between Stuart and me. "London's not cheap. No, I loved it for my undergraduate years, but yeah, I'm a bumpkin, a country girl I guess because I really missed this…this serenity. I don't know."

"Yeah, well, this ain't really way out in the country," Ian says.

Molly seems to regain her focus, blinking a bit and then shakes her head and sticks her upper teeth out and crosses her eyes for a second.

I'm sort of lost in this, just sitting, watching. These two are serenely into a low-profile elegance of some kind. Joni Mitchell could be their mother and Jesus their father. It's mesmerizing.

In slow passing time, we eat. It's a large salad with small boiled potatoes and the most delicious tomatoes from their tiny greenhouse. Ian made the bread. I ask who made the butter and get some laughs.

It's after seven. A few insects are buzzing and the light's cooler green-gray and indirect as we take a walk up the road, me holding Ally's hand. One reason for this walk is that Ian and Molly continuously played with her when she got feisty and Ally's actually been very well behaved. Ally seems to like them. Keith seems to like Gabe and Stuart seems to like everyone. It's absurd. They want to absorb us. It's some kind of Goddamned nice cult. They keep smiling at all of us and I can sense that they want to show our kids the school so the kids can go there and become introspective and cool and highly functional or something.

It was Stuart who suggested we walk up the road to the school. I'm seriously shadow boxing in my brain. We round the corner and on our left is the wooded campus lake with the school's boathouse off in the distance. There aren't any other buildings on the beautiful lake. There are cute little old stone houses here and there along the road as we walk. Some stone houses are on hills a couple of hundred feet back from the narrow, curving tree lined road. It's so seductive and I know Stuart's hypnotized, because a minute ago he turned to me and whispered.

"When the school was founded in 1799, it admitted girls and boys."

Molly's walking next to me and Ian's ahead walking with Stuart, Keith and Ally, as we walk into the main driveway of the school campus. Molly and I remain behind a few steps. On the left is a deep, broad, sloping lawn down a few hundred yards and then narrowing a bit between a lot of very tall evergreens, down into an outdoor grassy theater.

"We have graduation and things there," Molly says.

I'm stunned by how beautiful it is. All of it so far. I just told Molly that. There are old brick buildings, and some stone buildings ahead, but there's one large structure with a bunch of beautiful, tall brick chimneys and that gets my notice. Ian turns to me and stops until I reach him.

"Yeah, I was just telling Stuart about Main Hall. I guess it's our weird landmark or something. It's almost a quarter of a mile long."

"Really?" I say, twisting my neck, trying to take it in as we approach.

We've reached an angle where we can see the long, narrow flow of the three-story brick building that's bulging here and there along the way. It's Victorian and flows like a long Romantic red brick ensemble. It's humankind's answer to the firmament above, all that solid old red brick with white trim around lots of large beautiful windows. As we stand and look at it, Ian tells us that the ground floor is mostly classrooms and the top two floors are living quarters for students and some teachers.

We make our way inside, into the Main Hall's hall which runs down the center of the building. It looks long, but that's not what gets me. It's that it looks like a dream, some sort of shared archetypal dream institution that carries on and on. It's the classic school with tall antique walls of dark oak wainscoting and robin's egg blue plaster that we drift by.

On both sides are small classrooms with an oak table in the middle of each one and about twelve to fifteen chairs around the table. The rooms have tall sash windows with lots of panes because the building was built in 1888. And we walk along. There are a couple of hallways that meet our main one at right angles and lead to the library or dining hall. Everything is intimate and warm, not cold and institutional. The hallway walls have occasional pictures of graduating classes and large old landscape paintings here and there. When we reach the end, we walk down the steps of the back porch.

We're walking on South Lawn, according to a sign, around the Main Hall ambling back, sort of in the direction of Ian and Molly's house, I guess. We're passing a new building, the auditorium, where we see some kids standing. Molly waves.

A dark-haired girl shouts, "I didn't do my homework."

"There's still time, Cathy."

Another boy shouts, "I did mine." Then one runs over to Ian and says something to him about a woodworking project he's working on. There's rumbling noise inside the auditorium suddenly. It was there before but just at a lower volume. We walk on and Molly tells me there's a stand-up comic for the kids tonight. They have concerts and things on weekends, but this is special because of exams and graduation.

"Oh, I hope we didn't keep you from that. Who's the comedian?"

"Uh, Kim somebody. I don't know. He's South Korean and according to my students, he's a big deal." She sighs, "Oh, God, I love the kids and all but it's so nice to be with non-teenagers for a while, to be with adults who have kids and I can let down my guard and have a personal, serious conversation about your life and my life, not just their teenaged life. And you don't teach here and so we won't start talking about work."

I laugh and nod.

She goes on, "The thing about teenagers is that they just have so much charm. You know? It's hard to define."

"Cornuplethera," I say. They're cornupletheras of charm."

She laughs, her head back. "Wow! Okay. Yeah. God, that's about it. No really, it's the most incredible, genuine charm. And you love them and worry about them and they love you back. But it's so much about them and it's so temporary. They're gone in a flash, and new ones are in front of you. And it all happens again and again . . . the same worries about what subjects to take, what some boy meant when he said that, what they want to study in college."

"Wow. Sounds intense."

"No, sorry, I really don't mean to sound negative. I wouldn't do anything else even if I won the lottery. I might take a year off and live in Rome or someplace."

"Rome. Yeah, well, I love your house. And Gabe's great and Ian's amazing. We don't know why he's so cheap. Sorry, I probably shouldn't say that."

"Yeah, that's okay. You shouldn't. No, I'm always telling him he should charge more. So you're nice to say that, and he should charge other people more but he hates money. Really, he hates it. So he doesn't make much. That's why I married him. Too many of these kids now only think about money. Anyway, he just makes unbelievably beautiful furniture and he's cute, so what can I say?"

We're walking on, faster because it's twilight and we don't want some drunk car wiping us all out. I want to get going, get out of here, get away from all this high-minded integrity and intellectual stimulation or tranquility or something. It's all just too damned perfect. I have a shit job and Stuart can't get a job at all and all this is just making me feel worse.

We thank them and wave from our car.

Chapter Twenty-Six

THIS HEAT'S DESCENDING AND A ripe, fertile morning mist is rising from the endless thick fields of corn. An agricultural miasma. Driving on County Road to see Marvin and Ester Mae, I'm tired. It's nine in the morning and summer's here before spring's done. In fact, I drove Keith to school this morning for fun and felt sorry for him, remembering the sense of loss when I was a kid and had to sit inside and watch all of life's potential spending itself outside the school windows.

I'm tired of having lunch with people. I finished those lunches last Friday and won't offer that deal next year. It did get a bunch of dealers to put in Foster and Knolls displays and that's actually really good for business. It's good for the dealer's business too. I'm just tired of trying to make conversation with these guys. God, Rufus Stoltzfus and his thirty-year-old son, Daniel just ate and barely spoke at all, to each other or me. Ester-Mae was the only woman who's come along. Aaron Stoltzfus acted like it was a date or something. He was supposed to bring Hubert with him, but it ended up being just Aaron and me. I guess he was fine. He didn't try to touch me or say anything inappropriate. He just smiled at me a bit too much. We got a lot of stares at Gaebler's Table.

Now this weird morning. It started with me calling Marvin around eight-thirty to ask if they'd received their last order. I was surprised when I got Ester Mae. They had received the order, but she said someone stole a mower from them and they needed a new one for a customer. It was a big sixty-one-inch commercial mower. I tried to ask her for some details, but she sounded so uncomfortable talking on the phone, I just said I'd go to their shop as soon as I could.

The farms around me are growing taller and thicker and the pollen is thicker and thicker. I'm blowing my nose a lot.

Ester Mae's behind the counter as I enter. Her light blue cotton dress and thin white bonnet look summery. After slowly saying hello to each other, I ask how the mower got stolen.

"Oh, it was left outside, because the weather's good. We don't bring everything in every night. Whoever took it didn't take the other two, so that's good. It happened to us a few years ago. And, Lisa, I know you don't sell the mowers." She's looking flustered.

"No, I'm just driving around this week because no one wants to see me because they're all so busy. All the orders are in."

"Oh, we are so busy. Same this time of year, every year."

"Okay, then I'll get out of here and bother someone else."

"No-no. I like the company. Marvin is picking up the new sixty-one-inch mower from Elam Breuner because we think a landscaper wants it. We will see. Marvin is so busy he didn't eat much for breakfast."

"Oh, that's not good. Marvin likes to eat."

"Oh, yes."

"He'll lose weight and be thin like my husband."

She looks up at me and bits her lip, smiling.

"My husband is all meat and no potatoes. I call him the lean machine." I suddenly realize that could be construed in a sexual way. Where did that come from? Do I want to brag about us? Ester Mae's blushing and looking down. I step farther away and poke at a chainsaw on the wall.

"Marvin gains weight if business is good and he loses weight if business is bad," she says.

I nod. "So he's a human barometer. But, really, you seem to do a lot of business." I blush at the implication.

Ester Mae just stares, smiling politely.

Then she says, "Yes, we are grateful."

I look straight in her eyes and mumble something and sink back and away continuing to mumble inanities about needing to leave her to her work and wishing them luck with the replacement mower.

I carry my general irritation through the heat to the even hotter minivan. The car smells of the early stages of decay. Rug rot, old, spilled motor oil, plastic, are all off-gassing in the heat. I close the door anyway and turn on the engine. I, in fact, have nowhere to go., nowhere anyone would want to see me. There's nothing left to sell or promote, not for a couple of months when the fall season beckons.

I pull slowly out of the driveway. No ideas are coming to me.

I do get sort of desperate to connect with people, even with Old World people who see me as an other. Maybe I'm desperate for friendship, but I couldn't help them with anything and then started belittling her and her family with cute jokes. I was breeding contempt. Just shut up sometimes, Lisa. Jesus. Less is more with Amish and Mennonites and with all these dealers down here in old farmland. I'm driving on.

I'll stop in a few dealer's and try to not stay for long.

Chapter Twenty-Seven

I'M OFF ON ANOTHER DAY of wandering, aimlessly, fitfully – fitfully, aimlessly. I just took the old minivan through a car wash and vacuumed the hell out of the inside. My phone vibrates and rings and it's Ron. My first call from him, so it's a good thing I'm on the road, not that I'm not almost always on the road.

"Hello. How are you?" He says in his deep, protracted Pittsburgh accent.

"Fine. How are you?"

"Yeah, been better. Yeah, we got some bad news from Foster and Knolls yesterday. They're going to cancel us."

"What?"

"Yeah. Barry Jorgenson called us. They're consolidating, or downsizing. They're cutting the number of distributors down by half. And we're one of the ones they're eliminating."

"Jesus."

"Yeah, sorry. It sucks."

"But, Ron, what does it mean? That's most of of our business. I mean, what can you do?"

"Not much. It's up to them. Manufacturers do this sometimes and a bunch are doing it these days. So, yeah, they increase the size of centrally located distributors and get rid of the other ones to save money. So APL outside Chicago is staying. And so is FiveStar in New Jersey. Then Foster and Knolls will also sell direct to the big box stores and cut out a lot of the middle step."

"Mm. Yeah. So, but what does that mean? Am I out of a job?"

"No, not for now. I'll keep paying you."

"Keep paying me? Will you get another line to distribute?"

"Yeah, we're going to look for something. Foster and Knolls is the biggest. There are other distributors near us with other lines so we can't get those for now. We'll look."

"Oh God, Stuart and I just moved and, Jesus."

"I know. We'll look around for other lines. I can keep paying you the same salary while we do."

I just moan, "But you might not find another line."

"Nope. Nope. But I can give you a bonus. Uhh, forty thousand?"

"Oh." I'm trying to compute all this.

"Yeah. I'll send a check around the end of June when our fiscal year ends. Do you want me to see if any other distributors need anyone?"

As I'm saying yes, I'm absorbing the story in pieces. There's a real limit on the salary I'll *continue to get.* Jesus, I have no job left. I'm stunned into a hopeless silence. He waits.

I say, "I have to get off the phone."

Part Four

Chapter Twenty-Eight

Lisa's coming home. We have to get the hell out of here.

She was crying on the phone. She almost never cries. I have to try to do something for her. It's going on eleven in the morning and I don't know what to do or think. We're screwed. We're in trouble and Lisa and I have to look for jobs again. That's what Lisa kept saying on the phone, and then she couldn't talk.

I called Franny Smoltz down the road and she said she could come to our house and babysit Ally.

She's walking across our lawn. But it's not our lawn. I have to throw some seed on it to make it look more like a lawn if we want to sell.

She has that vague, unconnected expression of most sixteen-year-olds. It's reinforced in layers of excess skin everywhere, stuffed into cheap, tight jeans and a flimsy T-shirt with, *Punked-up* written on it. Her skin has no glow and her swollen eye sockets give her a jaundiced menacing look. In a few years she'll be obese I'm thinking, for a lost, nasty second.

"I have field hockey camp at two, this afternoon." Her eyes wander, unfocused, same as the last time, the first time she babysat.

Ally didn't seem to like Franny that time and right now Ally's standing behind me whimpering. My hand's back on her head and I want to tell her it will pass, but Ally's miserable.

We stand and I should chatter about subjects Franny likes at school, but I can't. I have to get away from Franny.

"Sorry, I have to get to something. Could you take Ally down to the swing?" I'm crouching and facing Ally. "It's okay. Mommy's coming home and I have to talk with her. Then we can all play. Just be good and let Mommy and Daddy talk. Okay?"

Too many words and Ally's just lost in tears. Finally, Franny and I urge her onward, down the yard and I turn and see Lisa pulling into the driveway.

We're in the living room.

Lisa sits and says, "I never really thought my family company would fall apart."

I just stand and try not to stare. When I did look before, her eyes were dark and sore.

She says, "This means we have to sell and move."

I nod. "Yeah."

"If we sell before living here for at least two years we have to pay capital gains, right?" She asks.

"Capital gains?"

She starts to smile crookedly, but reverts to the bloodless glare, the nervous shifting, not able to sit still. She stands and walks to the window. Jesus, I'm thinking, she looks damaged and I have to try to help.

She turns. "This is a real estate black hole, isn't it?"

"Yeah. The whole area around here is, I think."

"Yeah." Her eyes are still sore.

I'm pacing, waving my clenched hands. "We're stuck here now. Fuck. Now our resumes make no sense at all to anyone, anywhere. Fuck! It's a vicious circle!"

"I know." She looks crushed.

I stop myself and stand rigidly. We're both standing, stuck, unable to say anything.

After a minute of walking around the room, I ask, "He said the companies going bust. The whole thing is going under?"

"I don't know."

Lisa's shaking her head and biting her bottom lip.

We're speechless again.

Still standing, I say, "Well, I'm no help at all. I can finish some of the addition...I guess. If we do get that forty thousand. If we do move for a job somewhere, we'd at least be able to sell, I guess. I guess, I guess, I guess."

Lisa says, "What do we do next?"

"We have to find jobs and move."

"How? What jobs are we going to move for?"

I shake my head.

Lisa's crying.

I'm tired, exhausted from seething alone, seething in front of Lisa. I'm getting out of bed, trying to not wake up anyone. I'm creaking very slowly down the old stairs. It's been two weeks of this. I'm exhausted by not panicking and I hate watching Lisa try to not panic. I'm exhausted but can't sleep.

It's warmer and damper here, downstairs. The white plaster walls seem to have a sheen on them I haven't seen before. I walk to the front windows and open them and then I open the two side windows. The small fan might help. I look at my watch. It's almost three-thirty, but at least I'm not still lying in bed awake. Lisa doesn't need me staring at endless dark matter next to her. Any time she half wakes up and sees that she just wakes up.

I took that allergy pill to battle the breeding walls. Where am I? I turn on my computer.

Something about poking at real estate sites for Boston makes my laptop feel too hot so I put it on the floor and lie down next to it. The broad, varnished old pine boards feel cool under me, until they don't. If we sell this place for four-fifty or maybe more, like five hundred thousand, there might be some interesting houses to fix up in Massachusetts, maybe in Gloucester or Ipswich. Everything's wooden in New England, not stone. We'd have to have jobs. Jobs.

There are a couple of great antique fixer-uppers in Ipswich, but I have to stop looking. Now sitting on the floor with my back on the couch, I'm staring at the opposite wall. The deep windows reflect the inside light and walls and furniture, sucking it back out.

I walk to the front of the room. If I really fix-up this house, go all out, we might be able to sell it for more…five-fifty or more. But we'd have to put another fifty thousand into it. That would mean adding to our debt. Lisa would freak if I even thought out loud about that, obviously. Christ, we have no jobs and owe a hundred and fifteen thousand on the mortgage. We can't get a loan when we don't have jobs. I'm a dumb fuck. It's just that, with fourteen acres, a finished three bedroom, two-and-a-half bath, three thousand square foot house, an hour plus from Philadelphia, might sell for five-fifty or six hundred thousand in this market. And a miss is as good as a mile.

I walk outside. I have to look for a job and stop being an idiot. It's been two years of looking, looking, looking. When I look for a job, I feel like a desperate idiot. When I don't look for a job, I feel like an irresponsible asshole. Why do I feel so compelled to fix-up houses? It seems to be the only thing I can do. I'm traipsing through the summer night to the edge of our property and the road. The cedars I dug up from the field in back are starting to form a clean row along the road.

Chapter Twenty-Nine

ALLY WANTS TO ROLL DOWN the slope in the side yard while I stand and watch.

It's hard to pay attention. I have to get back to running around inside the house, fixing things up, tired or not. I have to finish painting the walls in the unfinished addition. Keith will be off school for the summer in a couple of days. I keep trying to not show Keith the panic inside me but it will be harder with him around all the time. Lisa's been great, I guess, going off to work, driving around doing her job like all's well, when most people would stay as far away from their soon-to-be ex-job as possible. Maybe it's a way of avoiding me. We don't talk to each other much these days. She spends a lot of time searching online for jobs at night and has even passed the word around at dealers.

I'm standing here on the side yard between the half-done addition and the boulders that border our property looking at Ally rolling down the gentle, slopping yard toward me. It's nine something in the morning and eighty degrees and we're waiting for Ian. I told him our predicament and that there wasn't going to be any more building going on.

But he said he wanted to come and see me. I'm not in the mood for socializing. Ally wants to roll more effectively than she's able to. At almost a year and a half she's doing really well, but she keeps raising her head and going off at angles. Then she stops rolling and wonders why. Life's one Goddamned metaphor after another.

I don't really know what that metaphor means. There's Ian pulling into the driveway.

He smiles at Ally and leans down and gives her a one-handed hug. Now she trying to show him her rolling skill but raises her head to look at him right away and stops. He claps and she gets up and runs to him.

"Hi."

"Hi to you, too," he says and picks her up. His cheerfulness is enough to make me nuts. He turns in a circle with her, then kisses her on the cheek and puts her down. She's off, running slowly down the yard to the swing near the spring house. I turn away from Ian and start walking down toward the swing.

I have to say something. "I got rid of her crank swing."

"Yeah?"

I want to thank him for helping me attach the smooth wooden plank to the hickory tree with two ropes, back before Lisa lost her job, but I don't want to talk.

"Yeah, that branch looks really sturdy," he says in a plaintive voice.

Ally wants to show us how fast she can run and she's watching her feet as she goes, and just manages to not fall. She straddles the wooden plank on her stomach and barely moves so we pick up our pace, walking down to push her.

"Hi. Push Ally. Push Ally." She's reaching toward us.

"I asked Molly if there were any teaching positions at the school for you guys, but I'm afraid not now." Ian says, about to push Ally.

"Oh. Thanks." I have to say something…he's waiting. "We don't have teaching backgrounds or whatever…certificates."

He's pushing Ally on the swing and says, "Yeah, well they hire people with different backgrounds if they like them. You know, if they think they'd be good. Some people get more degrees while they're at the school."

"I'm old and, what? I'd teach art history?"

He smirks at me. "Yeah, you might be old and useless, but I was thinking of Lisa."

I glare at the swing.

He laughs. "Man, you have to get a positive outlook. I was joking. We were thinking of both of you. But Molly asked and they're full-up for now. Sorry."

I'm repulsed by his desire to help and telling me he's unable to. My stomach twists.

He keeps pushing Ally on the swing.

Weighted seconds pass. To hide my anger, I grumble, "I'm not sure what we'll do, but we'll have to move. Sell this."

He looks at me as I turn to look over at the house. He says, "Can you get someone to look after Ally?"

"Look after her?"

"Or bring her along. I just can't have her in the truck in the front seat. Let me show you something…if you have the time."

I feel defenseless. Ian's probably never been unemployed for a Goddamned minute. I half shrug and, with great effort, slowly find myself walking up the yard, then getting in my car and driving.

The fifteen-mile drive seems to take all afternoon. Ian directs me instead of the GPS. We pull into an old mill building's parking lot, the only car there. *Larsville Antique Hardware* is stenciled in large white painted script on the brick and stone wall to mimic the old-fashioned theme. A four-foot square piece of varnished plywood with, *GOING OUT OF BUSINESS SALE*, painted in black is nailed to two posts on the grassy hill near the road. There's the narrow river or wide creek down there flowing by the building.

It's dark and cool inside and an old, portly, white haired guy says hello to us from behind an old oak table next to the door. It's a few thousand square feet of nineteenth century factory space only half filled with long oak tables and long rows of old oak shelving. There are sections of brass, glass, porcelain and wooden doorknobs, cast iron latches and hinges, copper sinks and porcelain sinks and all sorts of faucets. There are signs everywhere saying, *50% OFF.*

"We can take some more off sometimes," the old guy says still behind his desk at the door, twenty feet away. He's either tall or he's standing on something behind his table.

Ian and I nod at him and walk farther into the space. No one else is in the place. I'm holding Ally because if I put her down, she'll treat this place like a toddler's grab fest.

Ian says, "No, I know you don't want to spend money right now, but I thought these prices were so good when I came here a few days ago that you might get some ideas."

"Yeah, I get ideas all the time. Time for Lisa to put me in a special home."

Ian laughs and offers to hold Ally.

"More things downstairs. Old doors and some cabinets my son got out of old houses," the old guy says.

Downstairs is a dusty windowless version of upstairs. There have to be a hundred antique doors, all sorts of doors. They're supported by two long rows of two-by-fours along one wall. One row is exterior doors and one row is interior doors -- solid pine early nineteenth century doors, solid oak late nineteenth century doors, Arts and Crafts doors with stain glass glazing and raised panels. And the prices are low.

"Shit, and we need doors," I say.

"Remember you take fifty percent off," Ian says.

"What? That's right. Goddamn it."

He throws his head back laughing. "No, come-on! You can skip it. I just thought, if you were going to buy any of this stuff, anyway. I mean, what are you going to do with the addition? These are solid wood beautiful antique doors, not new composite crap."

"Yeah, I guess it would help sell the house."

We walk back upstairs and my heart's pounding and my brain's spinning.

Biting my lip, I approach Carl.

"Yeah, I might be interested in some things. If I get a few things, like four or five doors and nobs and latches and hinges…would there be a bit more off? Sorry, I know they're already good prices."

"No, sure. Tell me what and I'll give you a deal. My son, Brandon, doesn't want to have to pay for shipping too much of this stuff. He already has a warehouse full in Charlotte. And we have to be out of here, I don't know how."

Jesus. I feel a mix of guilt and wild exhilaration. He seems desperate to get rid of things and he has a baby face, a round face with round blue eyes and all of it encircled by white, fluffy bits of hair on top. I don't want to take advantage of this nice old guy, but some of those doors were amazing and I'm headed down there again.

Moving quickly, Ian follows with Ally.

Ian and I calculate the standard measurements of the addition's door frames and the measurements of some of these gorgeous antique doors. I settle on a bunch as Ian measures them and mumbles about how much they'd have to be cut down. We go for the closest fits we can.

I grab Ally and head up. I pick out new latches and old cast iron hinges and then a small old cast iron light for outside, next to the door. The exterior doorknobs are the dark

Victorian brass ones. There are some amazing old wooden nobs for inside doors. It's all so damned beautiful, I'm almost hyper ventilating.

We pile the nobs and hinges and latches on the desk in front of Carl, who starts making notes with a pencil on a pad of paper. We hand him our own hand-written list of doors from downstairs, copies of the item numbers and listed prices.

He scratches away and adds things up. "Okay, how's... let's see. With the fifty percent off, it would be around eighteen hundred for everything. Let's say, fifteen even. How's that?"

I can't believe it. I know he can see me getting worked up and I try to calmly just nod my approval.

"You take credit cards?"

"Yup. You going to get these things out of here? I don't have a truck," Carl says.

I look at Ian.

"Yeah, we'll come back. Maybe later today, or tomorrow," Ian says.

Chapter Thirty

I KNOW I HAVE TO explain my fit, my dangerous fit. What am I, fifteen? Lisa and I are walking on the side lawn and Keith's up in the magnolia tree in the middle of the front yard. It's seven-thirty at night and Ally's in bed.

"You didn't say much on the phone this afternoon about me buying all that stuff," I say, walking next to her, aimed at Gord's woods.

"I couldn't. We don't have any money. Or jobs."

I take a quick look at her. She looks totally withdrawn and gray. Her mouth is tight and her eyes duller than I've ever seen them.

There are no words I can say to this person. We walk along.

She says, "I know we have to try to sell the house, so we can get out of here. You said the things you got were really good. So when will I get to see them?"

"Tomorrow. Ian's helping me."

"We have to pay Ian if he helps."

"I know."

"Yeah, the super bargain bonanza of antique doors."

"Yeah, it was incredible. But I have to get those doors in. And the place will look amazing, even if it isn't finished."

"But we need jobs somewhere before we can put the house on the market," she says.

That word, *jobs*, stokes all the fear I have in my soul. I say nothing and just keep walking and facing the long, wide field between us and the distant woods. My whole body is clammy and it's hard walking because my leg muscles are clenching too tightly, or something.

We reach the fence at the end of the back yard. We stare at the useless fields.

"So where? It been a few weeks since I've even asked you where you're looking," I say.

"Where? No, I phoned Glen Young at Continental Chain in Minneapolis. I spoke with him a couple of times last year. He knows Ron and knew my father. He said he'd ask around. Yeah, I've emailed a bunch of people like that and haven't heard anything back."

I'm just listening.

Lisa adds, "It was bad enough last year but now, I'm in the outdoor power equipment field. What the hell?"

She stops speaking, still facing forward, like me. I have nothing to add.

She says, "So, it probably doesn't exactly help that I'm a woman...pretty much the only one. God, I don't know what we're going to do. I just feel frazzled . . . to a hair's breadth." The last part is barely audible.

She looks close to tears and just shakes her head. My heart sinks. I put my arm around her, and we say nothing for a minute. She stares out at the field again.

I step back and say, "Sorry. Am I making things worse by spending money on the house? I just think we have to finish as much as we can, as quickly as we can."

Lisa's shaking her head staring at me but definitely not seeing me. "You think we'll make any money selling it, if we finish more of it?"

"Maybe, from what I'm seeing online, we might make a bit. But who knows what the hell is selling or not selling way out here?

We turn and walk back up the yard and toward the front of the house. Keith's down from his perch in the tree, running around, kicking a soccer ball.

Somehow, we find ourselves in bed, frazzled.

Keith has two more days of school and I have to hustle. I can't panic. Today I have to concentrate on cement. I have the wheelbarrow out and start to pour in the mix. The dust surprises me and I step back and blow my nose and spit on the lawn. It's hot, really hot and my nerves are half dead from fatigue, so my sweating almost feels good. I pour some water from the hose into the mix. It's too much water so I have to add more mix.

I scrape some cement across the front porch floor. If I put a thin coating across the whole floor, then I can push it into all the old cracks and even it. Then, I'll paint it an old-fashioned dark gray.

Ally's taking a nap, so I have an hour, maybe, to do this. The three-foot-long two-by-four seems to be working, but I have to back-up on my knees like a medieval pilgrim and it's tearing at my old khaki's and hurting. I'll have to keep Finnegan from walking on this for a few hours.

Finally, I reach the end of the porch and scrape up the excess cement with the old two-by-four, my thick encrusted work gloves half on. My knees are a bit bloody, but the cement looks like it will work.

Maybe I can get some cement in the gaps in the dining room fireplace. First I have to kick and push at my shoes to get them off and run down to the basement to get a drop cloth…then, push the wheelbarrow through the kitchen into the dining room, open the old wooden doors to the three foot high, four and a half foot wide hearth…and clean out the layers of old grit and soot with a dust pan and broom. I hope Ally doesn't wake up.

I use a large trowel to shove cement into crevices on the old hearth floor. Some of the gaps are a few inches deep.

Ally begins to cry upstairs. I shove in the last bits of cement.

Tomorrow, I'll paint the porch floor. No, I'll paint the posts and window frames and sills in the porch and then paint the floor.

I'm vacuuming the basement. I can't quite stand up without hitting the top of my head and my back aches. The floor is half cement and half dirt, and I have to vacuum all of it. I can hear the machine coughing and dying. Tricia gave us this vacuum and it's the stand-up kind, for carpets. It doesn't work for us. It eats up the throw rugs and does nothing much on our old wooden floors. So I'll sacrifice it by finally cleaning all the old debris all over our basement.

My phone rings and vibrates in my pocket. I know it's Lisa, because it always is, but I have to turn off the screaming, grinding, dying vacuum cleaner and wrestle with my pocket to get the phone and sit down on the step.

"Hi." I twist my head and neck to release the twisted muscles in my back.

Lisa says, "Hi. How are you?"

"Uh, my system hasn't shut down. No, I'm fine…"

"Ron called. He said we're getting the bonus, but that the job will end July 31st."

"That's less than a month away."

"Yeah. Scary. He said he'd give me more money while I looked for a job for the next six months."

"Really. But give you more money while you're looking for a job? Your salary?"

"No idea. Yeah, I'm bad at asking him questions. I feel like I'm leaning all over him, asking for handouts."

"Well, anyway, it means we can finish some of the house." I'm thinking out loud.

Lisa says, "So, what's next?"

"He's retiring?"

"What?"

"Ron."

"No, he said they're going to cut back to a couple of industrial lines and keep it much smaller with no sales force. They're going to just use the website and phone or something. The Bears are going, though. I sent an email and asked them."

"Downsizing. Ron'll do fine."

"I have to go. I'm filling the car at a Wawa."

Chapter Thirty-One

HERE'S ANOTHER MIDDLE OF THE night episode I'm in, sitting downstairs trying to not cough. It's not any good, so I'm going outside into the cool fresh air. I can breathe. The long paces across the lawn and back again, back and forth usually feel good. Now I'm preoccupied and focused.

Ron.

The earliest information that Ron was alienated by us arrived at a party. We were having that party in Cambridge. That was before Keith was born. It was around ten years ago, and Lisa and I were living in our amazing apartment on Arlington Street. I don't know how I found that place. Avon Hill was one of the most attractive and expensive parts of Cambridge. Karen Lyman's house was tall and narrow, tucked into the top of the hilly, leafy street. It had a French mansard slate roof and since we got the top floor, we got the high, expressionist shaped ceilings. It was a two bedroom and divorced, fifty-something Karen was renting it to me for half the going rate in the area. She seemed to like the idea that I worked at the Museum of Fine Arts

We invited her to the party, four years later. We invited a lot of people from the Museum of Fine Arts and Ron showed up. He called out of the blue from the Pennsylvania Turnpike saying he was on his way.

Apart from having a couple of friends over for dinner, Lisa and I never had parties. That party was my idea. I might have wanted to show off the apartment. During the three years we lived there I painted everything and refinished the floors and Lisa and I combined our bits of furniture and, wow, it was a handsome damned space. Pumpkin pine floors, geometrically shaped ceilings around deep, wide dormer windows and a big square old kitchen with a window facing the side yard. The kitchen had a small nineteen sixties sink and two large chests of drawers and a bookcase for food and dishes. It was some sort of epitome of genuine.

I lectured Lisa about the need to invite a lot of different ages and shapes and sizes of people, play no music and only have potato chips and pretzels for food, maybe some mixed nuts. People had to bring their own drinks. They would talk and Lisa and I wouldn't be sidelined with anything. And, sure enough, a bunch came and yapped at each other and remarked on how they never socialized with people from other departments.

Cheryl Gersoni, new assistant manager of the museum film and video department, came. She was young, around mid-twenties, just out of graduate school at BU and talked to me about the need to increase public access to museum theaters. She looked like a young Diana Vreeland in her expensive saffron silk dress. The more she drank, the more lucid she became, except not about art as much as about sexual reproduction. She began looking around the room at guys, some of them half lit too.

"Boys. Where are the adult men?"

She pointed her nose at a couple of her favorite art historians. Then turned to me.

"I need a guy just like you. Find me one here."

I gulped, surprised. I had more wine in me than I was used to. I stepped back, looking askance. "Okay. But then Uncle Stuart has some requirements. You have to date without sex. Tell them that. Tell them you date. Tell them you have to get to know people, really know them over a long time, like Lisa and me. We worked together for two years, then lived together for two years, then got married."

"That's cute. She's lucky. You break up with her, you get me, wrapped around your finger."

I shook my head, "No. No. I was just telling you. Date. You need to take your time. Date."

She gave me a deep frown. I was sort of recalling the loss of sanity once alcohol starts taking over and turned to look for Lisa. She was talking with Ron, who had just arrived. I waved them over and introduced everyone.

Lisa shook Cheryl's hand and then Ron did, saying, "Hi. I'm Ron. I'm from Pittsburgh and I sell engines."

I laughed, but I was alone in that. Lisa and I stepped away. I was lusting after Lisa. She had on that white broadcloth blouse and gray flannel slacks that ended with trim, smooth Italian leather maroon flats. Plain, beautiful materials that showed off her trim, perfectly curved, smooth self. Her hair was very shiny, very dark brown, thin and straight to her shoulders. Jesus, she drove me crazy in her small old-fashioned button-down white shirts.

I leaned down. "What these people don't know is that you look even better naked. You're a ten with clothes on and a sex goddess naked."

"Umm, thank you. You're so sweet. I like you naked too. I like you drunk. I'm not used to it."

I had to control myself and not embarrass us, so we looked away from each other. Cheryl was excusing herself from Ron and he stepped a few feet over to Jun Lee and Bonnie Silverman, from East Asian Art.

"Hi. I'm Ron. I'm from Pittsburgh and I sell engines."

I looked at Lisa and she lost some of the blood in her face. She turned to me grumbling, "He keeps saying that. You think he's hating this party?"

I laughed, trying not to, then forced myself to stop, muttering, "Yeah, I guess."

Lisa looked concerned but just excused herself and walked away. She went into the kitchen and joined the huddle of three people from our, Art Collections Care Center. They were eating pretzels and drinking beer. It was Ellen Montez who had a background in archeology and Bryson Moore who did our matting and framing and Janet Slocum who was our conservator for works of art on paper.

Ron was still with Jun and Bonnie. I figured he looked good. He was around six feet tall with solid muscle from some gym pushing at the arms and shoulders of an expensive dark suit. He looked like a bloated businessman.

If he stood out in this group by announcing to everyone that he was from Pittsburgh and he sold engines, well he probably assumed this was a stylish group of cutthroat academics and aesthetes. Maybe he thought they had educations enough to take your breath away. But I glanced around. Not everyone had five-star credentials. Some of the people there went to local, yokel colleges and some only had bachelor's degrees. I had a weird, concocted background.

Jonathan Brice was there, the next-door neighbor who came to dinner once a month with different women each time. They didn't compare well with Lisa, his true love. He had on a very long, loosely knit blue sweater that he rolled up at the sleeves. He was over six feet tall and solid enough, so I don't know why he didn't fit into the sweater. He was an architect who had gone to Cambridge as an undergraduate and seemed more English than American. He grew up in Saratoga Springs, New York. Sure enough, he was talking to Lisa.

Ron was shaking hands with Darleen and Geoffrey. "Hi. I'm Ron. I'm from Pittsburgh and I sell engines."

The night went on and a few more people came, and the place was filled, and people were clearly having a great time. It wasn't just me. I knew I was right about this. You fill an attractive, quiet, comfortable room or two with adults and some drinks and they bathe each other in conversation or leave. Simon, from Classical, left after half an hour. The three from our Art Collections Care Center left, too, after an hour plus.

But Lisa couldn't get away from Ron's presence. His single line introduction was repeated again and again all night. I watched her grow more and more serious. Then around midnight she walked to the old boom box under one of the living room large dormer windows and put on a CD. Just one song by Bob Dylan, *Maggies Farm*.

I whispered in her ear after the party, saying that the music put the final touch on the party. Maybe music would have been good. She told me she thought Ron would like that song.

Ron slept on the sofa and left late the next morning. Lisa made him poached eggs on toast, first.

Chapter Thirty-Two

LISA IS OUT THERE DRIVING around every day deliriously, still doing the job she no longer has.

Meanwhile she hasn't received an email offering as much as an interview. I sent out more emails, essentially to the same people I sent them to before, mostly in New England. Nothing back. What the hell are we going to do?

Walking upstairs to our bedroom, I open the door slowly and check. Ally's asleep so I tread carefully through Keith's tiny room, that will soon be a hallway and a closet, and get to painting the wood paneling that outlines the new opening on the second floor between the old house and the addition. I'm painting it a color that's somewhere between olive green and celery. I mixed it myself from bits of left-over paint. I have almost a gallon down in the basement so it should cover the hallway up here. I'll have to buy some paint for the two small bedrooms and the bathroom.

I trudge downstairs into the basement, stir the gallon of paint I need, grab a stir stick and brush and head upstairs. The damned basement door is closed because Finnegan's in the house and we don't want him down here using it like a litter box. I can't get the door open. The old wrought iron latch needs to be pried a bit while I push at the humidity swollen board and batten door. It gives suddenly and my right hand jerks forward with the paint can and almost half the paint sloshes out onto the dining room floorboards.

I can't believe what I'm seeing. The perfect, time-honed old floor has a puddle of paint on it, with splashes in every direction. I run to the kitchen and grab the roll of paper towels cursing myself. I carry the kitchen trash bin with me... cursing, in a furious sweat.

Towel after towel gets saturated as I frantically toss them into the bin. After ten minutes I'm out of towels and I only have half the paint up. I open the Goddamned basement door and grab the pail and mop, run into the kitchen and fill the pail with water. It's a frantic slop fest as I slap at the floor and end up spreading the puddle even more. I toss the contents of the bucket out onto the lawn. I run into kitchen and repeat the crazy, mopping process for another twenty minutes.

Ally's awake upstairs. I stand, half coated in paint, paint all over my hands, arms, pants, shoes. I roar.

Ally's crying up there. There's a lot more mopping-up to do. I reach my wet green hand into my pocket and pull out my phone and as I smear green paint all over the phone, I push the button for Lisa.

"Hi, how are you? Rufus Stoltzfus just told me..."

"Lisa. Lisa, look, I just spilled paint. Ally's awake. Look, I have to do something."

"Spilled paint? Where?"

"In the dining room, on the floor. It's a freaking mess, but, no, I'll clean it up. I think. I hope I can clean up this fucking mess. Listen, Lisa, I have to get in the car and go to Boston. Okay? I have to get out of here and do this. Let me take Keith. I'll clean up here and go to Boston and look up some old friends. That's where our friends and contacts are and maybe I can get a lead on a job, if I'm just there in the damned place. We have to get out of these woods, Lisa. Jesus Christ!"

"Take Keith?"

"Yeah, I'll show him Boston. I can't take Ally. Can you take care of Ally for a few days?"

"No, that's fine. Good."

"You have to stop working Lisa, like you have a job. Ron fired you...or let you go. The douche bag doesn't know or care you're working here, Jesus, being conscientious."

"I'm not. It's okay. Go. Take Keith there. Will your car make it? I'll come home . . . be there in about an hour. I can stay home for the next few days."

Chapter Thirty-Three

LEANING DOWN AND FORWARD, I'M twisting my back from one position to another, sitting up and leaning against the steering wheel, then leaning back with my left arm supporting my lower back. Keith's finally asleep in the backseat. He watched a documentary on, "Famous Medieval Kings and Queens", that I found online for him. The night lights jab into my eyes on the highways. We went through New Jersey and now, we're on the long wend of Route 84 north. New York and Connecticut are behind us and we're heading to the Mass Turnpike.

I can see Keith in the rear-view mirror from the lights from the dashboard and cars on the opposite side passing us. I'm not staring at him. I'm just aware, very aware of him. I always am. I'm just as aware of Ally but she's still so small and Keith's getting older now. He's almost up to my chest when we stand and so he'll be aware of me, more and more.

My head aches. I used to like driving at night, but now the headlights all feel like they're too bright and straight into my face. Keith's awake.

"Are we near Boston?"

"About two more hours."

"How long have we been driving?"

"A little over four hours."

"Are we going to move there?"

"Yeah, we don't really know. You and I are going to go take a look at it. Okay?"

"Why's it so beautiful?"

"Beautiful? Uh, well, I guess because it's old. It's one of America's oldest cities and there was money there, lots of early industries there and schools and universities. So, yeah and they built a lot of very nice townhouses in Back Bay, the North End and the South End and Beacon Hill in the middle. Then Beacon Street and Commonwealth Avenue head west and yeah, we're staying there, on Commonwealth Avenue tonight."

I said way, way too much and lost him.

"We're going to stay in a hotel near Kenmore Square," I say.

Maybe he got that last bit.

The Stradford Inn near Kenmore Square is the only eyesore for miles. It's the flattened, open parking lot that's profoundly ugly. It's a holdover from the nineties. I barely look. We park in our indelible black parking space. Squatting in the middle of this old lot is the fragile little hotel building of pale-yellow brick and thin plate glass. The backs of prouder, much older red brick buildings are the main view behind the hotel-motel. Tall, innocuous late twentieth century Boston University dorms cloud the view in front.

I remember it all.

"Never thought I'd actually stay in this place." I mumble, standing behind the car with our one suitcase. "It's not much and it isn't even cheap." I close the trunk.

"Are we staying here tonight?"

"Yeah. And maybe tomorrow night. Okay?" I wonder if he'll like it. "It's close to everything, Keith. We're right in the middle of Boston."

"Yeah?"

He's excited. He usually loves hotels, any hotels. That thought makes me extremely aware of him.

We walk across the asphalt, under the blinking yellow streetlight that's meshing with the white florescent lights around the hotel's doorway.

Registered and up the elevator, Keith is getting worked up. I'm thinking about how he still likes to push the buttons for the elevator. Will he in a couple of years? As soon as we enter, I watch as he cases the room.

I put the suitcase in the bathtub, hoping we won't get bedbugs all over us. There is that heavy pall of insecticide somewhere. I head for the window and open it the three inches allowed. Then, I put on the air conditioner.

"What bed do you want, Keith?"

"This one."

That stopped him from poking any more at the coffee and tea maker.

"Can I have these? And this?"

He has some half-and-half creamers in his hand and he's trying to free his left hand to point at a packet of cocoa. Some of the creamers fall onto the floor.

I have to look away.

"Yeah. Just two of them though. Okay? If you make the cocoa – can you make it? Know how?"

"Yeah."

Of course, he does. He's done this a few times before in hotels like this. I look away again as he bounds into the bath-room to fill the black plastic pot with water. He's back with that and switches things on and then waits while bouncing on the bed in a seated position.

"No, you can't do that. Take it easy. Okay? There are people below us."

He heads into the bathroom and plays with the light and fan switches. Then he tries the shower faucets. Now he's out in the room looking at the air conditioning switches.

"Can I watch TV?" He's grasping the remote with both hands.

"Something halfway decent. Let's turn it off in an hour, though. Okay?"

Chapter Thirty-Four

I'M HARDENED TO THE NEXT task. "We're going to walk to the museum, Keith."

He slowly chews his cereal. Waiting is driving me crazy. I just have to. He's such a great kid that, no matter what's happening in the world, he's fine.

Walking out the hotel door into the hard-hitting sun, the aspirin helps a bit, but my head's in a haze.

I say, "This way. It's a long walk. That's Kenmore Square, straight ahead there. I don't want to take the subway because it'll take us inbound and then we'd have to get an outbound train. We'll take a subway later, if we can."

"Where? Is that Boston?" He's looking at the five and six story buildings of Kenmore Square ahead of us.

"Yeah, Kenmore Square. We're in Boston."

"Is that where the Boston Red Sox are?"

"Yeah, we're going to see the ballpark." The irony that we happen to be near Fenway Park has to stay muted. "We'll walk by it."

"Is that it?" He points to an old granite building ahead on our right.

"No. No, that's a Boston University building. Mommy went to college there."

He stops and looks down at a branch of a tree that's lying on the edge of the sidewalk. He pokes at it with his shoe.

"Come on Keith. We have to keep moving."

We walk on.

We finally reach Kenmore Square and wait at two different cross walks until the lights change and all the mid-morning traffic allows us to make our way to the right and onto Brookline Avenue. Keith seems so small, surrounded by so many adults. I have my hand on his shoulder and through the people and up the street we walk, slowly. The sun's on our backs at least. It must be in the high eighties already and my wrinkle free white shirt isn't breathing very well.

There are fewer people now. I stop walking to let Keith catch up.

"That's Fenway Park ahead up there, Keith."

"Whoa. Is that where the Boston Red Sox play? Are they inside there?"

"Yeah, they play there, but I don't think they're in there now. If they were playing a game now we'd see hundreds of cars and people all around here."

"How many people go in there?"

"I don't know. Yeah, no idea. A lot."

"A hundred thousand people?"

I shake my head at him, having a hard time talking. "No, not that many. Less than half that, I think."

We're walking right by the green walls of the stadium. He's guessing numbers and slowing down again. I look at my watch.

"It's nine-forty, Keith. We have to keep going. I don't have to be there until ten-thirty, but..."

It's hard to walk slowly enough. I keep stopping, waiting for him. There's Boylston Street a block ahead. Lisa and I lived near here for a few years and Keith was born at Beth

Israel Hospital up the street. Normally I'd talk to Keith about that. It's been a few years since he's been here with us and heard the stories and seen the apartment building we lived in until he was three. Why didn't we just stay in beautiful, leafy Cambridge? We wanted to be closer to the Center.

Right now, all I want to do is walk. Except Keith is slowing down.

"Getting tired?"

"Yeah."

I look at him walking a few steps behind me. Sandy hair in a bit of a mop because I haven't cut it for a couple of weeks. His face is smooth and round, his eyes blue circles. Old people always flip when they see him. He has on the blue jeans he always wears, the maroon T-shirt with the horizontal orange stripes that he always picks-out and an old pair of white sneakers.

He breaks my heart all the time. Normally, I don't want to cripple him or smother him with constant affection. I do hug him and tell him I love him. So does Lisa. But right now I don't know what to do, except try to get a job. We have to walk.

Across Boylston Street, we're in the West Fenway. This is the cheapest, "nice" neighborhood in the city. It's the starter neighborhood for some. Then there are the old people clinging to rent controlled apartments and a couple of buildings built for low cost housing. Do most of these people have jobs?

We're on Jersey Street, where four and five story apartment buildings from the early twentieth century, in various colors of brick, take up a third of a block each. The big restaurant franchises are behind us on Boylston Street. I remember there were some cool restaurants and a bakery. We could seldom afford them but didn't care because we were so wrapped-up in our important not-for-profit causes.

"We're more than halfway there, Keith." There are two young mothers with prams walking toward us on the sidewalk. They don't slow until they're right in front of us and then they wait for us to get out of their way, possibly walk on the road. Irritated, I put my hand on Keith's little shoulder and aim him ahead of me to give them room.

It's almost impossible for me to walk slowly enough to stay with him. I used to take walks like this all the time and never get tired. Friends told me I walked too fast.

"Sorry Keith, just keep walking. We should have taken a taxi or something."

"A taxi? Can we take a taxi?" he asks.

I shouldn't have said that. I look at my watch. It's almost ten o'clock. I hate being late, but all I really can care about right now is Keith. Five young people, probably college students, pass us and Keith squints through the sunlight at them and they don't see him, or me, at all.

"No, there probably aren't any taxis here now. The museum's just on the other side of that park. See the park?"

He looks but doesn't answer. He's looking really tired. We've been walking for about forty-five minutes.

"I thought it would take less time. We'll take the subway later, when we leave. Okay?"

God I'm feeling awful about dragging him along. Why did I bring Keith on this trip? I wanted to keep him near me, like I might lose him? Jesus Christ, it's hard enough looking for a job.

"Right across the park. See the museum across there?"

He doesn't look. He's tired and walking very slowly now. I wait. He shuffles to me. He doesn't look up but just stands next to me. I can feel myself well-up. It feels like a misguided effort walking this way. Why didn't I take a taxi from the hotel? I didn't want to spend the money? Tears are starting to form. And I know they'll pour. I jerk to the side to look away from Keith. Jesus Christ, what's wrong? I can't let Keith see this.

I grumble and gently pull at the material of his T-shirt covering his small shoulder.

But we do move a forward bit. The couple getting out of their car don't seem to look. Shuffling forward into the park, my tears seem to be unstoppable and I'm shaking a bit and it's hard to control this. If we keep moving, Keith might not look up at me. What the hell is wrong with me?

I keep trying to breathe in and calm down. I have to run. "Keith, come."

The bit of rushing air and muscle movement helps. He starts to run behind me. I turn, and he looks so damned small running slowly behind me. The only other people in the park that I can see are some guys playing basketball two hundred feet away and a young couple with a a toddler even farther away, sitting on the grass. I run off the path and onto the grass. Keith doesn't know what I'm doing but he follows me. I go in a circle around him and I'm feeling better and better even if my shirt is out of my pants and I'm working up even more of a sweat. The tears stopped. My face is encrusted from them, but I wipe at that with my sleeve and stop moving.

"Okay. Keith?" I walk toward him.

He was only halfheartedly running and now he's standing looking at my chest because the sun's behind me.

"We'll just walk a little more. I promise, okay?"

He nods just a bit.

We start walking again, me with my hand on his shoulder. We'll be at the small bridge that crosses the, Muddy River in a few minutes. Keith should like that. My phone's ringing. I pull it out of my pocket.

"Hello?" I stop walking.

"Stuart?"

"Yeah."

"It's Brian. Brian Marky."

"Hi."

"Listen, Stuart. I'm at the airport. I got a call this morning because Jenny Luce is sick . . . sorry, I'm all over the place. Jenny works for me and was going to DC to talk to some people, some foundations. I have to go. I'm so sorry. I wouldn't go but we have a meeting all set up in Washington and it's too important. I only found out an hour ago and I've been running and then forgot your cell number."

"Okay. Nothing you can do about it."

"No. But, shit, how are you? It's been a long time and I was looking forward to seeing you again."

"I'm fine. I'd be better if I just had a damned job." I turn away from Keith as I say this but I'm pretty sure he did hear me. Shit.

"Yeah. Yeah, I got your resume and stuff. I sent a copy to Human Resources, because there isn't anything in Development at this point but who knows what else there might be. I don't know if they got back to you – Tabitha Munrow?"

"No." I look down at the grass, then start to walk toward a tree to get some shade, nodding to Keith to follow.

"Oh, well, they will. I told her you worked at the museum a few years back and that we were friends. Are you looking other places?"

That question deflects me, off into distant space. "Yeah. I'm looking. How are you?"

"Great. No, I'm fine. Running around like a nut. We raised a pile though."

"Yeah, I read about it online. Hundreds of millions. God."

"Yup, for wings and endowment. Wings and endowment. As you know wings are easy, but not endowment. Anyway, Stuart I have to go, speaking of wings, but I was wondering, do you want to talk with Cindy, my assistant? I could call her and set up an appointment for today sometime."

The small deflections are adding up and I wince. "Uhh, you said there isn't anything in Development and you don't know about anything else, like in the administrative wing around you?"

"Anything else? No, Tabitha would know."

"Human Resources. I never, ever knew one person who actually found a job through HR."

"I know, I know. Really, I don't know . . . about any jobs. I wish I did. I will email you as soon as I hear of anything, anywhere. What about the Prints and Drawings Department? Emily Larsen and Geoffrey Marsden and Janice Cohen are all there still."

"Yeah."

"But, sorry, again Stuart. I won't be back for two days. Will you be around?"

"No. No, thanks anyway Brian. Go get your plane. We'll talk some other time."

"Yeah. Stay in touch. Email me with any news."

"Bye."

Nothing. I had the same conversation with Brian a year ago, me on the phone from Woodstock, him on his way somewhere, raising millions. I used to have lunch with him when I worked at the Museum but that was almost ten years ago.

Chapter Thirty-Five

I'VE BEEN STARING AND I don't know where or how long. I put my phone back in my pocket. Keith's so bored he's kicking the trunk of this old oak tree.

"Keith, yeah, my appointment's been canceled."

"We going to the museum?"

"Uhh, I don't know." I stand and look at the massive, classical revival building facing the park we're in. It's a long, horizontal pattern of handsome gray granite columns next to columns with long gray granite stairs in the middle and rows of tall windows all along the way. It's a very calm, symmetrical baritone on the outside. I remember the jumble of corridors winding everywhere inside and I remember I knew my way around years ago.

It's just about ten-thirty and I'm just standing in a park. What do I tell Keith we're doing? It would take another ten minutes, maybe fifteen to slowly make our way through the park and over the bridge and across the street to that Goddamned institution. I don't know what else to do but keep going in the same direction.

I'm almost sick to my stomach. It's hard to talk, but I have to. "Yeah, let's go Keith."

Keith's standing still, waiting and I start walking. More people are everywhere in the park now. Most of them are young and most of them are in the shade.

"Shade, Keith, as soon as we get to the bridge."

We keep walking, me trying very hard to take shorter, slower steps for Keith.

I grit my teeth. I can see if Janice Cohen's there. I haven't had anything to do with Janice or Emily for a few years, and this is a fucking awful time to be saying hello. I know I look like hell. Older and older. I haven't slept or eaten right.

We're almost in the shade of tall old trees that line the river that runs between the street and the park. Keith hasn't slowed down or stopped.

"That's the Muddy River, Keith."

"Why's it called that? Cause it's muddy?"

"Yup."

"What's the name of this bridge?"

"I don't know. Sorry."

He stands and stares at my chest.

"Keith, we have to get going. This has taken us all morning, just walking here and I don't even know why I'm here now. But, please, come on."

We make our way across the street. I still have my hand on Keith's shoulder.

"I guess you were pretty young the last time we were here. But you know how Mommy and Daddy met here, right." My chatter's a little manic, but I can't help it.

He just nods.

We're on the slow, long, low rising granite steps.

"You going to get a job here?"

"No, maybe, but really I'm just talking to some old friends."

"Friends you worked with?"

"Yes."

Jesus, my hold on this situation isn't strong. I never had a firm hold on a career here.

"I'm just talking to some people today." My voice echoes inside.

Keith's presence is not helping my equilibrium. I'm jittery.

"Tickets over there. Are you a member?" A guard asks us. His arm is out and he's ushering Keith and me and some other people toward the ticket booths.

"No. Thanks."

I hate having to pay. It's not cheap.

We're sitting on a leather upholstered bench facing some big, splashy Turners. I look at my watch and it's eleven-thirty. I'm exhausted and so is Keith, probably. This is the first time we've sat down for hours.

Now, what? No idea. I have to focus. I'm probably just headed toward the Department of Prints, Drawings and Photographs and don't want to admit it. I haven't spoken to Geoffrey or his crew there since I left around nine years ago. Except for Janice, good old Janice.

I don't have a choice.

"Keith, let's go."

"Go? Back home?"

"No, just go see someone. We can get some lunch with her. You hungry?"

"Yeah", he nods. We stand up and both reluctantly start walking again.

I'm going to try to avoid the conservators. I'm going to try to avoid Geoffrey Marsden, the Curator. They don't need to see me asking for a job at my age. They don't have a job for me.

The large heavy door looks the same. My head's feeling woozy as I open it.

There, at the desk where Simone Regourd used to guard the office workings of five assistant and assistant-to-the-assistant curators, is a new young woman. She's not as sleek looking as French raised Simone. She's not even as happy to see me.

"Hi. I was wondering, is Janice Cohen here?."

"No, sorry. Do you have an appointment?"

"No. I just happened to come here. I used to work here, uh, exhibition preparation years ago."

"Oh. Let me call her. She's at home doing some writing."

"No, no. That's okay. Some other time."

The phone rings and she excuses herself. I'm not listening as this young woman answers questions into her desk phone. I'm in a sweat, leaning against the door to leave.

"Stuart Macnayer! Wow. How are you?"

"Hi Emily. Fine. How are you?" Damn. There she is, short frizzy dark brown hair and freckles, all just a bit more faded and blended.

"Terrific. Busy, as you remember. Where do you live now? Last we heard you had moved to Connecticut." She's glancing at Keith.

"Pennsylvania at the moment."

"Lisa? And what was your son's name? Sorry."

"Lisa's great. And yeah, this is Keith. Lisa's at home with our baby daughter."

"Wow! Hello Keith. Oh my!" She shakes Keith's hand and stares at him.

"So are you here for any reason other than fun? Business?"

"Well, actually, I wondered if I could find a job."

Leaning back, she stares at me. "Well, wouldn't that be nice. Really?"

I nod, "I'm here prowling around looking for job."

Keith's hearing this.

"Are you looking here in the museum?"

Her face says she wants to help but she's the only person here who didn't write me a letter of recommendation last year when I asked. I have to persevere.

"Sure. Know of anything?"

She starts biting her lip. "Here, come and sit down."

Her small body is pointed at the large oak table in the center of the room. There's a young girl sitting there taking notes and looking at Rembrandt etchings.

Emily shakes her head. "Here, let's go back to my desk."

"I don't want to stop you from doing what you're doing," I say to the back of her head.

"No-no. I have a few minutes."

I put my hand on Keith's shoulder as we walk behind Emily. I should get him away from here, but not yet.

As Keith and I sit on small slatted oak chairs, she moves some papers off her own chair and then has to answer her phone, apologetically.

I look at Keith and he looks back. Why does he always behave so well, especially in public? Most kids aren't like this. I look out the window at the tall birches in the courtyard. It's almost too cold in here. Emily has a slightly mincing style on the phone, cooing to someone. She's around her mid-fifties now, so soundly secure in her job status? She was always so quietly competitive, but also always talking about her daughter, Kate. Kate wanted to hang out in Harvard Square and not do her homework. Kate got piercings all over her face, gained weight, dyed her hair light green, wore combat boots. Kate wanted to taunt Emily, who seemed to think her daughter was somehow empowering herself. Emily never rebelled.

Emily was always all hard work and smart thinking.

She's putting her hand over the phone. "Sorry guys. One minute." She rolls her eyes, dark brown eyes, and blushes.

She always wore conservative versions of the latest style and today it's something resembling a sari, I guess. It's colorful and wrapped around her, but to her waist. Then she has on off white chinos and black leather loafers. I always noticed she looked down when she walked, even through galleries.

She's hanging up.

"Where else are you headed today?"

"Uh, I had an appointment with Brian Marky in Development, but he got called out of town last minute."

She pokes at some books piled on her desk.

I say, "So, where's Kate, now?"

"Kate's at Amazon. Yeah, she works in their plant in Up-State New York. She loves it."

"Great."

She blushes and looks down saying, "How's Lisa doing? Where do you live now?"

"Eastern Pennsylvania, in the country. Lisa's fine. She's out of work. So, yeah, we're just looking."

"Um. But you're looking to come back here, to the museum?"

"Yeah, sure. I thought I should see what there is." My heart's pounding.

"I'm not sure there are a lot of jobs here, just now. Have you talked to Ray?"

"Sullivan?" My stomach tightens. Ray Sullivan, that earnest young guy who took over my position here, years ago. My lousy position.

"Yeah. He always needs help. Maybe you could do that while you look."

I can feel blood leaving my body.

She's a woman of few words and sits still, thinking, but not able to come up with anything more.

"Well." I'm unable to say anything.

"You could meet with Tabitha Munrow, but you know that. But tell her what you did here. We always need help with matting and framing!" Her words bubble.

My body is too weighed down with the past for me to compete here now, at all.

"Even if there were something, we can't move to Boston and live on minimum wages."

She blushes and shakes her head. Matting and framing was the only job for me, forever for Emily, no matter what academic or working credentials I added to my resume.

"We should get going," I say, standing up.

She's saying something apologetic. I keep walking, gripping Keith's shoulder, wanting to get Keith away from here. She follows us to the front of the room.

She pats my back. "Barbara could call a taxi, if you want."

"No. No." I'm shaking. I'm seeing odd flecks floating and I'm feeling lightheaded. I have to lean on the desk, Barbara's desk. I don't know her. She's looking up and over at me, worried that the strange old guy's going to die or something. I can tell in a blur, she's looking at Keith too.

I want to get Keith out, get away. I don't want to throw up.

"You okay Stuart? You look very pale," Emily says.

I'm standing upright as Barbara and Emily discuss what to do with me and I'm pulling Keith to the large oak doors and pushing through.

Noises echo and cool air whisks by as I stumble toward the Fenway entrance. Keith is silent as he gets pulled by me. It's too late to salvage much but if I can just get out of here. . .

Out through the big doors into the bright sunlight, blinking, looking. No cabs.

"Sit Keith. Sit here. We'll wait for a taxi." We sit on the steps and I try to get enough air.

"Taxi?" His voice is excited.

I nod. "Back to the hotel. I have to lie down. Just a little sick. I'll be okay."

Part Five

Chapter Thirty-Six

PITTSBURGH IS EVERYWHERE. THE NORTHPORT Inn off the highway, near Ron, is everywhere. An orange wall adjacent to a textured wall is vinyl.

His phone is ringing. And ringing. No answer. Shit.

"Ron, this is Lisa. I'm in town. Please don't tell Mom. I'm staying at the Northport Inn off 376. I need to talk to you so please give me a call as soon as possible. It's urgent, really urgent."

I throw the cell phone on the bed and walk to the window, looking out at the suburban wasteland. There's the bleak strip along Stanhope Road and then side streets with more crap all around. All the links in chain businesses are out there. Closing the curtain, turning into the room, I stand still. The walls are some kind of pale, cat puke orange in artificial textured light. I need a shower and a drink.

The question is, when will he call me back? There isn't any wine or whatever in a little place like this. Not like they have minibars.

Waiting an hour is enough to drive me completely nuts. The shower helped a bit. The hell with this. I tap the familiar number.

"Hi, Mom, how are you?"

"Fine. I was going to call you tomorrow, but this is perfect."

"Actually, Mom, I can't talk right now because I'm in the middle of work, but I needed to ask you for Ron's other cell number. He has that other one for private calls, right?"

"No, not that I know about."

"Uh, he does, Mom. You know, he's said something about it a few times. Look, I have to get in touch with him and haven't been able to."

"Oh, he's away. He's in New Hampshire or someplace. He needed to just take some time off. He's had so much pressure, just like you. It's terrible."

"Jesus."

"What? Why?"

"I'm getting off. I have to go."

I click off and throw the phone on the bed again. This time it bounces across onto the far wall, then a dull thud on the carpet. I sit.

Why did I assume he'd be here, now? He'll always be away, especially now that the family company's in so much trouble. And he's beyond all set for money.

The angry, frustrated feeling is growing, and I don't know what to do about it. I didn't even answer when Stuart called earlier. I sent him that text saying I was fine, busy and would call him later.

My phone seems to be all right.

What the hell am I going to do? It's seven-fifty. My phone's ringing. It's Mom. I toss it on the bed. If I didn't need it, I'd throw it out the window. I'll be damned if I'll start talking inanities, watering down my anger. And I won't tell her I'm here, not yet. It stops ringing. And I won't listen to her message. There's no way I'll waver, but what the hell can I do now that Ron's not even here? I walk around the room.

I think I'm sort of hungry. I ate some of that mix of raw nuts and berries and sunflower seeds a couple of hours ago in the car. I can't watch TV, that's for sure, but I have to call Stuart and I think he's the last person in the world I want to call right now. He's the first person I've always called.

"Hi," he says.

"Hi."

"You okay?"

"Yeah, sort of."

"Tell me."

"No, I'm okay. I'm just in a funk. Sorry. Kids in bed?"

"Yeah. They're fine."

"Yeah, Stuart, I just can't talk right now. Sorry. I have to get some sleep. I'll call you tomorrow. Okay? Yeah, I just wanted to call and let you know I got to the Northport Inn in Pittsburgh. I can't talk, but I'm fine."

"Okay."

"Bye."

"Bye."

Some tears come but I'm also so exasperated, I'm pulling off most of my clothes, lying down and I turn out the light.

It's three-thirty, the deadened middle of the night but I have to send Stuart a text, a long one.

> *Stuart – Sorry I hate the phone sometimes. Anyway, I'm also sorry I left so suddenly. I hope the kids are all right. I am. I'm fine and I'll be back in a couple of days. I just need a couple of days to sort out a few things. I don't know what I want to sort out precisely, not very*

precisely at all, but something. Anyway, I want some information and Pittsburgh seems like the only place for that right now.

You know what woke me up? I had this sudden desire to tell you to write. It might sound nuts, but I mean it. You wrote that novel years ago and you just have it on a shelf. Write some more. Do it. At night or whenever you can. I want you to.

And build whatever you have to so we can sell the house. Okay? I miss you and the kids.

Love...Lisa

Chapter Thirty-Seven

It's hard to wake up even though it's almost noon. I've been deep sea diving since room service knocked on the door at eleven. The sun's strong even if I'm not. Sliding to the side of the bed, I'm finally up. A shower will help after I put the, *Do Not Disturb* sign on the doorknob.

What the hell am I going to do today? I have to try to think, now that I'm clean.

Okay. I can eat my yogurt and the apple. Drinking the Inn's tap water with my yogurt and apple will keep me going for a while. The phone. Call Ginny, awful squeaky Ginny.

"Hi, Lisa, so nice to hear from you. Is everything all right?"

"Yeah, yes and no. Stuart and I are are jobless again, so…"

"Oh, I heard. I'm so sorry. Is there anything here? Does Ronny know anyone for you or Stuart?"

"Nothing yet. No, I'm calling to say hello and also to ask you something, since you've known my family so long."

"Oh, I know. Don't remind me how old I am. I was your mother's bridesmaid. I met her in high school. Isn't that amazing? She is such a gem."

This is her constant refrain, word for word. Squeaked and squealed, constantly, every time.

"Right. That's why I want to ask you…what did my mother and father say about the company being split up back when my grandfather retired? They'd never say anything to Ron or me, but they must have been surprised or something."

"Oh, yeah that seemed strange to me, Lisa. Yeah, I've pestered your mother about it and Larry too. But nothing. Now, you know what a busybody I am and I'm like a dog with a bone, but Tricia just always says Larry wanted it that way or that Norman felt Teddy and who? Well, whoever the other guys were who were working with your grandfather for years, they deserved a promotion, too. And I'm like, what?! I mean, you might give them a raise and some new positions, you know, like Vice-President or what are some of these things? Executive Director. You know?" She's trying to contain her tendency to squeak and squeal. She's still controlling herself.

"Yeah."

"Yeah, but no, he went and made them owners. I don't know Lisa, maybe your grandfather thought the company needed the money or maybe he did."

"Twenty thousand each, Ginny. Each new partner had to only pay twenty thousand dollars."

"No! Are you kidding?" she squeaks.

"No."

"Oh my God! That's so crazy. That's very interesting. No wonder you're asking! I'd be asking, too! So now, tell me Lisa, what about you? I mean since things seem to be sort of kaput."

I ignore her. "Did my father ever say anything, about retirement or anything?"

"Retirement? Yeah, I wasn't as close to Larry, of course, but I did ask him a few times if you kids were going to take over his place at OhPa. He'd just say, 'if they want to', you know in that quiet way your father had. I don't know Lisa. I don't know."

"Yeah, Ginny? Sorry, but I have to tell you, I don't buy it. Sorry, I just don't."

"What?"

"Well, yeah, look. Something had to cause my grandfather to screw over my father and something caused my mother and father to just take it. I mean, nothing makes sense unless my father did something and knew he was caught. Do you know anything you're not telling me, Ginny? Did my father cheat on my mother or something, so this all happened?"

"Oh my God, Lisa. Wow. You are upset."

"Just trying to get at a few basics here, Ginny."

"No, I know you must be very upset, not having a job right now and Stuart, same thing. I guess you could take some business courses . . . I don't know. Lisa, I was around then! If anyone would have known about something that upsetting to Tricia and to her father and all that . . . I mean, my God, Larry wasn't the sort of guy who could sneak around and then get caught or whatever you're thinking and then get everyone in an uproar. Especially your family, Lisa. Wow, everyone's so conservative and careful. You know what I mean?! Your grandfather would have fired Larry. I mean, why would Tricia even stay married if he did a thing like that!? No, I would have known something. You know?"

"I don't know."

"It doesn't make sense! So, Tricia's father, your grandfather, punishes his new son-in-law by dividing up the company!? Then he's hurting Tricia too!"

I'm pacing, shaking my head, biting my lip.

"Nope. Yeah. I get what you're saying. I should go."

"I'm so sorry your upset, Lisa. I hope you and Stuart get jobs. I really do. But you will or Stuart will. Maybe if you move here where your family is, we can all help somehow. What happened to Boston!? You were doing so well there."

"Oh, yeah, I don't know. We'll figure things out. But thanks Ginny. I'd ask you to not tell Tricia I called but I know you will. I don't care. Go ahead."

"No-no, I'll be discrete. I love your family. Barry and I and your parents were hand in glove. Your mother's been my best friend forever."

"Great. Again, thank you. I really have to go. I'll see you soon. Thanks. Bye."

I toss the phone onto the rumpled bed. I've never been able to stand Ginny. I just wanted info, so I had to call her? She always thought Ron and I were spoiled brats. We had more money than she and Barry and we lived in a bigger house in a better neighborhood. And Ron and I went to different schools from their kids and then I went off to Boston University and she heard about the Museum of Fine Arts. God, she got more and more challenged by the day and I'd hear it all from Mom. "Ginny wonders why you have to go all the way to Boston for college when we have fine ones right here. Ginny thinks you dress much too conservatively."

Now what? She'll tell Mom I think Daddy cheated on her, and I don't think that.

I should go outside and go somewhere, do something but I don't want to. There's actually nowhere to go now that Ron's not here and I don't really have anything left to say to my mother. I'll make lousy tea and eat some of those organic chocolate chip cookies I brought with me. I have some raw nuts and raisins.

I'm pacing. I'm in no mood to be yakked at by cable news. The world's in much worse shape than Stuart and I are, but I can't take a media catharsis right now. I'm just trying to get by.

I lean on the wall, staring down at the phone on my bed. Who do I call? People have a way of only seeing what they want to see.

And bullying lives on and on. It's an ugly part of life we have to navigate. Bullying and its quiet twin, shunning. I have to lie down again and close my eyes.

Waking up in the almost dark space of a hotel, I blink. It's a after seven. I sit up, rise and look out the window and the sun's setting on the vast hills of suburban Pittsburgh. All I can make out is a back parking lot, some raggedy trees and the tops of flat roofed commercial buildings. The air conditioning is hissing from the vent and sliding off the plate glass, brushing my face. I step back.

Okay, I have to go. I have to get out of this room.

Packing up is fast and I'm out into the hallway, soft cushioned step by step. Sagging downward in the stainless-steel elevator.

In the smelly silver van, I try to think about directions to the highway. It's almost eight o'clock so it's going to be a long night. At least the traffic isn't too bad this late. The GPS says I should be home at three-thirty. I won't tell Stuart I'm driving and have him worry about his crazy wife careening out of control. All I know is I'm driving East, on my way.

Maybe my mother was bullied by her father. Maybe she liked sharing the pain with her husband. Maybe he fought back by feigning indifference. I'll never know. I know what Mom and Ron do is shun all the time. They shun just about everybody. They, sure as hell, shun me and Stuart and our kids because we make them uncomfortable and we Goddamned well shun them back. Or maybe it's the other way around.

Pittsburgh's in the air rushing behind me, rushing backwards. Nothing back there but some money. No jobs, just someone else's money.

I put on Ravel's Quartet in F and drive and drive.

I stop and get gas, use the rest room, buy a wild berry smoothie and put on an old Car Talk CD. Anything to keep from thinking about jobs and money.

Chapter Thirty-Eight

THE DAMP SUMMER LIGHT PASSES over me and I feel the smooth white cotton sheet between my legs, and I take in more air from the beautiful old window. Sweet air.

I'm in no mood to sleep here with my family downstairs. I can't wait to get to Ally and Keith and I have to face Stuart. He knows we have to come up with a plan. Put the house on the market right away? Rent this house? Who would rent this house, here? Who would buy it?

The air in the bathroom is moldy sauna-like after my quick shower and I open the door and get dressed standing on the landing, hearing them all outside in the front.

I finally get downstairs. Now they're in the backyard, so I head out and walk around the half-finished addition. No more cement slab. I wave. Keith sees me first. Stuart's pushing Ally on the big tree swing.

Keith yells. "Mom!"

They all head up toward me with Keith running ahead and Ally following as fast as she can. We're all beaming. Why are Stuart and I beaming? I just manage to not cry.

The exchanges are all exhausted and I point my head toward the house.

"Pancakes? Organic buckwheat pancakes with strawberries? I think we still have those strawberries."

Lots of cheers. We head in.

It's just getting dark out and nighttime is sifting down. Twenty minutes of limbo after dinner for me and now I can hear his footsteps crackling down the stairway.

He appears in the living room looking tired and tanned. His old white broadcloth shirt is all wrinkled and the collar is half shredded. He's always used his old dress shirts for casual, knocking around, rolling up the sleeves. But now I see it as impoverished. He's stopped, looking at me blankly, waiting for whatever has to be said.

I ask, "Both kids are all set?"

"Yeah. They were both tired. Both asleep."

"Yeah, Ally fell asleep while I was reading to her. She doesn't usually do that."

"No."

I breathe in. "So, I don't have much to say about my trip to Pittsburgh."

"Yeah?" Stuart's looking uneasy on his feet.

"I'll tell you about it some other time. I didn't ask you much about Boston, but you looked so miserable when you got back, I didn't have to, I guess."

Stuart just shakes his head, his face fading away. It's the way Stuart gets in a crisis, quiet, thinking.

I say, "So, what's next?"

He shakes his head again. He leans against the door jam, looking at me and then the floor.

"We're going to have to move," he says.

"Move?"

"Yeah."

"Move where?" I'm looking up at him.

Head tilted down to the right a bit, he says, "Maybe I could make some coffee. I have a map. We can stare at it and see if we can see anything."

I'm gobsmacked. Normally, I would have laughed at that or made a dig or something. But not now. I just nod and raise my eyebrows and with it my whole face, as Stuart walks away toward the kitchen. I put my head back and close my eyes, to try to relax. Time manages to barely pass, provoked a little by Stuart making the occasional noise in the kitchen.

He finally comes in the room with a tray, a French press filled with coffee and two cups and saucers. He places it on the floor in the middle of the room. Jesus. Then he waves his hand a little as he leaves, indicating he'll be back. I stagnate completely.

He's back with a map, opening it.

"It's the US. It would be nice if we could include Europe and Canada and South America or something, but we can't, I don't think."

As he sits on the floor and starts to pour the coffee, I just join him on the floor, to be nice.

He spreads the map between us, and I watch as he looks at it. "East Coast first." He runs his index finger along the line that separates land from ocean. "Florida, Georgia, South Carolina, North Carolina, Virginia, Washington. Ever considered any of those places?"

I scratch my neck, my head up, my eyes down on the stupid map. "No, not really."

"You never did? Not even when you were looking at colleges?"

"Stuart, you know I didn't. I just wanted to get out of Pittsburgh. When I saw Boston, I was in love. It's what you say about England."

"Right, I had to come back. My visa was up. You never even thought of someplace else while you were in Boston, like Chicago? San Francisco? New York, Atlanta?"

"Stuart. We don't have any jobs or money. We can't just pick a place and move there. With two kids?"

He looks at me intently. After a few seconds, he says, "But maybe the point is, we can. We can't stay here. There's nothing here but this crazy half-house and this land we don't use."

Now, I'm the one staring intently. There actually is some barren, open-ended logic to what he's saying.

I say, "But what about getting jobs somewhere first and then moving?"

"What jobs? The jobs are where? Maybe we have to move somewhere we want and work low wage jobs and get by. I don't see any other way . . . not after over two years of these convulsions."

I have to get past the image of convulsions, but he's obviously aimed at something. His idea is dancing around inside me. I'm almost feeling giddy.

He's staring at me but actually focused on thinking. He says, "Maybe in some perverse way this means we're actually free to choose some of what we want to do."

We both lean back on our elbows, legs stretched out, and pause. I sit up and shift my eyes over the map, then he leans over it and looks. It is actually amazing to have the whole country spread out beneath us. I'm becoming more excited than I've been for years, maybe since getting together with Stuart. He stays silent while I point at San Diego and move my finger up the West Coast, past LA, up, up past San Francisco, past Portland to Seattle.

He's stretched out, leaning on one elbow, head supported.

He asks, "If you could live anywhere, where would you live? Money's no object."

I'm sitting with my legs crisscrossed, thinking for a second. "Chicago."

"Really!?" He sits up. "You never told me that."

"Never had a reason to."

He laughs and crouches and crawls over and grabs me and starts gnawing on my neck and squeezing me all over, groaning. We laugh and groan.

He says, "What a woman! What a woman!"

We stop grunting and snorkeling and he sits back a few feet and shakes his head at me, the way he does sometimes.

"I've been there a few times and really liked it," he says.

"I went there as a teenager a few times with my family."

"Jesus. Chicago."

I nod. "Maybe if we rent somewhere there for a while, we could see where we'd like to buy. We could buy a cheap condo after a while. You know, a three-bedroom condo. Where the schools are decent. The condo might not be great, but the area might be."

"Exactly. We'd both have to work low-wage jobs, with any luck not awful jobs. Maybe we'd get lucky and one of us would get a halfway decent job."

"One of us would have to be part-time to be with the kids."

"Yeah. Right. We'd have to see who gets what. But, so we have to sell this house."

"Yup."

"Yeah, I have to finish a couple of things. We can't put much more money into it at this stage. We need all the cash we can save for Chicago." Stuart picks up his coffee cup and raises it. "To Chicago."

I reach for my cup and raise it. "Chicago."

We sip some coffee and get up to go to the kitchen where we put the dishes in the dishwasher and head up to bed, tired and exhilarated.

Chapter Thirty-Nine

BEING SO FOCUSED FEELS SO good. I feel like I'm gliding toward something finally. I'll help Stuart again today by playing with the kids while he slugs it out in the addition plastering and painting. He wants to get to the floors by next week, put a few coats of that tung oil varnish on them and be pretty much ready to call a realtor. Chicago has been looking really good online for the past three days and parts of it look affordable. And maybe there are jobs. There definitely will be jobs if we're both willing to work for minimum wage for a while. We'll see what's what.

Stuart got that call earlier from Ian, who said he wanted to come see us before we sell our house and move. He's bringing Molly and I don't mind seeing them to say goodbye and I want to thank Ian for everything, even if it feels morbid. I wonder why they want to see us before we sell the house. I really can't help but wonder about that.

I've fixed a salad with all sorts of lettuce and boiled potatoes, fresh tomatoes, green beans sweet peppers and slices of tuna. I'll add olive oil and vinegar when they get here.

Stuart's calling my name from next door. I wish he put the French doors in between the addition and the old house, but that's too much money for us. The next people can do that.

I lean out the kitchen window and don't see him. I call him on my phone.

"Where are you yelling from?"

"The living room. The new living room. Sorry. I'm painting the trim. Ian called about twenty minutes ago, and I was up the ladder. Then I yelled for you and then I forgot. Yeah Ian asked if it was all right to bring Gabe. I said, yes, of course. But could you tell Keith? I haven't seen him."

My heart sinks. "God. Okay."

"What?"

"No, it's just that I hate doing this to Keith. We're leaving. You know."

"Yeah, no, I know. I had to say yes."

"No, of course."

"Yeah, I know. Keith won't understand any of this," Stuart says.

I sigh and then groan, and we say goodbye.

They're pulling into the driveway in a small, dark orange Ford of some kind. I was expecting Ian's pickup truck.

Keith and Gabe stand looking at each other awkwardly as everyone else says hello in the side yard.

"So I get to see the project," Molly says, putting her hand to her forehead to block the sun as she looks at the addition. "Wow, it looks so beautiful."

I say, "Want a tour? I usually think it's weird and vain to get tours of peoples' houses but…"

Molly says, "Ian's been involved."

We all speak at once about that.

Stuart and Ian are trailing behind and then disappear into the addition as I take Molly through the old house, eventually up to the attic, that she says is perfect. We walk down through the front door and then into the addition. I explain that there's a spot for French doors to connect the two parts downstairs and a hallway on the second floor would do that upstairs. She's filled with praises.

I'm thinking about how much more satisfying this tour is than the last one with my mother. It seems obvious they might like buying our house. Ian could finish it.

We sit in the dining room and eat and soon we tell Keith and Gabe they can run outside, maybe climb some trees. I notice they have on the same colors, Gabe and Keith. Both have on khaki shorts and white T-shirts and black sneakers.

Molly sees me looking. "I know, they dressed the same. I remember doing that with friends as a kid. But Keith and Gabe didn't even know."

I smile. "I see adults doing that. Fortunately, Stuart and I don't look at all the same. Maybe that's a few years away."

"Well, for Ian and me to know how that turns out you'd have to stay, or we'd have to Skype or Zoom," Molly says.

We all grumble and shift in our seats. Stuart seems to blush mostly and he's at loss for words. We're all lost for words, especially since Stuart, who usually has a lot to say, is seeming very quiet. We may all be forcing ourselves to be chipper, but he's not trying very hard. He's smiling in some forced way and just eating.

Were outside in the back yard after eating. Gabe and Keith are running around Ally. She keeps laughing and trying to catch them.

"Wow, you have so much land. That's so nice. Our yard's already too small for Gabe. We have to go up the road to the school grounds for him to kick a ball around."

"Want to buy our house?" I ask. "Then Ian can finish it. It's nice and close to Westtown, to your school."

No one says anything for a few seconds.

I say, "No? That's okay."

"It seems like a good house for you guys," Ian says. "Do you have to move?"

Stuart and I nod, and Stuart grumbles a bit, his head down, eyes drilling into the ground.

Molly steps in. "Oh God. Ian and I have asked around at Westtown and there just aren't any positions right now. I don't know if either of you even want to teach. It's not for everybody. But Ian has an idea. Well, not an idea exactly."

"Do you know John Kelly?" Ian's looking at me.

"John Kelly?"

"He owns Kelly Distribution in Wilmington, Delaware."

"Oh, sure. They have Firstline mowers and blowers and weed whackers…what else?"

"Yeah, he sent all three of his kids to Westtown and he's given the school some money and volunteered for a lot of things over the years. He's on the board now…a great promoter of the school. Anyway, I mentioned your name and he knows you."

"Knows me? Yeah, I met him once at an open house."

"He said he knew about you through some of the dealers he sells to around here."

"Oh, okay. Does he have an opening?"

"He actually does. He wants a salesperson in Lancaster and York, I think."

"You're kidding."

"No. I know you want to move and are all set to go to Chicago and no, I know selling outdoor power equipment to Amish farmers is not your idea of fun. So . . . yeah."

I'm unable to think.

"Sorry, I know it's not necessarily a great job. I just thought I'd mention it."

I'm just shaking my head. Stuart's staring at me, wide eyes glazed. His shoulders are squared off.

I stutter, "I did send them an email . . . and my resume . . . Kelly."

"Really?" Ian says.

"I'm going to sit over there in the shade," I say. They all follow. The kids are still running around. Molly's watching me. Stuart's head still seems hidden somewhere. We all sit on the grass. I smirk a bit and Molly and Ian shrug and smile a bit, waiting.

For reaffirmation, I ask, "So there really is a position?"

"Yeah." Ian nods, leaning back on both elbows, stretched out on the grass.

"I could call them," I say.

"Here's what he told me." He sits up. "The last guy who's been working for Kelly in that area, uhh, I don't remember his name."

I say, "Yup. Seth Nolte. Yeah, he's Mennonite. I've seen him around."

"Yeah, he's retiring. John said he heard from his sales manager that some dealers out there said all sorts of good things about you. So that's what you get for doing a good job, Lisa. But actually, I called him a couple of weeks ago and he looked into it. He's a good guy, John. So basically Lisa, the job's yours if you want it."

"John likes Ian," Molly says.

My head itches inside and I shake it back and forth. I glance at Stuart.

He looks like I feel, blindsided.

I'm driving to Wilmington, Delaware. It's Tuesday morning and hot and humid, reluctant to let go, late summer style. The GPS in this old van told me it would take just over an hour. I'll be driving past my territory with all those Old-World dealers. So this John Kelly said on the phone he wanted to interview me formally but that the job was mine. It's a job. It's the same bizarre job as before. But it's a job.

Made in the USA
Middletown, DE
23 November 2021

52756613R00149